A MATTER OF POSSESSION

Also by G. C. Scott
available from Carroll & Graf

The Passive Voice
His Mistress's Voice
Their Master's Voice

A MATTER OF POSSESSION

AN EROTIC NOVEL

G.C. SCOTT

CARROLL & GRAF PUBLISHERS, INC.
NEW YORK

Carroll & Graf Publishers, Inc.
19 West 21st Street
New York, NY 10010-6805

ISBN: 0-7394-0508-X

Manufactured in the United States of America

1

FLYING SOLO

A woman sits on the sofa. She wears a black corselet and shiny dark grey tights. Her hands are bound behind her back, her elbows drawn tightly together with white braided nylon cord. Similar cords encircle her legs at ankles, knees and thighs, drawn tight enough to indent the flesh beneath the sheer nylon. She wears high-heeled shoes with straps that encircle her ankles. A wide strip of adhesive tape across her mouth gags her, and more tape over her eyes acts as a blindfold. Her face, or what can be seen of it beneath the tape, reveals her fear. Terror might not be too strong a word. Yet at the same time she is in the grip of sexual tension, for she is helpless and dressed provocatively, unable to escape or see or speak. Unable to avoid whatever her captor decides to do to her. Anticipation is written in the tense lines of her body. Her name is . . . well, never mind her name. She is every man's fantasy victim, the woman upon whom he can make any mark, to whom he can do anything he wishes. She waits for him, trembles before him, yet passionately desires him to take her, use her, make her his slave. The light from the fire glows on her flesh, throwing highlights on the shiny nylon of her tights. The door opens, the creak startling in the heavy stillness of the room. She stiffens at the sound, knowing he is coming for her and knowing again her own helplessness.

The man holds a riding crop in his hand as he advances toward her. She turns her head, trying to guess from the sounds she can hear what he will do to her this time. The look of fear on her face makes her more desirable rather than less. She knows she cannot escape, but like a frightened animal she strains against her bonds, twisting her body in panic and fear. The muscles in her arms and legs stand out in relief as she struggles to break free. The man ignores her struggles, bringing the crop down with a crack across the tops of her thighs. The bound woman emits a strangled cry, a sound of pain and surprise. A red weal appears on her flesh under the smooth nylon of her tights. The next blow lands on her breasts, outlined under the tight black elastic of her corselet. She doubles over from the waist, shielding her breasts and thighs from the whip, but exposing her back. The crop promptly lands there, bringing a further muffled shriek from her. Her face is working, contorted by the pain, but at the same time her hips are thrusting back and forth, as if she can feel herself penetrated by a rigid cock that is arousing her intolerably. Because she *is* so penetrated. Inside her anus and vagina are rubber dildoes, held in place by the tight fitting crotch of her corselet and sliding in and out as she writhes under the lashing and twists in her bonds. Even as she cries out in pain she is being sexually aroused and is experiencing the onset of orgasm.

Barbara woke sweating and breathless. This was the second night she had had this disturbing dream, or one very similar. In each of them she had been helplessly bound and was undergoing sexual torture which she found intolerably pleasurable at the same time as she suffered the pain. Where did these images come from? She had never been in a situation like the one she dreamed about, yet as she sat up in bed she was aware of the stirrings between her thighs and the stiffness of her nipples. Wonderingly she raised her hands to her breasts, half expecting to find the marks of the lash. There was nothing there, but her nipples were so engorged they were painful, as if they would burst with the strength of her desire. When she felt her crotch, her hand came away moist with the evidence of her excitement. The odour of her arousal was strong in the close air of the bedroom. She was alone; the room dark, the house quiet. She knew the doors were locked and that she was safe from intruders. Briefly she felt regret: would her demon lover never come? Then she was struck anew by the bizarre nature of her dreams, and she wondered once again if she were not a little crazy. The aftermath of her dream had left her breathless and hot.

Barbara's hand strayed once again to her crotch, lingering this time, and rubbing gently and determinedly at the hard button of her clitoris. She was almost unconscious of what she was doing, as if her hands had a will of their own. She raised the nightgown above her hips so she could get at herself more freely, her fingers sliding into her vagina and kneading the small grape at the apex of her labia. She uttered a low whimper as she worked on herself. With her free hand she alternately cupped her swollen breasts and teased her nipples until they became intolerably sensitive beneath her touch.

As she rubbed and teased herself, Barbara tried to recapture the dream, to turn the fantasy she had imagined into the actual manipulations in her dark bedroom. She felt the familiar wave of pleasure as her orgasm swept over her, and she bit back the cry that trembled just within her throat. In addition to the desire to be bound and tortured, Barbara wanted to scream out her release, but this was a quiet neighbourhood and the noise would attract the attention of others. She surrendered herself to another orgasm, shuddering in the darkness and wishing it were some man doing this to her, making her writhe helplessly with desire and pleasure. None of the men she had known had done to her anything remotely like what she had dreamed these last two nights, and she thought that might have been the reason she had found them ultimately unsatisfactory. She had recently begun to be tortured by both sleeping and waking fantasies in which she was the helpless prisoner of a lover-sadist who put her through incredible torment which nevertheless drove her mad with sexual desire.

At length, exhausted, Barbara lay back against the headboard of the bed. She stretched her arms out and clasped the posts of the bed with her hands, imagining what it would be like to be bound so; her wrists and ankles lashed tightly to the posts of the bed, held immovably, herself unable to touch her breasts or her vagina or her clitoris, yet with all these vulnerable areas open to the touch of some mysterious, menacing *other*, someone who would show her no mercy, making her scream and scream and come and come. She slept fitfully, waking in the morning feeling exhausted. She was still spread out on the bed as if bound.

Barbara got up and made coffee. She would have to go to work as usual, but at least it was Friday, and she would soon be able to relax. She had no plans for the weekend, no date, that is. She didn't particularly mind that, especially since there was no one she particularly wanted to be with. No one she knew could quite take the place of the dream-lover she was beginning to think of almost exclusively. If she were going to meet *him*, now . . .

She ate toast and cereal and took a shower, hoping it would clear her head. Then she began to get dressed, still under the influence of her dream. She went to her special drawer, the one which held her collection of dildoes and bondage gear: handcuffs, leg-irons, gags, rope – the things she had assembled over the past several years as her fantasies took definite shape and grew stronger. As she selected a pair of dildoes from the collection she wished once again that there were someone she could confide in, someone who could help her realise her fantasies. But there wasn't. She wondered if there would ever be anyone, or if she was going to become increasingly more obsessed and unfulfilled. The only thing that made her feel better was the relative ease with which she had been able to purchase the items for her collection. If these things were so freely available, there must be others like herself who were buying them. She just didn't know how to make contact with them.

From her bureau drawer Barbara selected a black corselet like the one the woman in her dream had worn. Did she dream of this garment because she had it, or did she have it because she was unconsciously drawn to it by her dreams? She chose dark brown tights, the shiny sheer ones that had become fashionable again, an imitation of the silk stockings of an earlier era. Barbara smoothed the tights up her legs, enjoying the feel of the nylon and imagining her dream lover's hands doing this task for her. Just before pulling the top into place, she lubricated the two dildoes she had chosen with hand cream. Deftly she inserted one in each of her openings, and adjusted the panty part of her tights. Then she stepped into the corselet, working it up her body and settling the crotch tightly between her legs, holding the dildoes firmly inside her. She eased her full breasts into the brassière cups and smoothed the one-piece garment over her body. Not bad, she thought as she looked at herself appraisingly in the mirror. Good bod. Attractive, she thought. Not past it. The dildoes stirred inside her as she turned away, bringing a tiny flash of sexual pleasure as they shifted. She put on high-heeled shoes and a nylon slip before sitting down to do her make-up. As she sat before the small mirror Barbara wriggled slightly on the bench, enjoying the pressure of the dildoes inside her. When she was done she was panting lightly. She put on her skirt and blouse and was ready to go to work.

The editing post suited her in most ways, though she kept saying she wanted a crack at serious fiction. That was probably an inevitable effect of her university days, when she had read English literature for her degree. She had even contemplated writing a Serious Novel, but had been caught up (like so many arts graduates) in the sordid business of making ends meet. It only required two weeks of starving (metaphorically speaking) in a London garret before starting to look for work. Her first job was as features editor for a glossy women's magazine. 'Feature' in this case translated as freelance, which meant largely unpaid when they didn't print her stuff. So she went job-hunting again, with the vague idea of at least editing serious fiction if she wasn't actually writing it. She was offered the post of subeditor in a small publishing house which specialised in romantic fiction aimed mainly at women. At university she had scorned the formula writers who were turning this stuff out by the mile, setting her sights higher. Likewise she scorned the stereotyped roles women were allotted – shy virgin waiting for Mr Right and fending off all sorts of lecherous beasts intent only on taking her 'flower' (some of the writers actually used that word!) without paying the price of true love, matrimony and a mortgage.

While she still held the genre in contempt, Barbara was impressed by the amount of money it made, mainly for the firm and only incidentally for the authors, whose share hadn't changed materially since the days when Enid Blyton was penning her schoolgirl epics. Occasionally something more serious came her way and made her stay at her post (which she couldn't really afford to throw up anyway, lacking as she did the rich and indulgent father/family/husband/lover who made such extravagances possible in the fiction she edited). So on she worked, waiting for the break that seemed to take an unconscionably long time to arrive.

She was still waiting (and having the usual number of affairs and encounters with men) when she stumbled across a short story by an unknown French writer. It concerned a descent into an underground room via a long flight of stairs. As the narrator descends the stairs he sees first a female figure lying on some sort of dais at the bottom in the half light. As he gets closer he perceives that she is in fact bound to a stone altar by her wrists and ankles. When he reaches the bottom he realises that she is intended as the centrepiece of some obscure ritual. There the story ended, inconclusively, as most stories since Kafka have done. But the story crystallised her own attitudes and fantasies. As she read the story, Barbara alternately identified with the man descending the staircase and the woman victim at the bottom of it. Of course the idea of being the centre of a boring (and public) ceremony was not very appealing, but the notion of being tied up had instant appeal for her. She felt herself go hot all over as if her whole body were blushing, and her breath became ragged as she imagined the ropes being fastened to *her* wrists and ankles.

That was her first brush with B&D, as she quickly learned to call it. She had no idea why the idea of being tied up had such instant appeal for her, but she was eager to learn more about the matter. And once she was aware of the perverse desire, she found that she was not alone. There were any number of magazines, books and mail order houses catering to the B&D set. So, she concluded, there must be a lot of us out there. But she never figured out how to meet anyone who admitted to similar interests. What she did begin to do was order various types of 'restraint' devices, as they were so coyly called, from the mail order houses, all of whom promised both satisfaction and discretion.

The discretion they managed with the plainest of plain brown wrappers. So plain, in fact, that they practically advertised their guilty contents – or maybe that was just Barbara's own guilty reaction. As to the satisfaction, alas, that only meant that the handcuffs and leg-irons and dildoes and gags did what they were supposed to do, as she found out by trying them on herself. They did not, however, provide the partner who would use them so expertly and devastatingly on her. She saw some items that she longed to try out, but they were of such a nature that they couldn't be used without the help of another person. Such delicious things as the all-enclosing leather bag with the straps that went round the wearer after she was secured inside. Or the leather slimming-suit, as the catalogue called the armless leotard-like garment that rendered the wearer absolutely helpless once her arms had been crossed behind her back and the zipper and waist belt had been closed round her helpless, struggling body . . . Once again, the mere existence of these devices and garments argued the existence of people who would help people like her into them, and then close them up around the helpless prisoner.

True, there were 'contact' magazines that offered the names and telephone numbers of people – both men and women – who professed an interest in (or the practice of) B&D, but Barbara didn't think it wise to trust herself so completely to strangers. So she never replied to these ads. She learned that the chances of finding someone to help her among her acquaintances was vanishingly small. It wasn't the sort of thing you could just blurt out when meeting someone for the first time, and somehow she never got up the nerve to bring the subject up later. She couldn't find the right words, or the best time, and she didn't like to think of the consequences of asking the wrong person (of whom there were several types). If she told an unsympathetic man that she wanted to be bound and gagged and, and . . . She didn't even like to finish the thought. The consequences of misplaced confidence were too unbearable to contemplate.

So Barbara carried on with her editing, finding the work congenial enough if a bit predictable and sometimes boring. The salary was enough to allow her to rent a smallish apartment and to begin her collection of bondage equipment. She bought the panty-corselets because they were the nearest thing to a body suit or slimming-suit that she could don on her own. She grew to like the sense of confinement, of restriction, that they imposed upon her body. She felt safe and enclosed when she wore these garments. And the gusset was handy for keeping things inside her. Like the dildoes she wore today.

And lately she had begun to dream, quite lurid dreams like the one she had had the previous night. She felt a growing need to find someone to help her. The need grew stronger the longer it remained unfulfilled, but she was still no closer to a solution. She had toyed with the idea of placing one of those coy coded ads in a contact magazine: attractive brunette, late 20s, good figure, restrained and agreeable, seeks male partner to captivate her and carry her away. But her native caution had always prevented her. It was the old problem of trusting herself to an utter stranger when she was helpless. Anyway, she told herself, she would probably get an answer from a silver-haired older man who would think being 'carried away' meant she liked to tango.

And that was where she found herself on this Friday morning as she set off for work. She didn't have to go to the office. She could just as easily work from home (a feature of her job that suited her very well). But Fridays were usually hectic at work, and the crowds might still part and reveal to her startled gaze a handsome man whose piercing glance would penetrate to her soul and see how badly she wanted to be placed in bondage. Yes, and the same superman would penetrate her sedate outer clothing with his X-ray vision and perceive the tight corselet she wore. He would guess in an instant why she wore it, and what she longed for, and he would have a body suit in just her size as he ushered her masterfully into his luxurious apartment with the torture chamber in the basement. There was an equal chance that pigs would suddenly take wing.

After some practice, Barbara had evolved a means of partially satisfying her need to be helplessly tied. She had learned to chain herself so that she could get free when the game was over, ie, when she had brought herself to orgasm by writhing on the floor and struggling against her bonds. But the essential ingredient was lacking. She was still able to free herself. She wanted to be tied so that she couldn't escape, or be left chained with no way to get at the keys that would set her free. And that required help. Back to square one, she thought bitterly. And off to work.

The train was full as it usually was. Barbara played her game of imagining what *that* one would be like as a captor. How would he approach her? What would he do to her? The dildoes inside her anus and vagina felt good as they moved gently to the play of her interior muscles. She wriggled slightly in her seat so as to emphasise the in-and-out motion of the two plugs. What would he think of her game, what if he knew about the plugs inside her? But they were all hopelessly (if not happily) married – to the job if not to some partner, the new unisex word foisted upon us all by the feminists who had turned their ideological guns onto the language in the latest campaign to eradicate the differences between the sexes. And indeed, what would the bra-burners think of her if they knew what she wanted some man to do to her? Ostracism would be the mildest reaction. Worse, they might try to 'save' her by re-educating her in feminist values. Barbara didn't want that. She simply wanted to have sex and B&D.

At the office she settled herself into her chair, aware once again of the dildoes shifting inside her and the sense of being stuffed full where it counted most. Barbara tried to fix her attention on the manuscript she was editing, but the dreary formula writing and the outmoded sexual mores of the protagonist were hard to believe. Especially fixed as she was now. Did virgins really still exist, and did they still battle so vigorously to retain that status? Why? she wondered, thinking once again of her lurid dreams and fantasies. But the job had to be done, so she put aside philosophy and began to read.

Lunchtime was a welcome break. Barbara hurried down to the lift and made her way to her favourite watering hole, a pavement café in the French manner set down incongruously amid the English weather and their horror of eating in public. She found a table for two still unoccupied and sat gratefully under the umbrella sipping her gin and tonic while she waited for lunch to arrive. She was just about to lapse into a reverie that included dark strangers and ropes when a male voice interrupted her.

'Is this seat taken?' it asked.

Looking up, Barbara was blinded by the sun and had only an indistinct impression of a tall well-dressed man. Dark hair. Pleasant voice. At the same time she noticed that all the other tables were full. She motioned for him to be seated.

'Thanks. Tell me why someone as lovely as yourself has no escort for lunch.'

It was one of the oldest chat-up lines in the book, but the tone of his voice made her look at him again. He seemed serious. Barbara liked what she saw. He appeared to be in his middle thirties. Older than her by a few years at any rate. Tanned, as if he had just come back from a holiday to one of those fabled lands where the sun shone and summer was a matter of months rather than days; or maybe he patronised a sun-bed centre, though she preferred to think of him coming by the tan naturally. She wondered if it was an all-over condition. Barbara was reminded of her own pallid English complexion, but in that respect she knew she was like millions of other women. He had dark hair and laughter lines around the eyes, but there was a hint of something – could it be cruelty, she wondered? Or coldness, as if he could look into her soul. She shivered slightly, the dildoes shifting inside her, and she had a sudden flash of alarm, as if he could somehow know what she was doing.

But that was nonsense. She attempted to dismiss the alarm with a light response to his remarks, but she was undeniably attracted to him. They talked easily until it was time for her to go back to the office. She left without giving him the telephone number he hadn't asked for, feeling a regret as she did so and wondering how she might make contact with this definitely interesting man again.

That evening after work Barbara decided to do the weekend shopping so she could have the rest of the time to herself. She had a good idea about what she wanted to do, and once again she regretted the lack of a compatible partner. But she had been forced to work out an acceptable substitute – until the real thing comes along, she told herself. If it – or he – ever did. She wished he'd hurry, thinking once again of the stranger who had shared the table at lunchtime. Maybe she'd go to the same restaurant on Monday. They'd meet again. Their eyes would hold one another's gaze. He'd take her home. He'd . . .

Barbara drove to the local supermarket and parked alongside a family car filled with noisy kids, blowzy wife and tired husband. The way most people lived suddenly depressed her. Before she could turn the depression onto herself she hurried into the store and made the rounds, filling her trolley and enjoying her little secret. Not many of the women who were doing their shopping did so plugged as she was. The sense of being different was exhilarating.

At home Barbara put the shopping away and made coffee. She wasn't hungry. She was too interested in the time stretching before her and by the way she planned to use it. In her bedroom she took off her outer clothes and hung them up carefully. Then she went to the drawer that held her collection of B&D gear to select the things she'd want for the next few hours. To hell with it, she decided, she'd make a night of it instead. Sleep in the best (ie, the strictest) bondage she could contrive single-handedly. That meant she'd have to use her special lock box, the only item that she had had made especially for her by an acquaintance who didn't know what she planned to use it for.

The time lock was her way of making herself helpless for

a set period of time. It was simply a steel strong box that locked with a timer rather than with a key. Whenever she wanted to simulate as closely as possible the conditions of a real captive, Barbara set the timer and then locked the key to her chains inside the box, knowing that she couldn't open it again until the set time had elapsed. There was always a dropping sensation of excitement in her stomach as she closed the box and then locked the chains on herself. A moment like the one sky-divers described as they propelled themselves out the door and into the sky. Committed. Irrevocable. What if the timer malfunctioned, stopped before it unlocked the box? She would be unable to escape without help – which she was extremely unwilling to summon, involving as it would the unwelcome attention of strangers, the police and fire brigade at a minimum. The neighbours would probably get a glimpse of her bizarre amusements as well. Not good.

Barbara decided to keep the corselet and tights on, wanting to approximate the dream of last night as closely as possible. The faint smell of perspiration and of her own secretions combined to give the impression of a long confinement in which she was unable to take off her clothes or change them. That heightened the experience for her, made it easier for her to imagine that she was indeed the captive of her dark demon-lover. She chose a pair of high-heeled shoes with ankle straps. Once she had secured her hands she would be unable to remove the shoes. Barbara went to the toilet before beginning the bondage session; if she had to go again before she could release herself, she would just have to deal with the mess. This possibility set her heart to beating dully in her ears with renewed excitement. She had once had to lie in damp clothes for long hours because she had misjudged her will-power. Because it was both unplanned and inescapable, Barbara had been tremendously excited and had been able to make herself come again and again. At the end of that session she had been most satisfied with her method. But it was something that had to happen. She couldn't deliberately set out to do it.

Barbara made sure the doors were locked and set her telephone answering machine to record the calls she would be unable to take. She experienced a fillip of excitement whenever the phone rang while she was tied up. She imagined herself struggling to make her plight known to her callers, and failing. Their voices came in to her place of confinement. They were free and she was a helpless captive. She had to use a great deal of imagination to derive maximum pleasure from her efforts. Next she set the remote control for the TV on top of the fridge so that it would be out of her reach. It was important that she not be able to hear outside sounds, nor know how much time had passed.

Finally there were no more things to do. It was time to secure herself. Barbara had chosen to tie her legs with rope because she liked the way it bit into her flesh and reminded her of her helplessness at every moment. She would have liked to be able to tie her hands as well, but she couldn't manage that unaided. So she had substituted handcuffs, locking her wrists behind her back after she had applied a gag and (sometimes) a blindfold. Occasionally she put plugs in her ears, dulling but not eliminating outside sounds. She would have liked complete sensory deprivation, but couldn't manage that either. This was the best she could do.

Barbara sat on the sofa as she had done in her dream of the previous night. With the thin nylon cord she bound her ankles together, pulling the ropes as tight as she could and tying a square knot in the ends. She had learned that this knot was least likely to slip. She repeated the process on her knees. The ropes couldn't slip down past the swell of her calves. Finally she bound her thighs together midway above her knees, pulling the cords especially tight so that they indented her flesh and could not slip down her legs. If she did a sloppy job here, the experiencc wouldn't be as satisfying. It was important for her to immobilise herself and for nothing to slip loose. When she was satisfied, Barbara used another piece of the thin cord to tether herself to the coffee table by her ankles. She would be able to sit on the sofa or wriggle down to sit on the floor in front of it, but otherwise her movements would be severely restricted. She knew she could drag the table across the floor by hunching herself along, but there was no place for her to go if she did that. Sometimes she did it anyway, imagining herself being forced by her dark captor to move in that fashion for his gratification; he liked to see helpless women struggling to perform the pointless tasks he set for them after he had bound them.

For her gag Barbara used a ball of discarded tights which she first twisted into a scarf. She stuffed the ball into her mouth, distending her cheeks and trapping her tongue so that she couldn't speak. She used the scarf to hold the ball inside her mouth, knotting it tightly behind her head. Next came the ear plugs, the ordinary foam rubber cylinders used by mechanics and others who work in noisy places. The street sounds receded, allowing her to imagine that she was being held in a place far away from help and other people.

Barbara buckled a narrow leather belt around her waist. From a stainless steel D-ring at the front a short length of chrome-plated chain dangled. Her handcuffs were linked to this chain by a ring of welded steel that passed around the short chain between the cuffs. She wormed the cuffs between her thighs and up behind her back and settled the chain in her central groove, enjoying the feel of it in the sensitive areas of her crotch. Then quite suddenly it was time for the final preparations and the securing of the key. How long did she want to remain helpless? The question should have been how long did her captor want to keep her prisoner, but she was on her own.

Barbara had decided she would spend the night in bondage. She reached for the small, heavy box on the coffee table and set the digital timer for 9:00 a.m. She usually woke (and got up) long before that hour, even on days when she didn't have to go anywhere. She knew that she would wake up at her usual time and feel the tug of habit to be up and doing. But that would be countered by the tug of her ropes and handcuffs. She would have to lie awake and in bondage until the time lock allowed her to retrieve the keys. She dropped the key into the box and closed it. There was a decisive click as the lock engaged, and the key was out of reach until the next morning.

Barbara used strips of surgical tape to hold her eyelids shut. Then she groped in the dark, bringing her hands behind her back and fumbling the cuffs around her wrists. One at a time she locked them, feeling a pleasant sinking sensation in her stomach and crotch as they closed with distinct heavy snaps. Now she was helpless until release time. She shifted herself on the sofa, trying to find the most comfortable position. With her hands behind her back she wouldn't be able to sit back against the cushions or lie on her back. Nor would she be able to lie on her side for very long because her weight would cut off the circulation to the arm that lay beneath her. As she shifted Barbara felt the dildoes moving inside her, bringing a pleasant warm flush to her whole body. The chain that ran between her legs tightened against her crotch as she moved her hands. The short chain didn't allow her much freedom of movement. She had measured and experimented carefully to achieve that result.

In her self-imposed darkness and immobility Barbara felt both safe and excited. It was as if, by cutting herself off from the world of people and sights and sounds and movement, she had removed herself from its influences as well. On one level she knew she was not free of it. There could be an intruder who would choose her apartment this time. She shivered in a combination of apprehension and anticipation as she imagined what he might do when he got in and found her helpless on the sofa. That was her most frequent fantasy. There could be a fire as well. That wasn't a pleasant thought, for she would be equally helpless in that event. But there were few things in life that were completely risk-free. You have to take some chances, she told herself, or risk becoming a vegetable. And the element of risk added piquancy to the experience.

The only way she could judge the time was by the muffled sounds from outside. More noise told her people were up and moving, less told her that they had retired for the night. She had deliberately stopped the cuckoo clock from marking the hour so that she would lose track of the passage of time. That was an important aspect of her game. She wanted to feel cut off from the stream of time, lost in her own personal fantasy world. True, she could sometimes hear the chiming of the church clock in the distance, but if there was any wind she might not hear anything at all to tell her the time of day – or night. And she might be asleep when it sounded, and so miss the hour.

Barbara had taught herself to sleep in bondage for several reasons. First, because it was necessary if she were immobilised for any length of time, as she was now. Sleep also had the effect of disorienting her, of collapsing time so that she was unable to guess how long she had been in bondage or how long it would be before she could get at the keys to free herself. But most important, sleeping in bondage made her feel doubly vulnerable, doubly captive; not only was she helpless in her bonds, but she was also unconscious. She found this deeply exciting. Barbara had read that sleeping while bound and gagged was a widespread fantasy. She could vouch for that by her own reaction when she did it. But it didn't come all at once. It took practice.

After reading the short story about the man descending the staircase, Barbara had searched for more information on B&D. What she found, at first in bits and pieces and later in larger chunks, was that there were many others for whom the feelings of helplessness and vulnerability were deeply exciting. They claimed that the experience of being bound paradoxically made them feel free. It one is helpless, one has no control over one's actions or one's body. So there are no choices to make. And where there is no choice there is no responsibility and no guilt about what happens. Because things can only happen to the prisoner; she has no say in what is done to her.

Unfortunately, having no one to assist her, to make her a prisoner and subject her to their will, Barbara couldn't experience this freedom completely. What she did, she did to herself. She was still responsible. She wanted to feel the sense of complete freedom from responsibility she had read about. Along with the excitement of sex without her control, of course. And so she came back to her favourite fantasy; helpless woman driven out of her mind with pleasure while bound and gagged. Put that way, it sounded like a headline from one of the more lurid tabloids.

But now she had found a tolerable position on the sofa. She leaned back in the angle formed by the back and one arm rest, her hands more or less filling the space behind her. In this way she stood the least chance of cutting off circulation and getting cramped. Barbara wriggled slightly, testing the cords that bound her legs and liking the constriction. She tugged experimentally at her tether, feeling the rope come up taut between her ankles and the coffee table. Satisfied, she tried to relax.

Ideally, she would drowse and dream of being tied and gagged. Waking, she would find that she was indeed helplessly bound. Half awake, she could struggle to free herself, simulating panic or terror, and so bring herself to orgasm by writhing and twisting. The chain between her legs would saw at the area of her crotch as she jerked against the obdurate handcuffs. In turn that would cause the dildoes inside her to shift. And she could more easily imagine that she was impaled on some unknown man's cock, and that he was having his way with her helpless but responsive body. Heterodyning was the technical name for the process. But Barbara preferred to dwell on the pleasurable, rather than the technical, effects. And afterwards she would still be bound and gagged, unable to escape. And she could do it all over again. But how much nicer it would be, she told herself, to have someone else to share this with her. There was so much more that could be done to her. Barbara drowsed.

During the ten or so years since she had discovered and explored her *penchant* for B&D Barbara had read many books on the subject. Most of them emphasised the secret (and forbidden) nature of the subject and of those who indulged in the sport. Obviously, in a land where almost any sexual activity could land the interested parties in trouble of various sorts the moment their liaison became public knowledge, the B&D types went to great pains to preserve their anonymity while at the same time managing to convey the impression that there were quite a lot of them about. Come the day when they decided to emerge from the closet as the gays and lesbians had done, there had to be enough of them aware of their status and needs to make an impression on the rest of society. But that day had not yet come, and showed no signs of arriving soon. So the B&D groupies tended to keep a low profile.

Another thing Barbara had discovered was that the novels about bondage tended to be set in a fantasy world, either past or future, or on some exotic planet. And sometimes both. Or else they took place in the exclusive world of the idle (and therefore profligate) rich, who had the wherewithal to provide large manor houses with high walls – or in one notable case, an entire private island upon which the masters and slaves cavorted. Barbara wondered how that particular sex club would deal with low-flying aircraft equipped with long-range photography gear and manned (or womaned) by the prurient and the censorious – of whom there was no obvious lack. Even the classic *Story of O* took place mainly within the walls of a large secluded villa.

Where did that leave the rest of us, she thought. Or did the middle classes not think of B&D, leaving such obvious abominations to the licentious aristocracy? Barbara doubted that. There must be many more bondage freaks among the middle and working classes than in the ranks of the rich and the titled. After all, there were so many more of the former to begin with. But where was their story told? They had no entrée to secluded country houses or private islands. They must then be limited to stolen moments in their own homes, cramped and ill-suited to long vistas in which to chase or contemplate their partners. And with the pressure of work – the need to make ends meet from which the wealthy were blessedly free – the lower classes had less time to devote to the sport. And even less time to write about it. Which was a pity, because the information, even in fictionalised form, might have provided her with the means to make contact with a (male) soul mate who would torture her in the way she liked best.

Barbara knew that there were many women in the bondage and discipline game. Their advertisements were in almost every telephone kiosk in certain parts of the city. And they solicited in the contact magazines, alongside the other women who offered sex for sale in one form or another. She had gone to one such woman, because she was desperate and because she felt less threatened by a woman. That was probably why men went to women for their own B&D, especially those who had an aversion to anything resembling homosexuality. It had been a mistake on her part, but a perfectly natural one. She had been naive, imagining that the woman was seriously interested in the finer nuances of sexual bondage. Her operation was actually geared to the maximum throughput, and she herself seemed impatient and (what was worse) slightly contemptuous of her clientèle.

Perhaps the contempt and impatience had been all right for those who sought humiliation along with their bondage. But for Barbara, who had by then developed some quite elaborate fantasies involving long-term bondage and sexual torment, the impatience had been a major turn-off. And there were other problems associated with the transaction. The woman didn't really know how to deal with another woman. She had developed several (quite inadequate, Barbara thought) tricks that might work with men, but she had apparently never had a female customer. Perhaps she was surprised that any woman would seek bondage. And there was the embarrassment for both Barbara and the two male customers who waited their turns with Madam. They had all avoided one another's eyes.

When it was Barbara's turn, she had been conducted to a small windowless room with no furnishing other than a bed that looked as if it needed a change of linen. She had been dreaming of being tied spread-eagle fashion to a four-poster double bed in a large airy room with the sunlight streaming in from the window that overlooked a garden. This was a flimsy modern bed with no provision for tying anyone to it in any satisfactory way.

She had imagined that she would be sternly ordered to strip naked by an imperious woman who would bind her cruelly to the bed and deal harshly with her before leaving her alone to contemplate what would happen later. She would be blindfolded, perhaps gagged. There would be a whip of some sort to lash her with. She would writhe and jerk against her bonds as the lash stung her helpless body, her cries of distress muffled by the cruel gag. But no matter how hard she struggled, she would find it impossible to free herself. And no matter how she cried out in pain, the stern woman would not relent. Then, abruptly, with no warning, the lashing would stop. The door would open, and close again, and she would be left alone in the room in a haze of pain and sexual arousal, her whole body aflame with desire, waiting for the return of the dominatrix who would bring her to an earth-shattering orgasm.

But – where was she? The hours lengthened, the warmth of the sun moved on her helpless body, the others in the house passed the room in which she lay captive, ignoring her. Footsteps came and went, then silence fell. Had she been abandoned, left bound in an empty house? But no. The door would open softly, letting in a draught of cool air that made her naked body shiver. Footsteps would cross the floor slowly, so slowly. A soft, almost feathery touch on her belly, a hand finding its way between her parted thighs, a finger touching the small slippery grape-like swelling at the apex of her labia. Warm breath on her exposed breasts, then parted lips, a scorchingly hot tongue finding her nipples, tiny sharp teeth nipping them until they became taut and swollen. The finger sliding into her as she struggled futilely against the ropes . . .

Her dismay at the venue was heightened by the unseemly bargaining they had had over the price. That done (though Barbara thought that fifty pounds was high), she expected the rest of the scene to unfold hitchlessly. The woman was on the wrong side of fifty, with thinning, dyed black hair, that fell to her waist. She wore a leather corselet and tights designed for a much younger woman, though her figure was still good. Her face was not unattractive, but the sense of here-we-go-again almost caused Barbara to leave at once.

But worse was to come. 'Now, dear,' said the woman, 'what do you want me to do to you?'

Barbara had been expecting to be told what to do. The woman had advertised herself as an 'experienced mistress' who knew how to handle slaves, and she was asking Barbara what she wanted done! But instead of leaving, as she should have done, Barbara found herself stammering, 'I . . . I want . . . you to tie me up. And gag me. Leave me . . . for several hours before you come back.' She didn't have the nerve to say anything about wanting to be whipped.

The woman looked at her crossly and said, 'I can't leave you for hours. That's not how I operate. My clients usually have an hour. And what do you want me to do when I come back, anyway? I usually give hand relief to my clients.'

Barbara found the circumlocution baffling. But she repeated her wish to be tied up and gagged for as long as possible.

More gently, the woman said, 'Well, maybe you should take your clothes off.'

As Barbara hesitantly began to unbutton her jacket the woman turned away as if in embarrassment. She rummaged atop the wardrobe at the foot of the bed and produced a single length of rope which she laid on the bed.

Barbara was too dismayed to protest. She had been expecting to be tied up in imaginative ways, involving lots of rope. This bore no resemblance whatever to her fantasies. She took off the rest of her clothes and lay face down on the bed. Her arms were pulled behind her back and her wrists tied loosely and clumsily together. The woman had her roll over onto her side, and when she did, her knees were bent and the free end of the rope was used to tie her ankles. Barbara knew she could free herself from these loose bonds at any time. Where were the ropes that would bind her helplessly, immobilising her and leaving her at the mercy of she who (her adverts said) had none?

'I don't know about the gag,' the woman said. 'What should I use?' When Barbara said nothing, the woman went on, 'I suppose I could use a scarf.' She chose a head scarf from the bureau and approached the bed. 'Open wide,' she told Barbara. The scarf went between her teeth and was knotted loosely behind her head. 'All right?' she asked Barbara, and when she said nothing, she added coyly, 'What's the matter? Cat got your tongue? Don't go away. I'll be back soon,' she said as she left the room.

Barbara was mortified. She lay quietly listening to the noises from the TV in the front room. She distinctly heard the woman say to someone else, 'Silly cow wanted me to tie her up and leave her all day – as if I didn't have others waiting to use the room.' Another woman laughed at this patent absurdity, and Barbara's ears burned with something very much like shame. She was ashamed of herself for expecting something special when clearly she was going to get something quite ordinary, if not substandard. She didn't know exactly what she was going to get, but she suspected from the haphazard way in which she had been tied that it wouldn't be much. The woman just couldn't be bothered.

Less than an hour went by. Barbara could tell almost to the minute how long the woman waited because she heard the TV show end on the half hour. A few minutes later the woman came back and sat awkwardly on the bed. She seemed at a loss what to do next.

'Shall I play with your titties?' she asked. 'Would you like that?'

Barbara pretended that her gag made speech impossible. She said nothing, thinking that this would never end. But she had paid a lot of money for this, and she was determined to see it through. And she reproached herself at the same time for not having the courage to call it off and flee.

The woman took her silence for assent, and she fondled Barbara's breasts clumsily. The nipples took a long time to get hard. Barbara was seething with disappointment. She pretended to be excited, breathing slightly faster and letting out a low groan. She was hating herself for the pretence at the same time.

Encouraged, the woman bent to her task, using both hands. After a time she moved one hand down to Barbara's crotch, probing her labia and just missing the clitoris every time. 'Does that feel good?' she crooned as if addressing a baby. 'You like that,' she asserted. Maybe she believed what she said.

Barbara decided to end it with the least embarrassment to both of them. She shuddered and let out a loud moan, faking an orgasm she was far from feeling and hoping the woman would get the idea.

Apparently she did, for she produced a wad of tissues and wiped Barbara's labia before removing the gag and untying her. Mercifully, she didn't say anything as Barbara hurried into her clothes and fled, silently vowing never again. There had to be something better than that. Indeed, anything would have been preferable to what she had just done. She wondered if the male clients went away as dissatisfied as she. How did the woman stay in business? Then, answering her own question, she imagined that the men who went to her had no better idea of what it was about than the self-styled expert. Or maybe they were fleeing from something worse at home. If so, things must be pretty grim in the sex wars.

That dreadful experience had driven her to act out her own fantasies as best she could, on her own. Masturbation, she reasoned, is at least sex with someone you love. And she tried (and often found) release with men she met. Those encounters had been pleasurable, but the fantasy was always in the back of her mind. The man she really wanted to find was proving very elusive, and the ones she met suffered by comparison with the dream-lover, though she tried not to let them know how badly. The result was that, at the age of twenty-eight, Barbara was still searching for Mr Right.

Most of her friends were married, and had their homes and their children to occupy their time. Barbara had never felt the urge to produce smaller editions of herself and some male, and in view of her sexual preferences that was just as well. If she ever did meet the right man, children would be an obstacle she could do without for a while. Maybe forever; though she knew she would have to withstand heavy pressure from parents and friends to have the obligatory 2.3 (or was it 2.4?) children. In any case, it wouldn't do to let them see what she got up to in her private moments. Children can make the most embarrassing revelations to their friends.

Barbara came back to the present when she heard the telephone ring. The answering machine came on after three rings, and her recorded message played through: 'This is Barbara Hilson. I'm sorry I can't take your call, but I'm tied up at the moment. As soon as I can get free I'll call you back. Please leave your name and number after the beep.' Some people simply hung up when they heard the machine. Others waited for the tone and left a message. Barbara reckoned that if someone really wanted to talk to her they would leave a message. Those who hung up without saying anything weren't serious. It was her way of separating the gossip from the important stuff.

The recorded message was another of her devices – more hopeful than practical. She half-hoped that if Mr Right ever called, he would realise the message didn't sound quite right. He would instinctively understand that the message was literal and know that they were on the same wavelength. But not this evening. It was a friend from university whom she hadn't seen in several years. Barbara could hear the muffled voice of her friend and wondered what the woman would say if she could see who she was calling. The much-touted vision phones that were supposedly just around the corner might not be such a good idea after all.

As always when she was in bondage, the sound of another voice speaking to her from the world of normal people just outside her door gave Barbara a fillip of excitement. She couldn't say why exactly. Perhaps it was the contrast between the normality of the rest of society and her own bizarre circumstances. And perhaps it was the knowledge that she was prevented by her bonds from doing something she might otherwise like to do. Her friend said she'd be in town for another few days, so there was no urgent reason for Barbara to speak to her just then. Barbara made a note to call her when she could. Just when that might be she couldn't say. Already she had lost track of time. She couldn't guess how much longer her enforced immobility and helplessness would last.

The caller rang off and Barbara found herself drowsing. There was nothing else she could do. She couldn't see anything or hear properly. The low sensory input deprived her of the ability to concentrate. Disorientation and drowsiness were the results, even though she suspected it was not all that late. Not knowing the actual time threw her biological clock out of kilter. Maybe she should be sleepy after all. She couldn't tell. So when she felt herself nodding off she didn't fight it.

She was seated on her sofa, bound and gagged. Her ankles were tethered to the coffee table, but only half of it was visible. The part where the locked steel box rested was invisible, might as well not have existed. But she could see. There was no sign of the tape she had used to blindfold herself on the Friday evening.

She had no way of knowing how long ago that was. It might have been days. She was in a room so big and dark she couldn't see its full extent. It couldn't have been her own living room. It reminded her instead of a warehouse, empty and lit only here and there by overhead light clusters. There was the smell of damp wood in the air, perhaps the timbers of an old wharf she knew must be right outside. She imagined she could hear water lapping below the floor. One of the lights shone directly down on her, making it more difficult to guess who else was there with her. She knew she was not alone, and this both frightened and excited her.

For she was obviously there to undergo some sort of interrogation, a process which included both painful torture and painfully exquisite sexual pleasure. And she knew that it would be impossible to tell where one ended and the other began. It had been that way with her forever, seemingly, though a part of her recognised the danger and urged her to try to escape. Momentarily she heeded the warning, flinging herself wildly about and struggling against the ropes that held her – ropes that looked surprisingly like the ones she had bought to use on herself in her own private bondage fantasies. And as she struggled, Barbara realised that her wrists were bound behind her back by more of the same light braided cord. The handcuffs she had used on herself were gone. This was the fantasy she had entertained for so long.

She knew that she couldn't have done this to herself. Even her elbows were bound closely by more of the same rope. She realised at the same moment that by a kind of sympathetic magic, like calling to like, the things she had done to herself had carried over into this dream. Barbara knew it was a dream. Perhaps she was having this particular dream because of what she had done to herself. She was even dressed in the same black corselet and tights. She felt the shift and slide of the dildoes inside her, finding it hard to tell whether this was real, or simply another dream sensation, and not caring either way since the effect was the same.

As she ceased struggling, she heard a sound from the surrounding darkness. Her inquisitor, coming for her? In her other dreams there had been no questions. Only sensations, sometimes so acute that she awakened in a state of sexual tension, straining for release.

This time the man who came for her looked a bit like the dark-haired one who had shared the table with her at lunch. He said nothing, which made him seem more forbidding to her. Sometimes her dream-lover began by lashing her for reasons she never knew. This time, he began with sexual stimulation. He moved behind her, behind the sofa on which she perched nervously, her breasts heaving as her breathing quickened.

Casually, he rested his forearms on the back of the sofa, letting his hands hang near her breasts, but not touching them, teasing her. He could see that she was excited, wanting him to touch her, her breasts, her thighs, her sex, anywhere at all. She could feel his breath on the back of her neck, and she arched her back, trying to touch his hands with her breasts. Barbara knew that her nipples were erect even though he had not even touched her. Her legs flexed, the cords tightening as she tried to lever herself into a position where he could touch her.

With a thin smile, sensed rather than seen, the man moved his hands out of range, placing them on her shoulders, restraining her. She wanted to scream, 'Take me!' but her gag prevented it. She could only moan in frustration, knowing she was being toyed with. Her tormentor leaned closer and kissed her behind the ear, brushing her hair aside to touch the bare skin with his lips. Barbara almost jumped out of her skin at the contact. He kissed her neck, letting his teeth nibble gently at her. With one hand he turned her head and began to kiss her eyes, her cheekbones, her forehead, light feathery touches that nevertheless seemed to send an electric shock to her sex. Then he moved to her mouth, pressing his lips tightly against the tape that gagged her, making Barbara wish she could open her own lips to him. She wanted to open her thighs too, and she strained once more against the ropes that held them tightly together.

At last he turned his attention to her breasts, fondling them through the tight black elastic of her corselet, cupping and squeezing. Her nipples sprang into relief, and he used his fingers to tease and harden them still further. Barbara was moaning steadily now, twisting her body to offer herself to him. Without seeming to move he was suddenly standing in front of her. He knelt close to her bound legs. He began to kiss her knees, his lips warm and moist through the sheer nylon of her tights. His hands stroked the backs of her calves. His lips trailed up her thighs, kissing and nipping gently, until he reached her pubic mound. There he burrowed his face deeper, toward her sex. She could feel his breath on her legs, and she struggled to open herself to him. The ropes prevented her once again. She could almost feel his stiff cock entering her, sliding home. Or it might have been the dildoes she herself had inserted on the Friday morning as she got ready to go to work.

He stood up abruptly, breaking contact. Barbara felt dismay, and she strained toward him, wanting him to continue, to go further, to ravish her utterly. Instead he laid her roughly on the floor. Suddenly the sofa was gone, leaving her in an empty space. She was still tethered to something by her ankles, but what it was she couldn't see. He took up a position behind her, and began to lash her bottom and legs with a strap. Barbara tried to twist away, to avoid the blows that landed on her. She twisted onto her side, but he only turned his attention to her exposed breasts, lashing them as he had her bottom.

Abruptly her body shifted gears. The pain turned into sexual arousal, making her writhe and buck against the unyielding floor, driving the dildoes in and out as she thrashed about. She was making the sounds she always made when she was on the brink of orgasm. An almost continuous moan of pleasure came past her gag. Barbara felt as if a flame had been kindled in her belly and was spreading to the rest of her body. Her breasts, her nipples, her thighs, her crotch, all felt as if they were burning.

And Barbara found herself on the carpet of her living room, lying near the sofa on which she had been seated earlier, as the dream became Friday evening once again. She was thrusting with her hips, and she could feel the dildoes inside her. The chain that ran between her legs and back to her handcuffs was sawing at her crotch, driving her wild. The muscles of her bound legs tensed against the cords that held them together as she twisted and writhed on the brink of orgasm. And then she was past the point of no return, out of control. Barbara couldn't count how often she came, judging the result only by the pleasure she felt, and by the depth of the lassitude that claimed her afterwards.

Finally the storm was over, and she lay in a sweaty heap on the floor, her breath sawing in her throat as she sucked in great draughts of air through her flaring nostrils. She was dizzy with the combined effects of her wild thrashings and the after-effects of the racking series of orgasms she had induced.

Eventually her breathing slowed and the dizziness

passed. She felt a dampness between her bound thighs, in her crotch, and she knew it had to be her own vaginal fluids seeping out. Barbara was tired now, and wanted to rest right where she was, but that would almost certainly prove uncomfortable. In a short time she would begin to have problems. She had learned that the best position was sitting up with her head and shoulders resting against something. Preferably something soft.

She had ended up lying mainly on her stomach, but with a twist to her hips and shoulders that allowed her upper torso to rest on her shoulder rather than on the arm. She rolled over fully onto her stomach, the dildoes sliding wetly inside her. The movement caused more fluid to dampen her tights. She could feel the wetness spreading between her thighs. The ammoniacal odour of her release was sharp in her nostrils. The slight movement caused her tether to come up taut, telling her where the coffee table was and in which direction the sofa lay.

In her struggles Barbara had rolled away from the sofa almost to the full length of her tether. She bent her body at waist and knees and began to hunch herself along the floor. Her mental image of a bound woman struggling to move over the floor gave her a momentary excitement. Her back touched the sofa, and she rolled again until she could bring up her legs. Leaning heavily against the cushions, she managed to sit up. Barbara had to bend her legs almost double to worm her way up. She felt a thrill as the cords bit into her flesh again.

Finally she was sitting up with her back braced against the front of the sofa. She slid sideways until she felt the arm rest against the back of her head. Then she was able to brace her shoulders and straighten out her legs. That relieved some of the pressure from the ropes. Half leaning, half sitting, Barbara lay still while she recovered from her struggles. It was quiet outside, and she guessed that the hour must be late, but she had no idea of the time. She might have to lie bound for many hours yet. She slipped easily from waking into sleep, and this time there were no dreams, or at any rate she did not remember any of them.

When next she woke, there was a distinct chill in the room. It must be getting near dawn, she told herself, shivering slightly. She had no way to cover herself, and her feet felt icy. That may have been due to the temperature, but wasn't helped by the stiffness of her body. When she tried to move, she could barely feel her legs. They felt wooden and lifeless. The cords that bound her were dull lines of pain that encircled her legs. At least, she told herself, she had done a first-class job with the rope. Nothing had slipped loose during her struggles the previous evening. Barbara wondered if this was how a real (ie, somebody else's) prisoner felt as she accepted that she was still bound helplessly in spite of her efforts.

But she would have to move now. Try to get up onto the sofa and work some of the stiffness from her body. After several attempts which left her damp and breathless, Barbara managed to rise to her knees and shuffle forward until she felt the front of the sofa against the fronts of her thighs. The next trick was to get from her knees on the floor to her bottom on the seat. The chain that ran between her legs to her handcuffs prevented her from gaining any leverage with her hands, and the way she had tied her legs made her quite unstable. The insistent pressure from the dildoes inside her did nothing to help her concentration, nor did the movements of her hips and pelvis as she struggled to get up onto the seat. Almost before she was aware of it, she was teetering on the brink of another orgasm as she teetered on her knees. The combination of her movements and her mental image of a woman in bondage (who just happened to be herself) moving clumsily and blindly was sending her over the top.

Barbara allowed herself to fall forward so that her upper body lay on the sofa while she continued to kneel before it. Her breasts were crushed against the cushions, her nipples stiff with arousal. She rubbed herself against the seat, feeling her nipples harden still more. She began to pump with her hips, as if she were making love to the furniture (which didn't react at all, ungrateful thing that it was). That caused her dildoes to make themselves felt, and

Barbara helped things along by pulling against the chain between her legs. She wasn't really surprised to hear her gasps and moans. Almost clinically, a part of her observed the rise in volume and tempo as her climaxes took her. The rest of her was busy shuddering and thrusting to keep things going.

At the crucial moment she put too much weight into her thrusts, and the sofa slid away. Barbara was able to twist as she lost her balance, so that she fell on her side instead of her face. On the floor, she curled herself into a ball, bent almost double at the waist and with her legs drawn up as tightly as possible. She was trying to curl herself around her centre, trying to hold onto the really delicious sensations originating there. As the delightful spasm passed, Barbara allowed herself to straighten out. From that position she rolled over onto her stomach and her hips began to rise and fall as she thrust herself against the floor. She imagined that the dildo in her vagina were her dream-lover's cock. She felt herself coming again. And then again. The analytical part of her wondered how long she could continue. The other part of her said simply, 'Don't stop!'

In the end (because all things must end), Barbara lay gasping on the floor as the sensations from her sex and belly gradually subsided. As she regained her breath, it occurred to her that she would have a particularly interesting entry for her journal. She sometimes got excited all over again as she wrote down the details of her experiences and worked out new variations to try. And if she ever did meet her demon-lover she would have a whole range of experiences to show him. She imagined him reading what she had written (they would share all their secrets, of course) and then trying them out on her again. And working out his own variations. There were sounds outside when she awoke next time. Footsteps came to her door, sending a thrill of terror through her as she imagined someone walking in and finding her bound and gagged in what the police would no doubt call 'suspicious circumstances'. If someone came upon her like this she would be terribly embarrassed at the very least. The sound of the letter-box relieved her fears: only the postman. Then the milkman. There were the first traffic noises too.

Barbara now knew approximately what the time was. Only a couple more hours before the time lock would let her retrieve the key and free herself. Her legs were stiff again. Barbara rolled onto her side with some difficulty and began to bend at the knees and waist to get the circulation going in her feet and legs.

This time, when she tried to get onto her knees, her legs would not support her, and she felt a stab of fear. What would she do if she couldn't get at the key? The coffee table was too heavy to overturn when she couldn't use her hands in any way to manipulate it. She had to be on her knees to get any leverage with her legs, and she already knew that was out of the question. She imagined herself having to drag the coffee table hehind her to the door so that she could get her mouth near enough to the letter box to make a sound that might (or might not) attract someone. And even if she did manage to summon a passer-by, there was no guarantee that he would recognise her choked-back grunts as the sounds of distress. And then it would be a matter for the police and the fire brigade, and the secret would be out.

No, she told herself firmly. Get a grip on yourself. Think of something. But as she lay on the floor she could think of nothing. Some indeterminate time later the phone rang, startling her from her increasingly desperate thoughts. 'Ummmmmmff!' she said, thinking, illogically, that the caller might be able to hear her somehow. It came out as a low grunt, probably not even audible in the next room. In any case she would have had to answer the phone to make herself heard. And the phone was out of her reach in the bedroom, and she was tethered by her ankles to the heavy coffee table in the living room.

Barbara listened helplessly as the recorded message played through, willing the caller to take the content literally and come to her aid. It was someone from the office wanting to know something about a manuscript. It was all so ordinary she wanted to scream. 'Help me!' she shouted.

The gag turned her shout into, 'Llll-eeeee!' The caller hung up and she was sweating in panic. She jerked against the handcuffs and flung herself about without result. She succeeded only in getting sweaty and breathless again. She had done too thorough a job of tying herself to get free so easily.

Barbara forced herself to lie still until her breathing slowed again. Then she rolled onto her back, enduring the twinge of pain as the handcuffs were pressed into her wrists. With a great effort that strained her stomach muscles she managed to sit up. As if to mock her efforts, she felt the dildoes inside her shift tantalisingly. 'Not now!' she thought furiously. 'I've got more important things to do!' Barbara slid herself across the floor on her bottom, lifting herself fractionally on her knuckles and pushing with her legs, moving an inch at a time. After an eternity she felt the coffee table against her back. Not daring to lean too heavily against it, lest it slide away as the sofa had done earlier, she worked her slow and awkward way toward the end where her memory told her she had set the steel box. She leaned her head back and swept it from side to side, hoping to encounter the thing. Nothing. her head swept empty air. She swept again. Nothing.

A new panic threatened to overwhelm her. Suppose she had got turned around and was in the wrong place? She had to find the box. Barbara shifted further and tried again. Nothing. She fought down the panic and tried again. This time she touched something. Straining every muscle, she moved her head and felt the box slide. But she couldn't push it off onto the floor from that position. Once more she shifted, and pushed the box another fraction of an inch toward the edge of the table. After many awkward shifts she heard a dull thud as the box fell to the carpet beside the table. The box was on the floor! She rolled onto her side and began to inch her body toward the box. It was slow going with no help from her legs. Then, just as her head touched the box, the tether on her ankles came up taut. She could hardly feel it because her legs were too stiff, but she knew what had happened because she couldn't move any further.

Barbara fought down a fresh wave of panic and forced herself to think. She rested. She knew she would have to shift the coffee table itself if she wanted to reach the box. Once more she rolled onto her back and sat up. She strained to lift herself on her hands and drag her body along the floor. The coffee table was so heavy she thought she'd never move it. But it came inch by inch. By the time she touched the box with her hands she was drenched in sweat, the product of her exertions and her panic. Mingled with the sweat was the odour from her sex – all the fluid that had leaked earlier must have been dampened by her perspiration, and she could smell herself again.

But now she held the box. Her fingers scrabbled at the lid. It wouldn't open. Once more Barbara had to fight down panic. It was too early, she told herself. But a small voice asked her, what if the bump had put the timer out of action? She thrust that idea aside. Must think of something else. And at that moment her body came to her rescue. She smelled her own odour and thought, I smell this way because I can't do anything about it. Her helplessness was the trigger this time. Experimentally she moved her hips. This time she welcomed the slide of the dildoes in her anus and vagina. Her inability to use her legs increased her feeling of being powerless. That made her more excited.

Barbara thrust again with her hips, and again. She could feel the warmth spreading in her belly, the relaxation of tension and panic as she continued to arouse herself. She could feel her breasts getting heavy, her nipples stiffening as they became engorged beneath the lacy elastic cups of the tight corselet. The first climax was a small one, but she welcomed it. The next one almost swept her away. She heard the low continuous moaning sound she was making, but she didn't try to stop. The last orgasm left her gasping and shuddering. It seemed to her, when she recalled the incident for her journal, that she had never had such an intense sexual experience.

When she became aware of the present once more, Barbara tried the box once more. The lid opened immediately, and she felt weak with relief. She fished around inside until she found the key to her handcuffs. With shaking fingers she tried to fit it into the lock. It went in on the third or fourth try, and she screwed it home deliberately. The steel band on her wrist sprang open. She quickly opened the other one and rubbed the sore patches on her wrists. Her shoulders ached from being held so long in that unnatural position.

When she stripped the tape from her eyes, the light of early morning dazzled her after the long hours in total darkness. She removed the gag while her eyes adjusted. Next came the ear plugs. When she could see again, Barbara fell to work on the cords that bound her legs. They came free, leaving red indentations in her flesh beneath the sheer material of her tights. She almost cried out as the blood began circulating in her legs again. The corselet and tights had dark patches; her sweat and vaginal secretions from the smell of it. Barbara stripped everything off and removed the dildoes she had worn inside for more than twenty-four hours. Naked, she made her way to the bathroom, walking carefully because her legs still weren't working right. A shower first, she thought, carrying her soiled garments into the bathroom to be washed. Time enough afterwards to plan for the rest of the weekend.

The hot water felt heavenly after her night of cramped and fitful sleep. Now that she had overcome her panic about the key, Barbara thought that the whole thing had been worth the time and effort. And worth the panic too. That had added a piquancy to the experience. She knew that (barring the sudden appearance of her dream-lover) she would do the same thing again. Maybe even tonight. She would decide later. The only change she contemplated was leaving the box on the floor in case the same thing happened again.

She examined her legs beneath the warm water. They were feeling almost normal now, but the tight cords had left angry red indentations which looked as if they would take some time to fade. She touched the marks on her thighs experimentally, gauging the depth and tenderness of them. There was a soreness as she pressed her fingers into the areas where the ropes had chafed her during the long night. Maybe she should try something else tonight. Variety and all that. As she washed herself, Barbara decided to call her school friend, the one whose call had come as she was beginning her bondage session. A day out might give her a keener appetite for experiments later.

Among the envelopes lying on the mat were the usual bills and solicitations to buy this and that. Setting these aside, Barbara came across a smaller envelope that had seemingly been delivered by hand. It bore no stamp or postmark. Evidently it had come at some time during the interval when she lay bound and gagged in her living room. She felt a slight stirring of excitement, wondering who had been prowling around her door while she was helpless behind it. Probably nothing to it, she told herself. Nevertheless her fingers shook slightly as she opened the small brown envelope with care, as if it might be a bomb set to explode at the slightest touch.

Inside was a single sheet of ordinary note paper, folded once. The note said, 'Lunch with me on Monday, same place.' There was no signature, and the envelope yielded no clues about the sender. It sounded more like an order than an invitation, and Barbara realised it could only have come from the stranger who had shared her table the day before. The intriguing question was, how had he found out where she lived? But even as she pondered the question Barbara found herself imagining that this might be Mr Right, the dream lover she wanted so desperately to meet. Of course, she told herself at the next moment, this was usually how she felt when a new man came over the horizon. And she had always been disappointed. A fragment from Pope came to mind: 'Hope springs eternal'. Thus divided between expectation and disappointment, Barbara resolved to wait and see. And yes, she would keep the appointment. Nothing ventured and all that.

2

SARAH

Barbara arranged to meet Sarah at the same restaurant she had patronised the previous day, motivated perhaps by the note she had received. Almost superstitiously, she chose the same table, telling herself as she did so that it was all nonsense. By the time Sarah arrived, she was ready to tell herself it had all been a dream.

Physically, Sarah looked much the same as she had at university, and Barbara wondered if she could say the same of herself. But Sarah looked much happier than Barbara remembered. It was something that shone out of her eyes and betrayed itself in her conversation. As they caught up on one another's lives, Barbara wondered about the cause. At university Sarah had never been much of a social animal. She had been withdrawn, almost as if she were sitting in judgment on her fellow students.

That manner had gone, and Barbara looked surreptitiously for a wedding ring that might explain the change. Marriage often had profound (though not always salutary) effects. There was no ring, Barbara saw with something like relief. Sarah spoke often of someone named Elspeth, and her face lit up whenever she did. Barbara couldn't remember anyone with that name, so she asked who Elspeth was. She was taken aback when Sarah calmly replied, 'My lover.'

There was a challenging look in her eyes as she said it, as though daring Barbara to make something of it. Barbara wisely said nothing, but she did feel a certain envy of the obvious happiness her friend had found in the irregular relationship.

'Daddy and Mummy are of course outraged. He's refused to talk to me since I came out. Mummy's had any number of quiet talks with me, trying to make me see the error of my ways. I get the feeling she's more concerned about the grandchildren she'll never have than anything else. Both of them manage to give the impression I've let them down. At the same time they're asking themselves where they went wrong. So things are pretty strained at home. Luckily, though, I don't have to live there. Elspeth and I have a small semi near Glasgow. Her parents are taking it better than mine.'

Sarah chattered on as Barbara digested the information. It was a sort of revelation. A whole new person had emerged in place of the one she had known at university. The new Sarah would take some getting used to. But through it all there was no hiding the happiness her friend had found, and Barbara felt another stab of envy. She lost track of the conversation, thinking of how remote her chances were of finding the lover she sought. She became aware of her lapse only when Sarah touched her hand and said, 'Penny for 'em.'

'What?' Barbara asked. 'Sorry. I was miles away.'

'I noticed,' Sarah observed dryly. 'Want to tell me about him?'

'There's no "him,"' Barbara said without thinking. And she found herself telling Sarah about her search for the special someone who would make her happy. The confession was made easier by the fact that she was telling her story to another woman. And Sarah's own earlier 'confession' helped her accept her own need to Tell All. 'Last night's exercise,' she ended, 'is why I'm wearing trousers today. There's no way for me to go bare-legged without showing the world that I've recently spent a good deal of time tied up.'

'I wondered about your message on the answering machine,' Sarah said. 'It sounded just the least bit out of character. The wrongness was so subtle I missed it. So you want some man to tie you up and ravish you?' Sarah asked, using the old-fashioned word with deliberate irony. 'Better not let the feminists know, or they'll send someone round to pray over you relentlessly until you recant and accept the gospel according to St Andrea.'

Barbara made an impatient gesture, conveying at once her ignorance of the allusion and her lack of sympathy for the views of the rabid feminist mafia. She was about to put her opinion into words when Sarah interrupted her.

'If you're really serious about this, I may be able to help.' Seeing Barbara's look of surprise, Sarah continued, 'Now don't get carried away. I'm not offering to find you a guaranteed soul mate. Everyone has to find their own. But I can introduce you to a friend who is into B&D. And in turn he knows quite a few others who share your particular perversion.'

Barbara smiled at the irony in Sarah's tone. 'Pots shouldn't call kettles black,' she retorted just as lightly, but inside she was afire with all sorts of wild surmises. 'When?' she asked.

'Not today, if that's what you had in mind,' Sarah replied. 'I have to make a few phone calls to see if I can find out when he'll be home again. He's often away on business. Did I mention he's a publisher? Now if that's not a neat dovetailing of interests, I don't know what is. I'd have come better prepared if I'd known I was going to play Cupid's messenger. But maybe we can get you fixed up – or at least point you in the right direction.'

It all sounded too good to be true. The sudden change from despair to eagerness was hard to deal with. Changing the subject, she asked, 'Look, where are you staying? And are you alone? Elspeth not with you?'

'I'm in a decent enough B&B, a place I usually use when I'm in town. And yes, I'm alone. Elspeth had to stay at home to mind the store. We're partners in a small graphic arts business, waiting to be discovered by some big financier who likes to see small struggling businesses become large successful ones while remaining in the hands of the original operators. Only, the kind of angel we're looking for is rather thin on the ground just now.' Sarah smiled. 'Sort of like the Mr Right you're looking for.'

'Come and stay with me,' Barbara offered. 'I'm not in a position to help small businesses with large infusions of cash, but I can at least help the small businessperson (you'll note I'm being careful to use the politically correct term so as not to be accused of sexism) to save on hotel bills. I have a sofa that can be slept on, or we can share the bed unless you're afraid I'll try to seduce you. But I promise not to give Elspeth any cause for concern about your fidelity. And we have some catching up to do.'

Sarah smiled again. 'I'm not worried about your base instincts, but I could always tie you up if I thought you had designs on my fair bod.'

Barbara felt her heart leap at Sarah's words. It was something she had not thought of when she made the offer. But she said as calmly as she could manage, 'Does that mean you'll stay?' She didn't know if Sarah's remark had been serious, and suddenly she remembered her dreadful encounter with the female B&D 'expert'. Definitely not something she wanted to repeat. She barely caught Sarah's nod of acceptance and her expression of thanks. As they left the restaurant, Barbara found herself telling Sarah the story of that encounter.

Sarah nodded at several points in the narrative, as though Barbara's experience confirmed something she already knew, but she said nothing as she listened to Barbara. At several points in the story she laughed at things which Barbara had not thought funny at the time. Now she found herself laughing as well. It was a relief to be able to see that side of the affair. When Sarah said, 'I think I could manage the affair much better than she did,' Barbara felt her heart leap in excitement once again. Luckily, she didn't have to make any further comment, because she wasn't sure she could keep the excitement from showing in her voice. She might be taking Sarah's remarks too seriously.

As they were walking the last few blocks to Barbara's apartment, Sarah took over the conversational duties. She spoke of her earliest attempts to connect with a sympathetic soul. Her experiences had been more brutal than Barbara's because she tended to be the passive part of the duo, and because she had had several lesbian affairs, while Barbara had still to meet her match. As Sarah described some of her experiences, Barbara realised that her knowledge of lesbians and their life-style was seriously deficient, barely rudimentary for someone who thought of herself as an educated liberal person.

As the 'passive' partner, Sarah had encountered some women who were quite brutally aggressive. They tended, she had found, to take out their anger and frustrations on the passive partner much as heterosexual couples did. And for similar reasons. Some of them were outright sadists, a point Barbara had not considered. She had thought (realising that she never had) that women didn't go in for that sort of behaviour – at least with other women. As Sarah talked, Barbara found herself amazed at the variety of her friend's life. Barbara had tried out only one or two modes of sex. Sarah had tried out at least a dozen.

Barbara made the coffee and kicked off her shoes for a long talk. She spoke of her collection of B&D gear, and about her experience the previous evening, feeling her embarrassment melt away when her friend offered no censure, nodding understandingly as the tale unfolded. When it was done, Sarah said, 'Show me your collection.' Barbara took her into the bedroom and showed her the contents of her special drawer. Sarah's matter-of-fact acceptance of it all made Barbara feel much easier.

'Show me your legs,' Sarah said without preamble, and Barbara found herself lowering her trousers. Sarah touched the fading rope marks on Barbara's thighs, sending a shock through her body so that she jumped before she could control herself. Next, Sarah examined the braided nylon cord but said only, 'Maybe you need something thicker. This stuff cuts in too deeply.' When Barbara said nothing, she asked, 'Or do you like the feeling of thin cords?'

Barbara nodded at that. 'I like the way the cords bite. But I probably overdid it last night. Planned on too long, I mean. But I enjoyed it, even the panic when I couldn't reach the box. Well, anyway I enjoyed it afterwards, after I had got loose.'

'You like to get as close to the real thing as possible,' Sarah commented.

Again Barbara nodded, not trusting herself to say anything in case her voice betrayed her excitement. She was trembling.

Sarah came to a decision. 'Take off all your clothes,' she commanded. She turned to rummage in the drawer containing the bondage gear. Apparently she expected no argument. Barbara stepped silently out of her trousers and removed her pants. The silence was broken only by the light clinking noise Sarah made as she sifted through the collection of chains. When she turned to face Barbara, she held a pair of handcuffs and a set of leg-irons.

Barbara was in the act of removing her brassière. She turned a bright pink all over when she saw Sarah look her over. She tried to cover her embarrassment with a light remark, 'Will I do?' She didn't stop to think what she might do for.

Sarah said slowly and clearly, so that there would be no mistake, 'You're lovely. Always remember that. Don't let anyone tell you any different.'

These words, coming from another woman, made Barbara flush again, but this time there was less embarrassment and more pleasure. And a curious sense of well-being, as if she believed for the first time that someone else might consider her beautiful.

'Sit on the bed,' Sarah commanded. She knelt and locked the leg-irons around Barbara's ankles, stopping to kiss the marks made by the ropes at ankles, knees, and thighs, lingering there, as if waiting for a signal from Barbara. When none came, Sarah moved higher up and kissed her friend's labia, her tongue darting, seeking the centre.

Barbara sat still, hardly daring to breathe for fear of breaking the spell. She felt as if she were on fire, and only this brief bit of foreplay had been necessary to bring her to that state.

Sarah drew back, trailing her hands down Barbara's thighs and pushing herself erect. She held out a hand, and helped Barbara to stand up as well. 'Hold out your hands,' Sarah said. Silently Barbara did so, trembling slightly as Sarah locked the handcuffs onto her wrists. She put the keys into her pocket and, facing Barbara squarely, leaned forward to kiss her open-mouthed. Then, taking her manacled hands, she led her slowly into the living room so that she wouldn't trip on the short chain between her ankles.

Barbara followed docilely. She was excited but felt no need to hurry things. She felt safe in Sarah's hands, content to be led at her pace and in whatever direction she chose. There was no sense of urgency. She felt as if she were swimming in warm water that buoyed her up, cradled her and held her safe. Sarah led her to the sofa and let go of her hands. Barbara let them drop, making no effort to cover herself. She felt the steel bands on her wrists touch her *mons veneris*. It seemed as if a spark of electricity leaped straight from the handcuffs to her body at the contact. She lowered her gaze until she was looking at Sarah's shoes. Barbara felt a strong urge to take them off and kiss her toes, something she had never thought of before. But she did nothing, waiting for some direction from her friend.

Sarah leaned forward abruptly and kissed each of Barbara's nipples in turn, her lips sending more electric shocks to her sex. Barbara swayed, feeling her knees go weak with excitement. She moaned softly.

'Sit down, Barbara. You look as if you're about to fall anyway.' Sarah's voice sounded just the least bit tremulous as well. Apparently the excitement wasn't all one-sided.

Barbara sat with a feeling of relief, the cloth rough against her bare skin. She was breathing rapidly and there was a hollow, fluttery feeling in her chest. It had been some time since she had felt this way. Maybe back in her university days, just before taking an examination. But now there was none of the apprehension she remembered from those occasions.

Sarah crossed the room to lock the door. Barbara felt a delicious sinking in her stomach as the bolt shot home. Sarah, however, defused the moment by remarking, 'Elementary, my dear Hilson. Never get up to sexual perversions without first locking the door. The thought police are everywhere.' She seated herself in the armchair opposite Barbara and kicked off her shoes. 'When folksingers of the female persuasion take their shoes off on stage, it's a sign of their desire to become more intimate with their audience. Let's talk intimately about you. You've already bared your body. It's time you did the same thing for your soul, isn't it?'

Barbara's mouth was dry. She swallowed and licked her lips. Suddenly she found she had nothing to say. A shyness she had not felt before overcame her at just the moment she wanted to speak.

Sarah waited.

'I . . . I keep a journal.' Barbara was surprised to hear her voice uttering these words. 'You remember how our lecturers at university urged us to get into the habit, to write things down as they occurred to us? I guess . . . the habit stuck. I . . . put things down there I never tell anyone else. I'd like you . . . to read it.' She made as if to stand, intending to fetch the book. The idea of sitting quietly while Sarah read about her fantasies was suddenly very appealing.

Sarah waved her back. 'Where is it?'

'In the drawer below my . . . collection. Are you going to read it?'

'Yes, if you want me to,' Sarah replied.

Barbara nodded. As Sarah rose, she forced herself to speak once more. 'Sarah? Sarah, would you . . . gag me before you begin? Please?' Barbara felt a constriction in her throat. She felt as if she had to drag the words out, and there was a shuddery, all-gone sensation in her stomach.

'You don't want to be able to stop me once I get started?' Sarah asked. 'In case you get cold feet?' she continued with a smile.

Barbara nodded once again, and Sarah left the room. Barbara could hear the sound of drawers opening, the rattle of chain as Sarah rummaged once more in her collection. She fought down the rising excitement that threatened to choke her. Wait. There was plenty of time. There was the rest of the weekend. And more, until it was time for Sarah to go back to Glasgow and Elspeth.

Sarah came back with the familiar leather-bound notebook. 'You've kept this all those years? Sometimes I wish I had got into the habit.'

Barbara sat still as Sarah came closer, her eyes fixed on the things she held in her hands. Barbara recognised the gag she had used last night. Sarah had also brought a length of chain with a snap hook at each end.

'The rules have changed a bit. I didn't know I was going to be reading this.' Sarah indicated the journal, which she had set down on the coffee table. 'Are you sure you wouldn't rather tell me about it?'

Dry-mouthed, Barbara whispered, 'No.'

'Okay. Here's what we'll do. Once I get started you can't stop me. The gag will take care of that, as you intended. I don't want you to make any noise unless you're in distress. When I want you to speak, I'll remove the gag.'

Barbara nodded her acquiescence.

'I want you to sit here. I'll sit across the room, or move anywhere I choose. I'm going to chain your ankles to the coffee table to ensure you stay put. Sarah held up the length of chain and Barbara nodded once more.

'One last thing,' Sarah continued. 'I'm going to put your hands behind your back in case you're tempted to remove the gag. Judging by what you've already said, you'll probably find that more exciting anyway. All clear?'

Barbara nodded once again, the fluttery feeling making her feel weak all over. This was perilously close to her fantasy.

Sarah snapped the chain to Barbara's leg-irons and connected the other end to the coffee table. Then she took the key from her pocket and unlocked the handcuffs. Barbara brought her arms behind her, and Sarah turned her hands so that they were back to back before she replaced the handcuffs.

Barbara looked questioningly at her and moved her arms. This method was new to her. She had always cuffed her hands palm to palm.

'More comfortable that way,' Sarah explained, 'especially if you have to spend a long time in handcuffs. It doesn't work so well with rope because the veins in the insides of the wrists lie too near the surface and are too easily constricted.'

Barbara wondered where she had learned so much about B&D. Barbara herself had learned mainly by trial and error, aided only by the sometimes useful pictures she had seen in magazines. Barbara saw that she was about to be gagged. She moistened her lips to speak. 'Sarah? Would you . . . take off your clothes before you begin reading? I'd like to . . . look at you.' She indicated her handcuffs by moving her arms. 'I won't be able to touch you.'

Sarah thought for a moment, and then nodded. 'Okay. That seems fair. We'll both be naked. I'll tantalise you with my bod and you'll just have to sit there.' With a smile she added, 'I really don't care if you touch me, but just now we're playing your game. It'll be different when we play mine.'

Barbara opened her mouth to receive the gag at a sign from Sarah. She stuffed it in, expertly trapping Barbara's tongue behind the wad of used tights. Once again Barbara was surprised at her friend's grasp of the fundamentals. Sarah pulled the scarf tightly between Barbara's teeth, then knotted it behind her head.

She stepped back to observe the effect. 'Nice,' was all she said, but she smiled at Barbara as she picked up the journal and moved across to the armchair. She began to undress, facing Barbara so that she could look as much as she liked. Sarah began to undulate as she took off her clothes, the motions exaggerated like those of a striptease dancer.

She was a striking blonde. Her hair was worn longer than was fashionable, perhaps in keeping with her role as the 'passive' partner in the relationship. She wore a soft cotton dress that outlined her figure. Sarah reached up behind her to unzip it, then pulled it off over her head, her breasts tightening beneath her lacy bra as she raised her arms. She unsnapped the bra and let her breasts spring free. They weren't heavy, more pointed than otherwise, but they fitted her frame. No sag, and her nipples were set in wide dark areolae.

Sarah removed her tights and flung them in Barbara's

face, much as a stripper will fling some of her clothing into the audience. As the material struck her, Barbara caught a faint odour of healthy female mixed with perfume. As Sarah removed her pants, Barbara caught the gleam of something metallic between her thighs, half hidden in the blonde pubic hair. Her curiosity was aroused, but Sarah's rules (and, incidentally, the gag) prevented her from asking the obvious question.

Sarah sat down and opened the journal. She read silently for the most part, smiling occasionally to herself, and looking up at Barbara from time to time, as if trying to fit together the person sitting across from her and the woman revealed in the book. For a long time she was silent. Barbara shifted on the sofa with a rattle of chain and a creak from the cushion. Sarah didn't look up. Whenever Sarah shifted her position, Barbara caught the same metallic gleam between her thighs.

Sarah smiled, then chuckled. Finally she laughed out loud. Barbara wanted to make an indignant remark. Surely she wasn't that funny. But she remembered Sarah's rules (and the gag) and did nothing. Sarah looked up and spoke. 'I'm reading your account of the visit to the B&D expert. It must have been awful.' Nevertheless she burst out laughing again, and Barbara was mortified. Perhaps it hadn't been such a good idea letting Sarah read the journal

At length Sarah got up and crossed the room to kneel in front of Barbara. 'Poor dear. Let me kiss it better.' There was a tone of light mockery in her voice, but there was none in what she did next. Sarah looked directly into Barbara's eyes as she bent forward to kiss her on the mouth. Barbara's mouth was held open by the gag, and Sarah's kiss seemed to go right down her throat. She was almost choking with excitement. When Sarah bent lower and kissed her nipples, Barbara felt a spike of pleasure drive through her belly. She was going to come. She felt dizzy with the knowledge that she was Sarah's captive and couldn't escape anything the other woman wanted to do to her.

Sarah's hands were on her breasts, cupping them,

squeezing them, her fingers teasing the nipples. Barbara thought she would go out of her mind. Her head fell back, the cords in her neck taut beneath the skin. She was coming. She couldn't stop herself. A long-drawn 'Ummmmmmmnnnngg' began low in her throat. Sarah looked up quickly, as if to reassure herself that Barbara was all right. She saw immediately what was happening, and applied herself again to making Barbara come.

Barbara was twisting her body from side to side as the spasms in her sex spread through her. Sarah hadn't even touched her labia or clitoris but she was already out of control, moaning continuously. She was on the verge of passing out, but still she came.

Barbara didn't know how long it went on. When she began to take an interest in things again, Sarah had taken the gag out and was looking worriedly at her friend. 'So you're back with us,' she remarked lightly, belying her concern. 'I can't remember anyone coming as you did. You frightened me badly. I thought you were having a heart attack. How long did you say it was since the last one?'

Barbara drew a deep shuddery breath. She was lying back against the sofa cushions and Sarah was holding her. She was disturbingly aware of her closeness. Sarah hadn't removed the handcuffs, and she appeared to have forgotten them. Barbara didn't like to ask her to take them off. It might look as if she was ungrateful. She wasn't sure she wanted her hands free anyway, at least not just yet. In fact, now that there was someone around, she felt as if she could stay like this for days. She said only that she was all right.

She felt weak in the aftermath of the orgasm, amazed by the strength of her reaction, considering that Sarah had only fondled her breasts. It had to be the result of the bondage – her helplessness, someone else having control of her. Better than the best she could achieve with her own resources. Instant addiction, as she had thought it might be. And what would happen when her captor turned her attention to her cunt and clitoris? She trembled slightly at the idea, and thought 'good thing I'm sitting down'. But she was forgetting her manners. Barbara straightened up and kissed Sarah – her eyes, her mouth, which opened to receive her. 'Thank you,' she breathed.

'Does that mean you liked it?' Sarah asked with a smile. 'I couldn't tell just by your reaction.'

'Do you mean that all your partners pass out on you?' Barbara asked.

'Well, almost all of them,' Sarah replied. 'The rest are the real hard cases. They'll only admit that the earth moved and the stars were wrenched from their courses. But you can't please everybody.'

'Put me down among the more easily satisfied ones, then.'

The barriers were suddenly all gone. They were talking like old friends, and Barbara asked herself how she had let them drift apart. She resolved not to let it happen again. She remembered the flash of metal in Sarah's pubic hair, and she knew now was the time to ask about it. She didn't feel any of her earlier embarrassment.

Nor did Sarah. 'Think of it as my wedding ring,' she said. There was no blush or hesitation. 'Elspeth and I wear the same thing, so we can be reminded of the other whenever we're apart.' She stood up and spread her legs so that Barbara could get a better view.

Sarah's labia had been pierced and a series of stainless steel rings had been inserted on either side. Barbara counted eight in all. She had heard of erotic piercing. She had even considered it for herself, but rejected the idea. In her eyes, the whole point of the process was that it be done at someone else's request, or by oneself as a sign of devotion to another. Of course there was an aesthetic aspect to it, but only in private where one's partner could appreciate it. Sarah's erotic piercing was more elaborate, and served another purpose. Threaded through the rings was a light strong chain. In the top end there was a loop which was too large to pass through the rings. In the other end there was another loop with a small padlock through it. Barbara could see that it would just pass through Sarah's rings if the padlock were removed.

The effect was to close Sarah's labia against penetration

– a chastity belt for the surgical age. Barbara's first considerations were practical. 'How do you pee?' she asked. 'And what about . . .?' her voice trailed off.

'Sex,' Sarah finished the thought for her. 'I've given it up for Lent. Or for Elspeth, if you prefer. I've consecrated my bod to her, and we lesbians don't go in for casual affairs, so you needn't get any ideas. Anyway, you haven't got the right equipment.' Sarah's tone was light, self-mocking.

She continued, 'Since you've let me into your deepest secrets, I suppose I should tell you mine. Sit up properly and pay attention. Questions will be asked afterward.' She helped Barbara to find a more comfortable position before resuming. 'I told you there are some sadistic women about. Well, I met one. Her name isn't important. I want to forget her anyway. We had an affair. Like most affairs, it started out amicably enough. Later, when she thought I was properly hooked, she took off the velvet gloves. To give her her due, she took them off finger by finger, so gradually I hardly noticed the change.

'One day she took me to a Harley Street clinic (she wasn't hurting for the readies) without saying why. And I went along, not asking any questions. I don't know if I trusted her or feared her, but I said nothing. She left me there with a nurse. She had handed me over along with an envelope which I now know must have contained the instructions for my piercing.' Sarah indicated her crotch. 'They did the job under local anaesthetic, so I knew what was being done to me at every stage. I have to admit they knew what they were doing. There weren't any complications, and very little pain. Of course,' Sarah admitted with a smile, 'I had to walk bow-legged for a week or so until I began to heal.

'One day she came home with a chain like the one I have now. She threaded it through my rings and padlocked it just as you see. Then she told me to get dressed, that we were going out. Did I tell you that she kept me naked in her house? She locked up all the clothes when she went out. I suppose she thought I might run away if I could get dressed. Or maybe it was just her way of asserting her dominance over me. It hadn't crossed my mind to leave her at that point. I was so naive.'

Sarah paused as if collecting her thoughts. 'This is beginning to sound like the classic tale of the innocent maiden from the provinces corrupted by the cynical, worldly older woman. But I connived at my corruption, if that's what it was. The truth is, I liked most of the things she did to me, or rather the things I let her do to me, and the things we did together. The progress of the ruined maid wasn't all painful or forced.'

Barbara admired Sarah's calm detachment and her sense of humour and of the ridiculous – even when she was describing her own experiences. 'Oh, Sarah, my dear, this does everything crown/Who would have supposed I'd see you in town?'

Sarah picked it up, laughing as they finished the paraphrase of Hardy's poem in chorus: 'And whence such fair garments, such prosperi-tee?/"Oh, didn't you know I'd been ruined?" said she.'

And as they laughed Barbara remembered how they had laughed at the same poem at university. This was more like the Sarah of those days. 'I don't think we'd qualify as maids now – if we ever did. And we're certainly ruined as far as marriage and family life are concerned.

'Anyway,' Sarah continued, 'she laid out the clothes I was to wear. I was happy to have her make the choices for me, and I was happy to try to please her. You can see why, even now, I prefer the passive role. It must be something in me. Or maybe the desire to dominate has been left out of my character. She had decided to dress me like the fantasy girls who model women's clothes for male buyers. A mini dress with a tight skirt, crotchless tights, push-up half-bra so that I was presented on a plate, spike-heeled shoes. I should have started to worry when I saw what she was wearing. She chose a leather outfit for herself, very butch, more mannish than most men.

'On the way to the club in the taxi she made me raise my skirt and spread my legs. I was embarrassed because the taxi driver couldn't avoid seeing the display. I refused at first. A most unpleasant look crossed her face, then she slapped me, hard, across the mouth, forehand and backhand. My head was ringing and I felt terribly confused. She had never struck me like that before. She hissed at me, "Open your legs, bitch!" And I did. She snapped a lead to my chain and wrapped it around her hand. She held it taut all the way to the club. The driver saw it all but didn't interfere. He might have done if I had asked him to, but all I could think of was what would happen if I resisted her. She might throw me out. That seemed like the worst thing that could happen at the time. Later I learned that there are other, worse things.' Sarah smiled grimly at the memory.

'At the club – a place I had never seen before – she made me pay the driver. I fumbled some notes at him, avoiding his eyes. My face was burning with humiliation which, it turned out, was the object of the exercise. It also turned out that there was a lot more in store for me. She got out of the cab and tugged at my lead. I almost fell getting out. If she had really pulled hard, she could have injured me. I was led stumbling and crying across the pavement. A doorman held the door for us, paying no attention to me. He must have seen hundreds of similar scenes.

'It was dark inside, as such places had to be. I couldn't see anything for several minutes. There was music, and crowd noises. She led me across the floor and into the toilet. I was getting badly frightened by then. She had never treated me this way before. Sure, she sometimes tied me up, especially for sex. That didn't bother me, and she was always gentle and thorough, making sure I enjoyed myself. And when she left me chained at home while she was out, I knew she would take care of me when she got back. And I enjoyed waiting for her while she was away.

'But this was a totally different person. I was terrified. I pleaded with her to take me home, away from this place. She slapped me again.

'I felt dizzy and thought I was going to be sick, but she only told me not to dare spoil my clothes – or hers. She grasped my face with one hand, her fingers in the angle of my jawbones, forcing my mouth open. With her other hand she stuffed something inside my mouth. I saw her reach into her handbag and bring out a roll of packaging tape. I suppose I could have bolted, but I was frozen to the spot. I remember thinking, this can't be happening to me. But it was. She taped my mouth so I couldn't spit out the gag. I was hyperventilating by then, trying to fill my lungs through my nose, and almost choking on my gag.

'She twisted my arms behind my back and put a pair of thumb-cuffs on me. She must have had them in her handbag too. It dawned on me that she had planned all this very carefully, unless some women carry tape and thumb-cuffs around every day. She led me back into the main room, with me trying to keep up. I was still choking and crying, but she ignored me. She fastened my lead to a ring in the floor and left me there. The ring couldn't have been placed there for any other purpose than this. As my eyes adjusted I saw that there were other rings. And other people – men and women – tethered to them in one way or another.

'The crowd was mixed. I saw her talking to a group across the room. Every so often one of them would look in my direction, and my ears would have been burning if the rest of me hadn't been afire with shame and fear. It was obvious that I was the topic of conversation.'

Barbara wanted to hold her friend in her arms, to soothe away the distress that was so evident. But Sarah had not seen fit to remove the handcuffs. The only thing she could do was to lean forward and rest her head on Sarah's shoulder.

Sarah reached up and let her hands rest lightly on Barbara's hair. They sat like that for several minutes before Sarah was ready to resume the narrative. Before she did, however, she helped Barbara shift so that her head was lying in her lap. Sarah seemed to draw strength from the contact. Barbara was content to rest there for as long as necessary. In fact she felt comforted as well, though against what she couldn't say.

Sarah continued, 'Eventually one of the men she was talking to came over to me. Saying nothing, he unfastened my lead and pushed me ahead of him, out of the room and down an even darker hallway. There were doors opening off both sides. He opened one of them and pushed me into a room containing only a table and a bed. It wasn't too hard to figure out what he was going to do. There was a pile of rope under the table which he used to tie my ankles to two of the table legs. I was spread out wide. He raised my skirt. I was too numb to struggle. Somehow I knew he would take no more notice of my reluctance than she had.

'I knew what was coming, and I tried to make myself indifferent. With the front entrance blocked there was only one place for him to go. At least he used a dab of petroleum jelly to make the penetration easier. But I was still so tight he had to slap me to make me relax. When he entered me I thought I'd split. I was making muffled sounds of distress, but he must have known he was hurting me. Too late, I tried to twist myself away. That excited him without helping me.

'Finally it was over, and he withdrew. Before he untied my legs he inserted a plug up my anus, to "keep the fizz in," he said. He took me back to the main room, collected my mistress and drove us to her house. I wore the gag and thumb-cuffs the whole way, and the plug inside me made it very uncomfortable to sit. Just as important was the psychological discomfort. I knew his semen was still inside me, and I wanted to wash it away.

'He dropped us outside her house, she tugged me out of the car by the lead, and he drove away. Once again I thought I'd die of shame, but luckily it was late by then and there was no one about. I came and went almost daily in the neighbourhood and couldn't have borne it if one of the people I spoke to had seen me leashed and gagged being dragged into my lover's house. She led me into the front room and tethered me by my lead to the newel post of the stairs. She went upstairs, and came down almost immediately with a strap. She must have had it ready even before we left, knowing she would use it on me.

'She had beaten me before, but just enough to sting, as a prelude to kissing the light marks and sending me over the moon with pleasure. This time it was in earnest. The gag prevented me from screaming. None of the neighbours heard the muffled cries. It was just another quiet, ordinary evening in the neighbourhood. I thought I knew what pain was, but she taught me a thing or two that night. And as she beat me she called me whore and bitch, accusing me of enjoying sex with men. As "proof" she drew the plug from my anus, allowing a thin stream of semen to run down my legs and stain my tights. She seemed like a madwoman.

'When the fit passed I was leaning against the post, ready to collapse, held erect only by the knowledge that my lead would come up short before I hit the floor. And then she tried to kiss it all away, to make me come, to make things as they were before. It didn't work. Something was broken and it couldn't be fixed. I think she knew then she had gone too far, because she never let me free after that. Afraid I'd run away, even if I had to do it naked. I don't know if I would have taken off in the altogether,' Sarah said in a stronger voice, as if she was regaining her sense of the ridiculous. 'It would certainly have given the neighbours something to talk about,' she finished with a chuckle.

Barbara knew that she was coming out of the depression that telling her tale had brought on. 'I can see why you don't like men very much. You might even be forgiven for having a low opinion of women as well. But tell me, how did you come to meet Elspeth and fall in love with her?'

'Through her,' Sarah replied. 'Or you might say in spite of her.'

Barbara didn't need to ask who the vehement 'her' referred to.

'I hadn't been out for months. Aside from the fact that she kept me naked, I was kept chained to the newel post of the stairway. It was a long chain, not too heavy. I could reach the loo and the kitchen. And there was the TV if things got too boring. She made me wear handcuffs and leg-irons – extra insurance against escape, I suppose. When I woke up, I was already in chains. They never came off until Elspeth rescued me.

'I suppose I could have broken a window and screamed for help,' Sarah continued. 'I really don't know why I didn't. Maybe I was becoming too accustomed to my prison, feeling safe there and afraid of the outside. And there was always the embarrassment factor. Not only did I not want to be seen naked and in chains; I didn't want people to know I had become so abjectly dependent on this woman. Then there was the fear of the publicity that attends on any case involving lesbianism. And deep down I suppose I kept hoping the other person would re-emerge, and things would go back to the way they had been. But it never happened.

'When I had been her prisoner for more than two months, my warder thought I had been tamed. I never protested at anything she did to me, though fortunately she never beat me again as she had done on that awful night. I think she had frightened herself too. Anyway, she decided I could be safely taken out in the right company – other gays and lesbians, of whom she knew many. So one evening she announced that we were going out.

'I spooked at once, remembering the last time we had gone out. No, no, nothing like that, she assured me. Just a private dinner party and drinks at a friend's house. I could even choose what I wanted to wear. It had been so long since I had worn clothes, let alone had the chance to choose them, that I agreed at once. She insisted that I have my rings padlocked, but she did take off the handcuffs and leg-irons. They were hardly suitable attire for a *soirée*, she said.

'Elspeth was one of the guests. She was seated right next to me, and I was immediately attracted to her – a fact not lost on our host, who hadn't an unmalicious bone in his body. He lost no time in calling *her* attention to me and Elspeth *tête à tête*. The thunderous look that came over her face was priceless, but there was nothing she could do until she got me home. And just then I knew I had no intention of ever letting her get me home again.

'If Elspeth hadn't been there I might never have plucked up the courage to leave. Just by talking to me she showed me that I was interesting to other people, and she showed me that another way of life was available to me if I had the courage to seek it. It's so easy to get into a rut. I would have returned to that house and lived in fear of another outbreak of her madness. I knew the handcuffs and leg-irons were waiting for me when we returned, because she had already told me she liked me in chains.

'There, Barbara. Don't get so excited. I'm describing *hell.* Though you might not think so,' Sarah said with a smile. 'I hope you find the right person for your fantasies. Otherwise you'll be in serious trouble. Then again, you might not think of it in that way. *Chacun à son enfer*.

'Elspeth and I happened to be in the loo at the same time. Or maybe it wasn't so accidental on her part. Anyway, I was having some trouble aiming the golden stream because of my rings. She couldn't help but notice. She helped me. We exchanged confidences. True love was born. We fell into one another's arms and lived happily ever after.' Sarah paused for effect, then continued. 'Well, not quite. Their loo – any loo – is not the best place for romance to flower. But it is the approved, even the preferred, place for hatching plots, as any reader of spy novels can tell you. We decided to spring me. Elspeth offered to let me spend the night at her place, and decide later what to do.

'The only problem was the key to me. My mistress kept it on a chain around her neck. But Elspeth solved that problem easily enough. We agreed to keep apart for the remainder of the evening so as to make her less suspicious, while Elspeth asked our host to help get my erstwhile lover more than a little drunk. This he readily agreed to do, being as malicious as the day is long. He loved the intrigue, too. She had to be poured into a taxi for the ride home. She never noticed the friendly lady who helped me get her from door to door, and then safely inside her own. The key to me changed hands (or rather necks) en route.

'Elspeth helped me arrange a suitable exit. We were having fits of hysterical laughter as we packed my clothes and hers. We didn't plan to keep hers, merely to borrow them to return at a later date, after certain events would have (quite publicly) transpired. My mistress was snoring inelegantly as we stripped her naked and tumbled her into the bed.

'Elspeth and I bowed elaborately to one another, making sweeping you-first and after-you gestures toward her. In the end we worked together. We spread-eagled her on the bed and tied her wrists and ankles to the four posts. Not original, but highly effective when you don't want your captive to get loose. While Elspeth gagged her, I went to the larder to retrieve two rather large and fragrant salami sausages. These we stuffed well up into the obvious places, tying them with grocery twine so she wouldn't be able to eject them prematurely.

'It was Elspeth's sense of fun – one of the things I love so much in her – that carried the whole thing off. As we were about to leave for the last time, she thought of a final touch. With a lipstick, she wrote on the mirror, "The door is open and the police will arrive soon after 14.00, so don't worry. In the meantime, enjoy the salami." *Then* we ran off together to fall in love. She was duly found, and rated a short column in the daily papers the next day. We put her clothes into a storage locker and mailed the key to her. I've often wondered how she managed when she found herself without a stitch of clothes in the house.'

Barbara could tell that Sarah had reached the good times. Sarah's face lit up as she described her exit from the old life and the beginning of the new. She smiled more often as she spoke. 'One thing, though, Sarah; why are you still wearing the rings?'

'That's mostly due to procrastination. You see, that night Elspeth and I were rather busy making the move to her place and arranging the surprise for my old lover. We only got around to unlocking me when we got to her place. She laid the chain and lock aside. I thought she threw them away. Then she laid me in her bed and laid me. It was heaven. Just like coming home again without having your parents nag you about what you ought to do. And things stayed that way, whenever they weren't getting better.

'I thought I'd go one day and have the rings removed –

get rid of the past and the memories. Elspeth never mentioned the rings. She left the decision to me. I feel about doctors the way most people feel about dentists. The weeks dragged on and I found one reason or another to put off the job. In that time Elspeth and I were growing closer. We decided to move back near Glasgow. She had better contacts there, and I had only bad memories of London. And as I said, her parents were more understanding than mine. So we went.

'But just before we went Elspeth went through a period of withdrawal. It was nothing to do with me, or with us, she assured me. I was worried, but she put it down to the hassle of moving from one end of the country to the other. Then about a week before the move, with everything half-packed and chaos everywhere, I came home with a Chinese take-away meal, only to find the place in total darkness. I thought she had run away. She had been acting strangely. But the explanation was more mundane. The electricity company had mixed things up and cut the power a week earlier than we had agreed.

'Elspeth was sitting in front of a coal fire in the nude. She was waiting for me, and when I came in she rose and took me in her arms. I was damp from the bus ride and the walk, and she was warm from the fire, the light glowing softly on her bare skin. I melted, as they say in the romantic novels. It was so good to be with her, to have her back with me. But it got better almost immediately. She took the packages from me and laid out our meal before the fire. Then she lit candles and set them on the table. It was all cosy and romantic. I took off my own clothes while she was doing this.

'We sat opposite one another, cross-legged on the carpet, and I caught a gleam of metal between her thighs, in her crotch, exactly as you saw me today. She was watching me, waiting for my reaction, and she spread her thighs so I could see exactly what it was. She had had herself pierced as I was. Her "withdrawal" had been the healing period. I couldn't speak for a moment. She had gone through that for me. Elspeth said simply, "Now we match, Sarah." I didn't know loving could be like that. It never was, with boys, or with the woman who had pierced me.

'That night, after we had made love for perhaps the hundredth time, Elspeth got up from the bed and fetched a small jewellery box. When I opened it, there were two chains for closing our rings. One of them I recognised from the bad old days. I thought she had disposed of it. I handed her the other one, the new one, but she insisted on taking my old one. She said she was taking the bad memories on herself. I was to have the new chain to remind me to look forward, not back, and to remind me of her, not the other woman. I cried, and so did she, and we fell asleep in one another's arms.

'Now, whenever we're apart, we ceremoniously lock the chain for each other. She keeps the key to mine, and I to hers. And sometimes, to remind ourselves of the bond we share, we sleep chained together by a longer chain that locks onto our individual chains. We are joined, centre to centre.' Sarah got up and fetched a photograph from her handbag. Sarah and Elspeth stood with their arms around one another's waists. They were both nude, and a light chain joined them, looping down almost to their knees.

Barbara found herself crying a bit at the conclusion of the tale, and at the photograph.

Sarah said, 'I hope those are happy tears.'

Barbara didn't know. She moved her head until she could kiss Sarah's stomach, just above her pubic hair. Sarah held her tightly for a long moment, then announced it was time to get up. She got the keys and unlocked Barbara's handcuffs and leg-irons.

Barbara sat up and stretched her cramped arms and shoulders. 'Telling stories makes me hungry. Let's have something to eat. I can offer you ham sandwiches Barbara or omelette Barbara. If you're prepared to wait, I can do something more elaborate.'

'Chinese take-away,' Sarah said. 'Have a holiday.'

'That means one of us will have to get dressed,' Barbara replied.

'Then let's both get dressed and have a sit-down meal instead.'

So they did, laughing at one another's jokes and enjoying the sense of shared fun. Barbara knew she would feel regret when it was time for Sarah to go, but she also knew it wasn't right for her to interfere in her friend's life – especially not for selfish reasons. And her reasons would all be selfish. She had nothing to offer even remotely like the relationship Sarah and Elspeth had. She was looking for something as permanent as theirs seemed to be, and at the same time she was looking for a fundamentally different type of relationship, with a man. She might be able to visit Sarah and Elspeth. She probably would do so. But she would be an outsider. She had to make her own way. But there was no reason not to enjoy Sarah's company while she could. So the dinner party for two was a happy one.

On Sunday morning Barbara and Sarah made love. It was Barbara's first lesbian encounter, though she didn't say so. She didn't want to make Sarah feel as if she were opposed to the idea. But she had no clear idea of what she was supposed to do. Sarah had to guide her. She manoeuvred them into the sixty-nine position, with Barbara on the bottom.

'Let me lead. This time I'll be the butch one, and you can play the part of the shy, timid virgin – if you can still remember the lines. It's easier that way if you don't know what to do. You lie there and enjoy until you get the idea.' Sarah straddled Barbara and lowered her face to Barbara's crotch.

The alienness of the experience almost put Barbara off. The ambience was all wrong. Sarah didn't use the kind of foreplay her men companions employed. And there was something disturbing about being in bed with a woman doing *it*. Things didn't improve until Sarah applied her lips and tongue to the small slippery button at the apex of her friend's thighs. Thereafter things improved rapidly, from Barbara's point of view. Sarah's own crotch hovered invitingly above Barbara's face, and she raised her head to apply her own lips to the target. She nad forgotten the chain that Sarah wore. There was no way she could reach Sarah's clitoris with her tongue. But she could worm a finger into Sarah's cunt. That seemed to be a good idea, if Sarah's reaction was any guide. She was moist and receptive. Between what Sarah was doing to her, and what Barbara was doing to Sarah, they both managed to enjoy several very satisfactory climaxes.

Afterward, they talked. Sarah appeared to feel no guilt at being 'unfaithful' to Elspeth. 'We're not all that exclusive,' she explained. There's always room for a friend. Or two.'

Barbara had enjoyed the experience, but not as much as she had enjoyed even her own self-induced orgasms the day before. The element of bondage and domination was lacking, even though Sarah had taken the lead – been 'dominant'. Barbara still wanted a man to share her fantasies, even though she liked Sarah and enjoyed her company. The idea of being bound and raped by her dream-lover still made her go all shivery inside. She hoped that Sarah's friend could help her realise that fantasy.

On Monday morning they both got ready to go out, Sarah to attend to her business, and Barbara to go to the office. For her part, Barbara felt an undercurrent of excitement as she thought of meeting the stranger for lunch. The anticipation buoyed her up through the morning, and when lunch time came she found herself hurrying to keep the appointment. 'You're only meeting another man,' she told herself. 'Keep calm.'

He was already at the table. A good sign, Barbara thought. She didn't like the idea of waiting for him in public. He stood as she approached, and she thought he was even more handsome than she remembered. She began to wonder if this was going to be her lucky day.

'I'm Frank. Frank Richards. We didn't get around to introductions last time, unfortunately. I had to track you down.'

'How did you find my address?' Barbara wanted to know.

'I followed you back to your work place and asked the receptionist. She was enough of a romantic to want to help others out.'

Barbara said nothing about her excitement at coming across his note amongst the post. The fact that she was here should be enough to show she was interested.

He interrupted the conversation about jobs and interests to tell her that he had already ordered for them. But would she like a drink before lunch arrived?

She felt a momentary irritation at his taking charge without consulting her.

It must have shown, because he added quickly that he was a regular here and knew the chef and the menu. 'Besides,' he said, 'I wanted to impress you with my *savoir faire*.' The remark made him seem boyish and eager to please.

Barbara relaxed and they resumed their conversation. Frank was 'in stocks and shares,' as he phrased it. He was rather vague about it, and Barbara didn't know enough about the subject to ask intelligent, probing questions. At least (judging by his dress) he seemed to be doing well enough. She found herself warming to him as they ate. This time he asked for her phone number and he promised to call before the end of the week.

The rest of the day seemed like an anticlimax after the lunch-time rendezvous, but the prospect of going home to Sarah rather than to an empty flat made her feel better. She decided to work from home the next day. She intended to prepare a nice meal for Sarah.

Sarah had already started on their tea when Barbara got home. The aroma of pasta and meat sauce greeted her when she opened the door. Sarah called out to her to come through into the kitchen. She had bought a bottle of Chianti, and there were two full glasses standing on the table. Barbara sat down gratefully and picked up her glass.

'Open your mouth and close your eyes,' Sarah recited as she turned from the stove with a spoonful of what she was simmering.

'Ummmm,' Barbara said. 'When can we eat? I'm starved.'

'You like it?' Sarah asked. Before Barbara could answer she rushed on, 'It's my first attempt at spaghetti Bolognese, the only Italian dish the English recognise.'

'I'm glad you told me that. After I'd tasted it I was afraid we were in for some Third World ratatouille. It's so nice to know what one is eating. No, it's really good. I don't often get that adventurous when I'm cooking for just myself.' Barbara began to hum a tune as she made the salad, not really aware of it.

'Did you meet someone nice today, or do you just like to make salad?'

'His name is Frank,' Barbara said. She went on to tell Sarah the details of their luncheon. When she came to the matter of his ordering for them both, Sarah broke in to remark that he seemed quite assertive. Barbara thought about her own feeling of irritation. Could he be trying to take charge even at this early stage in the relationship? From there it was a short step to asking, was he trying to be dominant? And then, was he the one (at last) who would do to her what she wanted so badly? Barbara surprised herself at the quick string of mental associations that sprang from Sarah's careless remark.

But Sarah merely warned her to be careful before letting him assume too much control too soon. 'Don't let him see the handcuffs in your eyes,' was how she put it.

The thought so closely paralleled Barbara's own that she blushed. 'God, am I that transparent?'

Sarah smiled broadly. 'Only to those who have normal eyesight. But don't let it worry you. I won't tell a soul. I hope it works out for you. And if it doesn't, be sure to let me know. My friend may still be able to help you. You'll get what you want eventually. Go now and get into something more comfortable. We can eat when you're ready.'

When Barbara came back in her housecoat Sarah had set the table and was pouring out another glass of wine for them. She had turned out the lights and set lighted candles on the table. The effect was softer. More romantic, Barbara would have said in other circumstances. With another woman the effect was more disturbing. There were strange undercurrents in the room.

Even more disturbing, Sarah set the bottle down and began to get out of her clothes. When Barbara did nothing, she said, 'Don't be so cubical.'

Barbara took off her housecoat and hung it on a vacant chair, feeling her nipples tighten as she did so. She didn't look at Sarah, not trusting her own reactions. When she looked up, Sarah was approaching. The candle-light glinted on something metallic in her hand.

'The minute I saw these in the shop window I knew you'd like them.' 'These' were a pair of thumb-cuffs. 'I noticed you didn't have any in your collection.'

Barbara felt her heart turn over. Such a small thing as this could be used to make her helpless. She knew about thumb-cuffs from her reading, but had never expected to have the real thing. She had never seen any for sale, and here was Sarah offering them to her after only one day's visit to *her* town.

Sarah noticed her expression but said only, 'Explanations and directions later. Let's get you into these and we can go on from there.' As she spoke Sarah was moving behind Barbara. She pulled Barbara's arms behind her back and placed her hands palm to palm before locking the tiny cuffs around her thumbs. 'Hold still,' she cautioned. 'I have to double-lock them so they won't tighten and cut off the circulation. You wouldn't be much use to anyone without thumbs. And don't wriggle. You can't get loose.'

'Maybe not, but the captive is required to struggle against her bonds. It's done in all the best stories, and is intended to demonstrate virtue. After she knows she is truly helpless she can relax and enjoy what comes next.'

'Just take my word for it this time,' Sarah said. 'Whatever you do, don't use them when you're alone. Even if you have the key you couldn't use it. There's no way to hold it with your thumbs out of action.'

Sarah's hand on her shoulder urged her to sit. She sank onto the chair, the wood cool against her bare bottom and the backs of her thighs.

Sarah drew her chair closer and set the plates handy. She loaded a fork with spaghetti and sauce, offering it to Barbara. 'You first,' she said.

Barbara bent forward and Sarah thrust the food into her mouth, feeding her like a child. Barbara found the experience both novel and exciting. Being fed made her feel more helpless. A forkful of the sauce slipped down to land with a plop in Barbara's crotch. She jumped and squirmed as the food slipped between her legs.

'Hold still,' Sarah admonished her. 'I'll clean you up later.' She grinned and licked her lips suggestively.

Barbara flushed warmly but held herself still. The strange and exciting meal went on, neither of them saying very much. On Barbara's part the relative silence was partly due to her rising excitement. She wondered if Sarah found the experience as delightful. 'Where did you get the idea of feeding me?'

'My old keeper used to do this to me regularly – her way of letting me know I was dependent on her for everything. Unless she used the whip on me while she ate and I went hungry.' Sarah gave a shudder as she spoke. 'I'm so glad I escaped that. I could tell you some tales guaranteed to make you think twice before turning yourself over to someone else. But then again, they might only make you more eager. There's no accounting for taste.'

The meal ended and Sarah stacked the dishes in the sink. Barbara sat on at the table watching as her friend cleared up. Then Sarah strode purposefully back to the table, kneeling before Barbara's chair. 'Spread your legs,' she commanded. 'It's time for dessert.'

Barbara felt her legs trembling as she moved her thighs apart. Her nipples were hard and tight, crinkly with excitement. Her breasts felt heavy and warm, and she was beginning to breathe rapidly, as if she had just run a race.

Sarah reached for the taut nipples that stared her in the face, and Barbara gasped at the touch. She closed her eyes as Sarah caressed her swollen breasts, cupping them and planting a string of kisses all over their upper and lower slopes. She took the nipples between her fingers and squeezed them. At odd intervals she used her finger-nails to nip the taut flesh.

Barbara had never had someone pay so much attention to her breasts. Sarah was in no hurry to get to the other bits which Barbara usually found so arousing. She was being introduced to another sort of love-making. A whole gourmet course, in fact. It was hard to hold still while such things were being done to her, and Barbara showed her appreciation by shifting and squirming on the chair.

Sarah was kneeling in front of the chair, between Barbara's parted thighs. Without taking her hands from Barbara's breasts, she bent down to kiss her friend's *mons veneris* and her labia. Barbara spread her legs even further, trying to make things easier. Her breath caught on a gasp as Sarah's tongue found her sex. Barbara was beginning to take a keener interest in lesbian sex now that she had been exposed to more of it. It might have been that she was getting over her initial nervousness. And it might have been that Sarah had chosen the better approach the second time around.

Sarah now released Barbara's breasts so as to pay full attention to the rest of the territory. She rested her hands on the tops of Barbara's thighs, caressing gently. She slipped her tongue between her labia, finding Barbara already wet and parted. Her clitoris hardened under the gentle but insistent probing of Sarah's tongue and the nipping and nibbling of her teeth.

Barbara was whimpering tensely, gasping with pleasure whenever Sarah's tongue or teeth found a sensitive spot. Indeed she felt as if her whole body was one great sensitive spot, but she was glad Sarah was concentrating on her crotch. She was teetering on the brink of her first orgasm. Sarah pushed her over the edge with her busy mouth, and she cried out as the waves of pleasure spread from her centre to her belly and thighs. She felt as if she was rocking on the crests of successive dark waves, each one raising her higher than the last. Barbara closed her eyes tightly in order to concentrate on inner matters. If her hands had been free, she would have been holding Sarah's head against her.

But there was no need. Sarah wasn't going anywhere. She was doing her level best to make sure Barbara enjoyed herself – exactly as a good friend would. Her arms slipped around Barbara's waist and pulled them tightly together.

She used her hands to hold Barbara's behind her back, quieting their frantic twisting and jerking as she came. The next time Barbara cried out in pleasure Sarah paused for an electric moment, raising her head to spread kisses across her lower belly and the tops of her thighs. Then she bent her head once more to the wet cunt in front of her.

Barbara closed her thighs, holding Sarah's head and face against herself. She showed no sign of getting tired. Instead she held herself tensely, alert for the onset of the next orgasm. It didn't take long, and Barbara cried out again as she came.

Sarah came up for air and let her head rest in Barbara's lap while she caught her breath. Barbara saw that her face was flushed, and she felt a momentary pang when she realised that Sarah was doing everything to her and she couldn't reciprocate.

'Sarah, let me up so I can do you. It's not fair this way.'

Sarah smiled and shook her head, no. 'I want to do this. I want you to enjoy it all. We can worry about me later, if you insist on worrying. But I am enjoying this. Truly,' she added as she saw the doubting look on Barbara's face. 'Relax and let me handle it.'

Barbara could do nothing to alter things, but she resolved to do something to please Sarah later when she was free.

Eventually things slowed down, and Sarah stood up in front of the chair. Barbara didn't think she could stand just then. Her legs were distinctly wobbly. Sarah used a teacloth to dry Barbara's crotch. When she was done, she held the cloth to her nose and inhaled deeply. She smiled into Barbara's eyes and let out a deep sigh of appreciation: 'Ummmm! Fresh essence of sex.' Sarah helped Barbara to stand, then guided her through into the living room. She deposited Barbara on the couch and turned the TV on before going to make coffee.

Barbara squirmed into a more comfortable position and settled down to wait. When Sarah came back with the coffee she removed the thumb-cuffs and showed Barbara how they worked. 'When you find your dream partner, get him to use them on you. Then you can think of me while he drives you out of your mind. If you can think of anything,' she said with another smile.

The two women sat on companionably watching TV. When it became chilly in the room Barbara got up and brought the duvet from the bed so they could snuggle together under it. They talked and watched TV until bedtime. Barbara was too tired to do anything more than fall into bed and go to sleep. Tomorrow, she vowed silently, she would do something nice for Sarah – to Sarah – whichever applied. She hadn't any real idea what that might be. So long as she wore the chain and lock there would be no access to her cunt, so the kind of thing she had done for Barbara that evening was out. But there was always the back door, Barbara thought as she drifted off to sleep. She hoped Sarah would like that.

In the morning she got up first, intending to begin to repay Sarah's kindness by making breakfast. When Sarah came into the kitchen and saw what Barbara was doing, she brightened up. 'You'd make someone a good wife, but don't let him know how eager to please you really are. If you're thinking seriously about the tall dark stranger from the restaurant, be especially careful. He sounds like the kind who takes advantage of the too-willing.'

'For heaven's sake, Sarah, I've only just got round to giving him my telephone number. He hasn't even called me. He may never call.'

'You forget, I know what you're thinking of,' Sarah replied.

They began to get dressed in silence. Sarah glanced at Barbara from time to time as though gauging her mood. When she had got to the underwear stage – a pair of tights, a bra and a half-slip – Sarah stopped her. 'Wait there. Don't move.' She fetched the leg-irons and handcuffs that had been lying suggestively around until they were needed. She locked the leg-irons around Barbara's ankles and the handcuffs on her wrists. She double checked the manacles and stepped back to observe the effect.

'You should be able to work that way, Barbara. You'll

just be a little slower with the word processor, but you can entertain yourself by imagining that you've been taken prisoner and are doing forced labour. And you can imagine what will happen to you when I get back. Isn't that what you wanted?' Sarah asked innocently. 'You look fetching enough. Would you like me to call Frank and tell him where he can find you?' She was deliberately trying to excite Barbara with words, enjoying the effect it had on her.

Barbara began to breathe deeply. Her nipples erected themselves beneath the sheer see-through material of her bra.

'See – I told you you were transparent.' Sarah finished dressing and left a few minutes later. She made a show of dropping the keys to Barbara's chains into her handbag. Barbara heard the door lock and realised she was alone and in chains. This was different from the self-inflicted bondage she had been practising. Sarah had taken the keys away with her and there was no way Barbara could get free by herself. She could not leave the flat, nor even answer the door. She really was the captive of someone else and would have to wait for Sarah to come back to free her.

Barbara washed up the breakfast things, awkward in her handcuffs. Then she made herself a cup of coffee and settled down to work on the manuscripts she had brought home. Sarah had been right; she could use her word processor, albeit slowly and awkwardly. She liked the sense of working under duress, a prisoner in her own home. A hostage, she fantasised, letting her imagination loose. Her captor would come for her soon, and he'd . . . The ringing of the telephone startled her from her reverie.

It was Sarah. 'Just jerking your chain,' she said when Barbara answered. 'I was checking to see that you were all right. You never can tell who might walk in on you when you can't escape. I see you haven't managed to get loose.' Her voice hardened in mock-threat, 'You'll never get loose. Don't even try. I expect to find you just as I left you whenever I get back – or else. Enjoy your day.' She hung up.

Barbara pondered the 'whenever.' Sarah hadn't said

when she might return, and so she might be in chains for a long time. That idea excited her anew. She returned to work. Lunch time came and went, and she made herself a sandwich. In mid afternoon the phone rang again. Barbara moved awkwardly to answer it. This time it was Frank. She flushed when she heard his voice. Suppose he guessed she was dressed in nothing but her underwear and her chains? But of course he couldn't guess that, could he? She tried to make her voice seem normal despite the pounding of her heart.

He asked if she was all right. He had been to the restaurant hoping to meet her and when she didn't show up he took a chance and called her at home. Was she free on Saturday night? Barbara knew that Sarah was going back to Glasgow soon, and she wanted to spend as much time with her as she could. But she also wanted to see Frank. In the end she agreed to meet him on Saturday. He had tickets for a concert. 'Just some boring old Wagner,' he said apologetically. He didn't even know if she liked classical music, and they didn't have to go if she didn't want to, but . . . He sounded both eager and diffident at the same time, as if afraid she might refuse. Barbara agreed that that was fine, and she agreed to meet him as planned. Was there any danger she wouldn't? she asked herself. Not likely. No coy maidenly refusal, or even a pause for thought.

After she put the phone down Barbara found herself unable to work any more. She was too busy thinking of the coming Saturday evening. She went to her wardrobe and tried to choose what she would wear. Something attractive, of course. But what? First impressions were important. Some sexy underwear. Best be prepared, she thought. Seduction wasn't totally the result of male planning.

Barbara brought herself up with a jerk. Time enough to do all this later. If she did it too soon she would have too much time for second thoughts. And she was acting like a schoolgirl on her first date. She glanced at the clock. It was getting towards the time she would expect Sarah back. It was getting dark outside. Did she intend to come back that evening?

It got later and later, and still no Sarah. Barbara became increasingly worried and excited. When she finally heard the rattle of keys in the lock, she was fit to be tied – which she was already. Fit to be tied tighter? Never mind, she told herself, the exact phrase wasn't important. Her condition was. Sarah brought fresh French bread and salad things for them – the results of her safari in the wilds of Sainsbury's. 'I see you didn't manage to get loose. Did you try?'

'No. I already know I can't get out of these things without the key. And anyway you know I like this sort of thing. I enjoyed clinking around the place avoiding being seen at the windows. But you could have called. I was getting worried.'

'That was the idea. But you are a proper little slavey, aren't you?' Sarah taunted her. 'Don't let the feminists learn about you. They'd be beating a path to your door trying to raise your consciousness. Though I think you'd be a tough case for them. You already know what you want. But let's leave the ideology and eat.'

Since Sarah made no move to unlock the handcuffs and leg-irons, Barbara concluded that she was expected to prepare the food in her chains. She did so, awkwardly, but enjoying the restricted movement every time her leg-irons came up taut between her ankles, or whenever she had to use both hands because of the handcuffs. She imagined herself the slave girl waiting on her master who would either punish her or make dizzying love to her according to the whim of the moment. When she thought of these things, she could feel her nipples tighten with excitement. The sexual tension was so thick she imagined it would become tangible.

Sarah noticed her agitation. 'Thinking wicked slavey thoughts, are we?'

Barbara blushed and nodded.

Sarah was sitting at the table watching Barbara. She beckoned her over. 'Let's see if we can't make things a bit more exciting for you. Don't move,' she commanded. Sarah rose and opened the larder. She searched for a few moments, then gave an 'Ummm' of satisfaction. She returned with a nearly full jar of honey. Standing behind Barbara, she unsnapped the bra and slid it part way down her arms. Sarah smeared the thick honey onto Barbara's nipples, making them both sticky and erect at the same time.

Barbara caught her breath on a gasp as the thick smooth liquid was massaged into her breasts and over the sensitive nipples. She stood still as Sarah had ordered, but she couldn't prevent the little shudders of excitement that ran through her.

'Like that, do we?' Sarah asked unnecessarily as she continued to arouse her friend. 'Just let me know when you're about to come so I can stop abruptly and leave you hanging.' She smiled as she spoke, and seemed to be enjoying the game as much as Barbara was. But Sarah didn't wait for Barbara to say anything. She gave her nipples a final rub and then pulled the bra back into place over the heavy breasts, pressing the sheer material against them so that it clung wetly. Barbara's breasts were wickedly outlined. For good measure Sarah rubbed more honey over and through the cups.

Barbara was dizzy with excitement and breathing in quick short gasps. She could smell the odour of honey rising from herself. When Sarah knelt before her and eased her tights halfway down her thighs, she didn't have to be told what to do next. She automatically parted her legs for Sarah to reach her crotch.

Sarah dabbed her fingers into the honey and smeared it over Barbara's pubic mound, pausing every now and again to slide her sticky fingers inside and leave a thick film of honey on the sensitive lining of her sex. When she brushed the clitoris with her fingers, Barbara's knees buckled.

'Ohhh,' she sighed. 'Sarah, I'm going to come if you don't stop. Not that I'm asking you to stop, mind you,' Barbara managed to gasp out in a desperate attempt to take her mind off what was being done to her. She had forgotten completely about her resolve to do something nice for Sarah. She hadn't thought about the erotic uses of honey.

It was just as well that Sarah finished then. She pulled the tights back up, pressing them into the sticky substance and caressing Barbara through the sheer nylon. She applied more honey to the insides of Barbara's thighs, over the tights. 'Do you have any ants about the place? You're about ready to be staked out on an ant hill. The little buggers would love you. But never mind. I'll save you for dessert. *I'll* enjoy you, little slavey.'

Barbara's head was spinning and she could barely stand unaided. Her knees kept threatening to buckle.

Sarah was relentless. 'Get on with it,' she commanded. 'I'm hungry.'

Barbara moved tentatively back to the work top. She was acutely aware of the bra clinging to her sticky breasts, and the thick honey between her thighs made her tights slippery and sticky at the same time. Somehow she made salad and sandwiches for them. In the process she managed to get honey onto the insides of her arms whenever they brushed against her sticky bra. By the time they finished eating she was a sweaty, sticky mess. Sarah turned to her with a carnivorous grin.

'Should I force you to clear up the dishes and wash everything before we have dessert, little slavey? I wonder if you could manage. But I won't be a cruel mistress. I'll leave that to your dream-lover. Come here.'

Barbara rose and teetered over to Sarah, who forced her to stand still while she inspected her, stringing out the process unbearably. Finally she rose and motioned for Barbara to take the chair she had vacated. Sarah took the keys from her handbag and unlocked Barbara's handcuffs. 'Hands behind your back,' she ordered. When Barbara complied, Sarah pulled them through the chair back and locked the cuffs again, leaving her chained to the chair by her wrists. Next Sarah unlocked one of the leg-irons and manoeuvred Barbara's ankles until she could run the chain behind the legs of the chair. When she locked the irons again, Barbara was left with her thighs spread widely and her ankles drawn back on either side of the chair. She was unable to rise from the chair or to prevent whatever Sarah intended to do to her. She had lost control over the situation once again.

Sarah began to tease Barbara's nipples through the sheer sticky material of her bra. Barbara whimpered with excitement almost immediately. She had been aroused during the meal, restraining herself only with difficulty. Now that she was helpless and the moment had arrived, she surrendered herself wholly to Sarah. 'Ohhh, God,' she gasped. 'Saaarahhhh!' She moved her shoulders, offering herself to the fingers that caressed her breasts and nipples. The honey made her slippery and the sliding sensation was driving her frantic. Barbara's hips began thrusting backwards and forwards as if she were making love to someone. The muscles in her calves and thighs tightened and relaxed as she moved against her chains.

Sarah let her hand rest on Barbara's crotch. It was warm to the touch. She bent down and began to lick the honey which covered the tights and the insides of her thighs. She moved her hands back to Barbara's breasts as she applied her mouth to her crotch.

Barbara was frantic by then, whimpering continuously and flinging herself about as far as the chains allowed. She wanted to offer her breasts and her sex fully to Sarah, to thrust against those hands, but the handcuffs and leg-irons held her rigidly to the chair, adding to her excitement and torment. Then suddenly it was all too much. The maddening hands and her own helplessness drove Barbara screaming over the edge. She came, shuddering and gasping. She couldn't catch her breath and her cries were strangled, choked back in her throat as she tried to fill her lungs.

And Sarah kept on.

Barbara had neither the breath nor the will-power to ask her to stop. This was beyond her wildest dreams of sex and bondage. She came and came, jerking against her chains, until she thought she could come no more. Then Sarah showed her that she could. And she did. Barbara lost track of time, her surroundings, how often she came. She was wild with desire, freed of her inhibitions, something she had never expected with a woman. She was drenched in sweat, and the mingled odours from her sex and the honey filled her nostrils.

When she began to notice her surroundings again, she was alone in the kitchen, still chained to the chair and covered in sticky honey. Now the sweat was chill on her body, and she could smell the odour of her rut rising from between her thighs. Her wrists and ankles were sore from jerking against her chains. Barbara could hear the sound of the TV from the front room, and she croaked, 'Sarah!'

Sarah came back smiling. 'Back among the living at last, I see!' She moved behind Barbara and dropped her arms around her shoulders, bringing a hand to rest familiarly on each breast, unmindful of the sticky mess.

Sarah gave a gentle squeeze and Barbara gasped at the touch. 'Ohhhhh! Sarah, please . . .'

'Please what? Please stop or please, more? I wonder where you get the strength.'

'And I wonder where you get your ideas,' Barbara replied. 'I've never come like that before. Only my manners and good breeding prevent me from begging for more. My mother warned me not to be greedy.'

'Your mother has nothing to do with what we do. Nor have you, for that matter. I still have the keys to your chains. You're in my power. You can't stop me from doing whatever I want to do. There's no responsibility and no guilt and no greed involved so long as you're helpless to resist.' As she spoke Sarah's fingers were toying with Barbara's nipples. Abruptly she reached down and unsnapped the bra, baring Barbara's breasts to her touch. Sarah cupped the heavy mounds, and Barbara groaned helplessly as her nipples stiffened under the touch.

Sarah moulded Barbara's breasts with her hands, watching intently as the veins that supplied blood to her nipples became engorged and the breasts grew heavy in her hands. With her fingers Sarah traced the faint blue lines, circling the stiff nipples and suddenly squeezing them.

Taken by surprise, Barbara jerked erect in her chair. 'Saaarrrrah,' she groaned.

'I love it when you gasp out my name in the throes of passion,' Sarah said with a smile. 'It gives me such a sense of power over you. I could get addicted to that. Don't go anywhere. I'll be right back.'

Sarah left the kitchen and Barbara sat gasping in the chair. She was going to come again. She knew it at the same time as she wondered where the strength came from. It had to be the excitement of what Sarah was doing to her. She was living out one of her fantasies with her friend's help.

When she came back Sarah had another surprise for Barbara. It was the largest dildo she had ever seen, black rubber at least two inches round, and it seemed to go on forever.

'Definitely not the lady's handbag model,' Sarah said with a grin. 'This model was designed to revive the flagging spirits of even the most sexually exhausted lady. My friend at the sex shop wondered who the lucky person was going to be. I told him she was waiting for me – or for this – even as we spoke. He told me then I'd better hurry on home. And here I am. And here you are.'

As she spoke, Sarah was busy taking down Barbara's tights. When they were hanging below her knees, Sarah stooped and slid the instrument into her sex.

The honey provided the initial lubrication, but Barbara didn't fight the impalement. As the dildo slid home she felt each little touch on her clitoris. 'Ohhh, God, it's serrated!' she groaned.

Sarah nodded. 'I thought you'd notice that. It's nice to have someone so discriminating to work with. Glad you like it.' She stepped back to admire the effect.

Barbara sat erect against the back of the chair, bare breasts presented to Sarah with the nipples stiffly at attention. Her tights were down around her knees, hobbling her, and the huge black dildo was planted firmly inside her. Her eyes were closed and her mouth was open. There was no mistaking her state of arousal.

Barbara was startled by a bright flash of light and a whirring sound. She opened her eyes to see Sarah standing poised to take another picture with her Polaroid camera. 'Oh, Sarah, don't!' she protested. 'I look horrible like this.'

'On the contrary, you look very attractive. I wanted some pictures to blackmail you with. Just kidding,' Sarah said when she caught the alarmed look on Barbara's face. 'These are for you. Something to remember our reunion by,' she said as she took the next picture. She moved between photos, catching a slightly different pose and angle each time. 'You can close your eyes if you like. It makes you look as if you were lost in the throes of passion.'

'That's not very far from the truth,' Barbara ground out. She was still breathing heavily from Sarah's earlier manipulation of her breasts and from the full feeling the dildo gave her. She rotated her hips on the chair, feeling it slide in and out as she moved. The movement brought little spikes of pleasure that shot through her as the instrument moved against her clitoris. She threw back her head and groaned aloud.

'Perfect!' Sarah said as she took the last photograph on the roll. 'The captive maiden overcome by her passions. Just what the porn magazines want to see. You'd be on page three of the national newspapers if they weren't so prudish.' She put the camera down on the table and spread the photos out to dry. 'We can have a look at them later, after you've calmed down a bit. And who knows, they may even make you excited again. Some people go for that sort of thing.'

Sarah knelt on the floor and grasped the dildo, sliding it in and out of Barbara's sex. She didn't touch Barbara in any other way. The only contact between them was the rubber shaft. Barbara moaned with each stroke, and Sarah went faster and faster as she became more and more aroused. Her breasts were bobbing and shaking, the nipples almost crying out to be taken, squeezed, kissed, but Sarah paid no attention to them until Barbara seemed ready to burst. Her face was red and her mouth was open wide as she gasped for breath. Then, at the crucial moment, Sarah began to use one hand and her mouth on Barbara's tits. Barbara came at once, shuddering and moaning. Sarah must have thought she'd never stop.

Barbara didn't think of anything except the waves of sensation spreading from her breasts and sex. Finally she slumped in the chair, held erect only by her handcuffs. She felt limp, utterly spent.

Sarah unlocked the chains and removed the dildo. It came free with an audible sucking sound. The honey was smeared thickly over it. Sarah sniffed the mingled odours of honey and the clean salty smell of Barbara. She held the dildo under Barbara's nose, like a dose of smelling salts.

The smell brought her back to the present. Barbara opened her eyes and focused on Sarah's face. She leaned forward deliberately and kissed her friend on the mouth, an open-mouthed kiss that Sarah returned. 'Thank you,' she breathed into Sarah's mouth.

Sarah held her for a moment and then helped Barbara to stand. 'Let's get you into the shower. I think we can let you off any more sex for the evening.' She guided Barbara toward the bathroom.

Barbara moved slowly, hobbled by her tights which were still down around her knees. It seemed as if she were swimming through glue, and the familiar features of her flat seemed alien, as if seen for the first time. She leaned heavily on Sarah's arm. The honey had got smeared everywhere during the sexual gymnastics, and she felt sticky all over. When she got into the shower, she stood with her hands braced against the wall and her head hanging between her outstretched arms. From a great distance she was aware of Sarah taking her tights off and slipping the bra down her arms.

The warm water sluicing over her revived Barbara. Sarah used plenty of soap, and stroked her body tenderly as she washed away the traces of the recent sexual marathon. Barbara was unsurprised to see that Sarah was nude, in the shower with her. She stood passively, grateful not to have to move. Sarah even washed her hair, standing behind her and letting the warm soapy water run down her body and between her legs. Barbara was conscious of the warm firm body against her back and of the hands that washed her, but she was much too tired to feel anything but gratitude. If this was what women got up to when there were no men about, she had been missing something.

She let Sarah dry her off, sitting on the closed top of the toilet while her friend attended to her hair. She took the bath-robe Sarah offered her and watched while Sarah showered herself. The light glinted on the golden chain that ran between her legs. Idly, Barbara wondered what it would be like to be pierced herself. She made a mental note to ask Sarah for the name and address of the clinic before they parted.

They went into the living room and sat together on the sofa. After the last day or so it seemed like the most natural thing in the world. No longer one on the sofa and the other across in the armchair as they had on the day when Sarah read the journal and Barbara sat in chains opposite her. Old friends now, once again. The experiences they had shared and the confidences they had exchanged in the last few days made the intervening years seem trivial.

It was time for the evening news, Barbara saw with some surprise. It should be earlier than that – or later. She had quite lost track of time since Sarah had come home. She watched the daily recital of disaster and violence and felt glad to have found this island of silence and relative peace in a world that seemed so at variance with their last few days together.

As if reading her thoughts, Sarah said, 'I'll leave one of the photos with you when I go to remind you to think of me. And,' smiling mischievously, 'I'll use the others to blackmail you into writing to me. Each time you send a letter I'll reply and enclose one more photo. But miss one letter and I go straight to the tabloids with my sordid tale of sex and submission in suburbia. But let's not lose touch again as we did. We don't have that many friends we can afford to lose any of them. Come and visit us too – whenever you like. Both of us will make you welcome. Promise.'

The prospect of continued contact made Barbara feel better. A visit could be arranged easily enough. And Sarah would probably be able to visit her again. But she wasn't sure about her welcome in Glasgow. Sarah was her friend, but Elspeth was Sarah's lover. She might resent another woman. But that could wait. For now it was enough to have Sarah here.

'Do you intend to go into the office tomorrow?' Sarah asked.

'I don't have to go. I have enough to keep me busy here. Why? Do you have another day like today in mind?'

'Little slavey,' Sarah teased her. 'Mustn't be too greedy. But I had a day's shopping in mind, and lunch, and some time at the V&A. I need to see some of the older patterns in wallpaper. I need some fresh ideas, and what better way to get them than to raid the blessedly uncopyrighted past? And I thought I'd take you to meet my friend at the sex shop. You never know when you'll need the advice of someone like him. He's okay. He'll tell you what you need to know – even who you need to know. And he'll sell you whatever you need without awkward questions. If he hasn't got what you want, he'll probably know where to get it. All in all a valuable contact for a budding little slavey like you.'

Barbara liked the idea. It had been some time since she had done any serious shopping, and like all women she found the prospect of spending some money an exciting one. They went to bed on that note, Barbara once again too tired to do anything else. Sarah didn't seem to mind, or to feel hard done by.

The visit to the V&A yielded some notes for Sarah's illustrations, and afterwards they had the obligatory overpriced tea and buns at the museum café. They consoled themselves with the thought that some of the money would find its way into the museum's general fund and would be used to maintain these dim and musty rooms for a few more moments. Then they went shopping.

Barbara introduced Sarah to the wonders of crotchless tights, which she had not been aware of. They both bought several pairs, Barbara in the hope of showing them off to her dream-lover, and Sarah intending to surprise Elspeth with yet another way to be undressed while dressed. Both of them decided they had enough frilly-lacy gear to be getting on with, and there had been no daring breakthroughs in the lingerie line to titillate the male (or the female) libido.

It was getting on for lunch time when they had had enough. Eat first, they decided, and visit the sex shop afterwards – a sort of dessert to end the day. They bought sandwiches, crisps and tins of drink from Marks and Spencer and took them to a nearby park for an *al fresco* meal. The lunch-time crowd was out in full force, munching their packed sandwiches and trying to forget the grimness of the nine-to-five world they inhabited. The pigeons darted and flew about gathering up whatever crumbs fell, and the troopers exercising their horses cantered rigidly by, striving to ignore the civilian throngs as discipline required.

Sarah told Barbara to hike up her skirt as if she were sunbathing, and see what happened when the next troop came by. 'Does your Mr Right ride a horse? In your dreams, I mean. It's surprising how many women are attracted to horses. I don't mean they actually want to be mounted by them, though there are those sorts too. It's just the erotic notion of having this great animal labouring away between your legs. It sends them potty. Even the vicar's daughter is affected. If only Mummy knew – or could remember her own girlish dreams. She'd forbid her daughter to take riding lessons if she could do so without looking ridiculous, or admitting that she knew the real reason why women ride. My friend Colin – who I intend to introduce you to when he gets back – is a harness maker by trade. He got into publishing quite by accident. He tells me he gets quite a bit of extracurricular business from the female members of the horsey set. He has made some rather special harnesses for them – not for their horses. Would you like him to make a harness for you? I'm sure he'd be delighted to whip up something after I tell him all about you and what you like.'

'Don't do that!' Barbara said, alarmed. 'You can't go around telling strangers the sort of things we get up to.'

'Colin isn't a stranger. I know him well, and I know he's discreet to the point of reticence.'

'But I don't know him, and he doesn't know me,' Barbara protested.

'He will, after I tell him about you. I'm an inveterate matchmaker, and I think you two would get along famously.'

Barbara gave up. Sarah would do what she said she'd do in spite of her objections. She found it exciting that they sat among the crowds of office workers talking about a subject that fully half of them knew nothing about. And which the other half would doubtless consider an abomination.

After lunch they visited the sex shop, which like all such establishments in modern, enlightened Britain was obliged to carry on its business from a store front with no windows and only one door, which carried not government health warnings, but the corresponding caveats for the morally sensitive. They went into the darkened interior.

Sarah greeted the proprietor by name. 'Chris, this is my friend Barbara – another sojourner in the vast sexual desert that is modern England. She and I were at university together, and I can vouch for her. She is a genuine practising sex pervert like me, and I promised to continue her education by introducing the two of you. She lives hereabouts, so you'll probably see more of her than you do of me.'

Chris offered his hand and Barbara took it. It didn't feel slimy or scaly.

'I've missed Sarah since she moved up North. She and Elspeth were always in and out of here buying something to surprise the other with. There's been a recession since they left. And I'm always glad to meet a friend of theirs.' He gave them a tour of the shop and then left them to browse. He seemed to know about the embarrassment that often accompanied his customers through the door. He remained there to offer advice if it was needed. Sarah began a low-voiced conversation with him while Barbara looked around.

She saw a duplicate of the dildo which Sarah had bought for her. She also saw that it formed part of a set of similar instruments. The set consisted of a half-dozen tools in graduated sizes fitting onto a base that could be strapped to the wearer's hips and waist. Among the sets there was a pair of matched dildoes intended for the cunt and the arsehole. Just the thing for Sarah. Barbara overcame her embarrassment and bought the set, to Sarah's amusement. Chris made no comment.

There were various restraint devices for sale, among them a leather strait-jacket which strongly tempted Barbara. She felt herself go hot all over as she imagined herself being laced and buckled into it. But she knew it wasn't a solo garment. It would need the help of a willing assistant. Regretfully she filed it away as something for the whenever.

The body harnesses looked more promising, and Barbara seriously considered one for herself. Sarah noticed her interest and silently shook her head, no. Barbara laid the leather aside reluctantly. There was nothing else she wanted at the moment, and soon thereafter they both left the shop. Barbara carried the plain brown package which she was certain shouted its guilty origin and contents to the passers-by.

As they walked Sarah explained, 'If you're into harnesses (the pun is deliberate), wait until you meet Colin. His are much better. They're custom made for each individual, and he can build in many features the mass-produced ones lack. He's a real artist with leather, and he doesn't do all that badly with steel. You'll like him. I'll give you his phone number before I leave. And I'll tell him *everything* about you when I see him – including your phone number and the way your nipples stiffen when someone rubs honey over them.'

They made their way back to Barbara's flat. Inside, Barbara announced that she was going to 'do' Sarah that evening. She felt that she was guilty of taking advantage of her friend's good nature and wanted to pay her back.

Sarah said, 'Why wait for a certain time? The time for sex is whenever you feel like it. But I wouldn't want to rush you if you're not in the mood. After all, you did all the heavy breathing last night. I only helped you along.' There was no resentment in Sarah's remark. She was merely stating facts.

Barbara opened the package from the sex shop and examined the apparatus she'd bought. The harness seemed straightforward enough. There was a belt that went around the waist and buckled at the back. A vee-shaped strap hung down from that and went back up between the wearer's legs. It ended in a buckle that was intended to join the strap hanging from the neck collar. That took care of the supporting arrangements. At the apex of the vee there was a provision for fixing two dildoes – one facing inward and intended for the pleasure of the wearer, and the other facing outward, obviously intended to give the same pleasure to someone else. The dildoes all fitted the same base and could be worn in any combination.

That looked promising. Barbara began to undress, dropping her clothes in a heap in the middle of the floor. Time enough later for tidiness. She selected a large rubber dildo to fit herself, remembering the way she had been able to accommodate it last night (and how nice it had felt). This felt just as nice as she stuffed it inside and buckled the straps. Sarah helped her with the buckles behind her back, but the harness was designed to be got into by oneself if necessary.

Barbara fitted a slimmer dildo to the outer fitting on the belt. She looked around the room for a suitable work area. It was Sarah's turn to look apprehensive as she gazed at the instrument of her own impalement. Barbara had selected one that she thought would fit Sarah's arsehole, since her sex was laced shut by the chain. Barbara looked across the room at Sarah. 'What are you waiting for? Get undressed.'

Sarah took her clothes off slowly, looking all the while at the dildo Barbara wore. 'I'm afraid it will hurt. It's so big!'

'You never thought of that last night when you did me,' Barbara said. 'But I won't force you. I won't even insist on tying you up, though you deserve it. But I'll make it easier on you.' Barbara went into the kitchen to fetch the jar of honey. She came back and sat on the carpet, beckoning Sarah to join her in the cleared area in front of the couch. Barbara was sitting cross-legged, the black rubber dildo jutting up incongruously from her lap.

Sarah sat tentatively beside her. Sarah's nipples were stiff and crinkly with excitement. Apparently she was losing some of her inhibitions. On impulse she grasped the shaft and caressed it, causing its twin to move inside Barbara's sex.

She sighed gently at the internal massage, and her own nipples stiffened in response. Barbara simultaneously got a grip on herself and reached for Sarah's tits. This was supposed to be a repayment for all Sarah had done, not the incurring of a further debt. Barbara caressed the delicate pink nipples, enjoying the way they grew stiffer beneath her fingers' ends.

Sarah's breath caught on a gasp and she jerked spasmodically.

'Did that make you come?'

Sarah nodded. In a shaky voice she explained that her breasts were especially sensitive. 'That's why I spent so much time on yours, I guess.'

'You're certainly quick on the trigger.' Barbara continued to caress her, cupping Sarah's breasts as if weighing them, pulling gently and watching them elongate in her hands, nipping at the pink buds with her finger-nails.

Sarah grew flushed and warm.

Barbara took one of the nipples into her mouth, sucking gently. Her teeth nipped from time to time.

Sarah said, 'Oh!' in a surprised tone. Then a longer 'Ohhhh!' as she came again. This one lasted an appreciable time. Sarah was whimpering almost continuously, shuddering as the spasms took her. Her eyes were tightly shut.

Barbara's hand moved down to her friend's pubic mound, touching the metal ring at the top of Sarah's chain. Gently she pressed the metal against the soft flesh. She must have come down directly on the clitoris, because Sarah cried out loudly as she came again. Barbara continued to kiss her breasts and press down on the chain. Sarah was racked by another long series of shuddering orgasms. She bit her knuckles to keep herself from crying aloud.

When she subsided, Barbara applied some of the honey to Sarah's nipples and began to suck them in turn. She licked them clean and applied more. 'This is what I call a high-calorie fuck,' she laughed.

Sarah wasn't laughing. She was becoming frantic all over again as Barbara licked and nuzzled her tits. She whimpered and bit her knuckles again.

Barbara gently took her hands from her mouth, making her hold them flat on the floor. 'Scream if it makes you feel better, Sarah. To hell with the neighbours.' She resumed caressing the bare pink tits and Sarah moaned loudly every time she came.

Barbara got up and helped Sarah to kneel. She had Sarah bend down with her forearms flat on the floor and her bottom sticking up in the air. From that position Barbara applied honey to the pink rosebud of Sarah's arsehole and began to lick it away. While her mouth was busy with Sarah's bottom, her hands could reach Sarah's downward-hanging tits. Sarah screamed this time – a ladylike scream, but a scream, not a whimper or a moan. Her clenched fists were beating a tattoo on the carpet.

Barbara knelt behind Sarah and applied some of the honey to the dildo. She placed the end against Sarah's arsehole and pushed gently against the clenched ring. Sarah stiffened and cried out, but Barbara could feel her trying to open herself. She used her hands to spread Sarah's cheeks, and the shaft slid part way in. Barbara didn't force it when she felt the resistance. She waited patiently for Sarah to relax, then she pushed in a bit further until the next spasm caused the muscles to clamp down. By a series of pushes and pauses she eventually got the dildo fully home. Sarah relaxed limply with her bottom resting against the fronts of Barbara's thighs.

From this position Barbara was able to fold herself forward spoon fashion with her belly and tits against Sarah's back. Once more she took Sarah's tits in her hands, and at the same time began a slow rocking motion that caused the shaft to slide in Sarah's rectal sheath. And of course the other end of the shaft was moving inside her. Barbara sighed gently as she felt herself grow warm and moist with the movement and the penetration.

She felt the beginnings of her own orgasm. Barbara pressed her tits against Sarah's back, grinding her hips against Sarah's bottom as the other woman bucked beneath her.

Sarah was losing control once again. She cried, 'Ohh, Barbara! Ohh, God, ohh God, don't stop!'

Barbara tried to hold herself back, thinking this should be Sarah's show, her pleasure, after she had given so much pleasure to her.

Sarah sensed the mood and cried harshly, 'Come with me, Barbara! Come now!' She nearly made it, but Sarah had too much of a head start. Sarah shuddered in her own release. Barbara followed closely, bucking against Sarah's bottom.

They ended with Barbara's full weight pressing against Sarah's back. They were still joined, and Barbara felt the black rubber shaft inside her like a spear. Sarah's muscles were straining to support them both.

Barbara put her arms around Sarah and leaned slowly backwards, drawing the other woman up until she could roll slightly and land with a bump on her bottom. Throughout this manoeuvre Barbara was careful to stay joined to Sarah. They finished with Barbara lying on her back on the floor and Sarah on top of her. She fondled Sarah's breasts and twined her legs with Sarah's so that she was able to spread her friend's legs as she spread her own. Now Sarah's entire weight was on Barbara, who began a slow rocking motion with her pelvis to drive the shaft in and out for both of them. Her hands were busy with Sarah's breasts.

Sarah's own hands were once more beating softly on the carpet as she came. Barbara held her tightly so that she couldn't roll off. She was determined that they stay joined, penetrated by opposite ends of the long spike. This time Barbara didn't resist when she felt herself about to come. Sarah thrashed and whimpered and Barbara held them together. When they finished they were still joined.

Sarah appeared to be dozing, but she spoke as soon as she felt Barbara move beneath her. 'Are you all right?'

'Not sure,' Barbara mumbled. 'Let me get back to earth – if it's stopped moving.'

Sarah freed herself from Barbara's embrace and sat up, causing pleasant sensations from the shaft joining them. She rose slowly, her end of the shaft being drawn out of her backside as she stood.

Barbara was fascinated by the length of the rubber spike emerging from Sarah. 'I didn't realise it was so long.'

'Nor did I,' Sarah replied. 'But it's all right,' she hastened to reassure her friend. She bent down to kiss Barbara's mouth and to brush her hair from her face. 'Come along to the shower now,' she urged, helping Barbara to rise to her feet.

Barbara stood, the black shaft bobbing between her legs. She made an attempt to undo the straps that held it inside her.

Sarah noticed and stopped her. 'Do you think you can stand to leave it there?' she asked. 'I have a plan for later on. And ... I find it a ... turn-on. I mean, seeing that thing sticking up and knowing what's inside you.' Sarah seemed almost shy as she made this request.

'Of course I can stand it. Especially if I know it gives you pleasure.'

Sarah blushed and nodded her thanks. She led the way to the shower and Barbara followed, one dildo sliding inside her and the other bobbing in front of her.

Sarah took charge in the shower, facing Barbara and soaping her thoroughly. She paid special attention to the dildo, making it slippery with the soap and then caressing it as she might have handled a man's penis. The gentle tugging and pushing made Barbara come again, whimpering softly. She was terribly excited by the novelty of being handled like a man. She almost came again as Sarah dried the dildo and the leather harness.

When she put on her bathrobe, the black rubber spike stuck out the front. Sarah grasped it like a handle and led Barbara to the couch. Barbara sat down and Sarah sat on the floor between her knees, sitting sideways so she could grasp the rod as they watched TV. In that way she made

Barbara come several more times throughout the evening, gentle shudders accompanied by soft moans of satisfaction. In between times Sarah laid her face against the inside of Barbara's thigh, licking the dildo and her friend's soft flesh now and again.

Finally Sarah stood up. 'Bed time, Barbara.'

Barbara followed her into the bedroom, the rubber phallus standing rigid beneath the bathrobe. Once more she made as if to remove the harness, thinking the evening's frolics were over. And once more Sarah stopped her.

Barbara shrugged and removed her robe. She put her night-dress on. It had no opening in front, and the dildo made it stand out from her in front like a tent pole.

Sarah took rope from the drawer where Barbara kept her collection of bondage gear, the same thin cords that she had used to bind her own legs the day before Sarah came to visit. It seemed like a lifetime ago. She's going to tie me up, Barbara thought. Sarah's going to use those ropes to tie me up. I'll be helpless all night, with this shaft stuck up me.

'Do you snore when you sleep on your back, Barbara?' In response to her puzzled look, Sarah went on, 'I'm trying to decide whether to gag you after I tie you to the bed.'

'I don't know. I usually sleep on my front, but I won't be able to do that so long as this is stuck up me,' indicating the dildo between her legs.

'No, I don't suppose you can,' Sarah said. 'I plan to tie you on your back. We'll see about the gag later. Lie down in the middle of the bed and raise your arms above your head.'

Barbara did as she was told, her heart thudding against her rib-cage.

'Now push your hands through on either side of the central rod in the headboard,' Sarah directed.

When Barbara did so, they discovered that the bed was too close to the wall and would have to be moved so that Barbara's hands wouldn't be jammed against it. Together they wrestled the bed a foot from the wall, and Barbara lay down again.

This time there was enough space for her hands, and

Sarah was able to stand between the wall and the headboard to tie them.

Barbara felt the cords around her wrists, binding them together around the bedstead over her head. Sarah made a thorough job of it. Barbara tugged futilely at the cords while Sarah watched.

'That'll do,' Sarah said as she moved to the other end of the bed. 'Feet through here, please,' she directed, guiding Barbara's feet through on either side of the central rod in the footboard. She used more of the thin cords to tie Barbara's ankles together. When she was finished, Barbara was left lying on her back with her wrists and ankles bound to opposite ends of the bed. The black rubber dildo now almost exactly resembled a tent pole as it stood erect under the sheer nylon of her nightie.

Her voice shaking with excitement, Barbara asked, 'Where will you sleep?'

As she turned out the light, Sarah answered, 'Here beside you, of course. Unless you snore too loudly. There's room for two friends in the smallest bed.'

Barbara saw her undressing in the light from the street lamp. Apparently Sarah slept in the raw. Or she was doing so this night.

Sarah got into bed, drawing the duvet up over them both. The shaft inside Barbara held the bed clothes up like a tent pole. The weight of the quilt pushed down ever so slightly, and she felt the pressure inside her. She pushed back with her hips, and felt the dildo shift as she rose and fell.

Sarah noticed. 'Not still randy, are you?'

Barbara could hear the smile in her voice. 'It's not every night I'm tied to my bed with a great shaft inside me.'

'Poor you,' Sarah said, snuggling against her side and putting her arms around Barbara. 'We'll have to make the best of tonight then, won't we?' She grasped the rubber spike and moved it gently up and down. 'Are you snug enough?' she whispered in Barbara's ear. 'Would you like me to slip out of bed and tie your big toes and your thumbs as well? That's supposed to be ever so sexy.'

'Maybe later,' Barbara gasped. 'I don't know if I can stand much more of this.'

'Of course you can. Just lie back and think of your demon-lover – if you positively can't think of England.' Sarah fell asleep, one arm around Barbara and one hand grasping the shaft.

Barbara had somewhat more trouble falling asleep. She was much too excited. She twisted and heaved but the cords held her tightly, and the great rubber dildo exerted an insistent pressure which kept her on the brink of orgasm for what seemed like days. This was very close indeed to her favourite fantasy of being the helpless captive of her dream-lover. Barbara now had nothing against lesbians. One of my best friends is a lesbian, she told herself wryly. But she still wanted a man to do these things to her. She twisted restlessly against the cords on her wrists and ankles, and Sarah grumbled sleepily, 'Lie still!'

Sometime during the early hours of the morning Barbara woke up to find Sarah hovering beside the bed. She had drawn the duvet down and raised Barbara's nightie. She was in the process of coating the projecting rod with hand cream from a jar on the bureau. Barbara lay still so Sarah wouldn't suspect that she was awake. She had the impression that Sarah wanted to begin this while she was still sleeping – as though Sarah wanted to rape her sleeping victim. Or at any rate present her with a *fait accompli* when she woke up.

Sarah put the jar down and climbed onto the bed with her back to Barbara. She spread her cheeks and slowly lowered herself onto the upright spike. She had to be careful because the bed was none too steady a platform, and the room was dark. She had to do most of it by feel, but finally she was lined up. She lowered herself with a sigh as the rod slid into her. When she was fully impaled, she called over her shoulder, 'Wake up, Barbara – if you're not already awake!'

Barbara grunted, 'How can anyone sleep with a naked sex maniac like you in the same room?'

Sarah set the pace and controlled the motion since Barbara was immobilised by her bonds. She rose and fell gently, causing a similar sliding sensation in Barbara's cunt as she fucked her own arsehole. She reached behind her and found Barbara's breasts, the nipples already stiff. She caressed them until Barbara thought they would burst.

She wished fleetingly that her own hands were free to find Sarah's breasts, but on the whole she was happier they were not. It made her terribly excited to know that there was nothing she could do to alter or affect what was being done to her.

And Sarah was not to be deflected. She was beginning to whimper herself as she slid up and down the rubber shaft. Her hands tightened on Barbara's engorged breasts as she had her first orgasm. She didn't seem to need any further stimulation. Perhaps her fantasy was as vivid as Barbara's. She came again, crying out on a rising note. Her movements became wilder.

Barbara was being driven to her own orgasm by the combination of her fantasy and the motion Sarah imparted to the dildo inside her. She jerked at the cords on her wrists and cried out as she came. And came again. She couldn't hold herself back and she couldn't stop Sarah. She too went wild, her cries joining with Sarah's in the dark bedroom. She could feel the sweat trickling down her ribs from her own exertions as she thrashed on the bed. Sarah's bottom felt slippery and sweaty where it touched her.

Barbara was exhausted by the time Sarah had finished. She was only aware of a tug on the harness as Sarah freed herself from her anal penetration.

Sarah stretched out beside Barbara, curling lazily like a cat against her damp flank. She rested her hand on Barbara's cunt and massaged her gently, causing a series of deep disturbances inside her. But she made no move to untie Barbara or change her position in any way. At length she rose and drew the duvet over them as before, snuggling against Barbara and taking her friend in her arms.

From the gentle buzzing sound she presently made, Barbara could tell that Sarah had fallen asleep again. She herself lay awake for most of the night, excited by her helplessness and the stirrings inside her cunt whenever one or the other of them caused the duvet to shift on its tent pole. The windows were getting grey with the dawn when she finally drifted off to sleep.

Barbara woke up bursting for a pee. She could hear Sarah in the kitchen, and she raised her voice to call her. Sarah was still nude, and Barbara wondered if the neighbours could see her as she flitted past the windows. Barbara decided that she didn't care what the neighbours saw or did. Sarah was too good to be with.

Sarah untied her wrists and ankles as soon as Barbara explained the problem. 'Can't have a damp bed, can we? It takes a lot of the fun out of sex.'

From these remarks, Barbara guessed that there was more on the menu. She felt not the least aversion, but wondered where Sarah got her endurance. It didn't occur to her that she was the one doing most of the work, if that was the proper word to describe the pleasurable exercise of the last few days. After her visit to the loo, which she managed with some difficulty because Sarah had insisted she leave the dildoes in place, Barbara joined Sarah in the kitchen, still sticking up rudely under her nightie.

Sarah had already made breakfast for them. Barbara's only contribution consisted of pouring two cups of tea. That hardly counted because Sarah had already made the tea. During breakfast Sarah informed Barbara that she was going to call in sick that day. Sarah carefully didn't say what she would be doing. Sarah brought the telephone through and told Barbara to make her excuses to the office.

Barbara stumbled a bit when she told them she wasn't feeling well. She was having trouble keeping her mind on the conversation with Sarah hovering nearby, stroking and tugging at the rubber shaft as she tried to talk on the phone. Barbara was panting gently when she put the phone down.

Sarah wore an innocent smile. 'You clear up while I get dressed,' she told Barbara.

When Barbara began washing up, she found that she had to stand sideways at the sink because of her projection. She wondered what men did about washing up when they had a hard on. Probably they did something besides the washing up.

Barbara dried her hands when Sarah called her to come into the bedroom. Sarah was dressed to go out, and she had laid out some things for Barbara as well. When she saw the preparations Sarah had made, Barbara knew she wasn't going out that day. Sarah had laid out a new pair of her crotchless tights. They were black and sheer, the new shiny look that was coming back into fashion after years of dull, matte-finish stockings and tights. Silently she sat on the edge of the bed and began to put the tights on. She had no trouble smoothing them up her legs, but needed a third hand to manoeuvre the dildo through the crotch opening and get the top part in place.

Sarah helped her with that part, then asked her to choose a pair of high-heels, preferably in black, and preferably with ankle straps. And did she have another of those sheer bras in black? 'You know, like the one we got honey all over the other day?'

Barbara found the shoes and the bra Sarah required.

Sarah helped her get into the shoes, kneeling on the floor to do up the ankle straps. 'I understand why some men have a shoe fetish. There's something very sensual about helping a woman ease her feet into a pair of high-heeled shoes.'

Barbara reached for the bra next, but Sarah shook her head.

'First we package you,' she said as she approached, dangling ropes. She wound a length of the cord around the base of each of Barbara's breasts, pulling it tight and knotting it so that her tits stood out tautly. Her areolae were stiff and shiny with the tension. Sarah fitted the bra to Barbara's distended tits, stuffing them into the cups before doing up the clasp. She shortened the shoulder straps next, lifting the heavy round breasts inside the sheer cups.

'So far, so nice,' Sarah said. 'Now for the rest of the packaging.' She selected two short pieces of cord and tied the middle parts together so that there was a four-ended piece with a knot in the centre. She positioned this carefully between Barbara's legs, pulling it snugly into her crotch. 'Hands by your sides,' Sarah directed. She took two of the ropes' ends and tied Barbara's left wrist to the outside of her thigh, pulling the cords tight enough to bite into the flesh of her leg and her wrist. She repeated the process on the other wrist, leaving Barbara with her hands bound to her thighs.

Next Sarah used more cord to bind Barbara's elbows to her sides just above her waist. These she pulled tight as well, leaving no slack. Now Barbara's hands and arms were immobilised, and she was breathing heavily with rising excitement.

'You can sit on the bed now if you'd like. In fact I recommend it highly,' Sarah said gaily. 'You look as if you're ready to fall anyway, and I'm not even finished with you.'

Barbara sat on the edge of the bed while Sarah knelt to bind her legs at ankles, knees and thighs, exactly as she had done for herself a few days ago. Barbara thought this was much more satisfying than tying herself up. The stiff black rod stuck up rudely and insistently from between her bound thighs, through the hole in the crotch of her tights. The internal end of the shaft moved inside her as she wriggled to keep her balance on the edge of the bed.

'There's just the gag,' Sarah said. 'Open wide. We'll need that when I get back if you're to be quiet while I do some wild things to you.' She stuffed the wadded-up tights into Barbara's mouth and tied them in place with a scarf which she pulled between her teeth and knotted tightly behind her head. Sarah applied a dab of perfume to the pulses on each side of Barbara's neck, to the hollow of her throat, and behind each knee. 'You smell delicious,' she said as she replaced the bottle on the bureau.

Barbara grunted through her gag.

'Yes, you look nice too. Now quit fishing for compliments. You can sit there or lie back on the bed if you prefer. I'm going to leave you sitting up because you can lie down any time you wish. Getting back up again might be a problem. A matter of gravity when you can't use your arms or legs. I'm off out. See you later. Enjoy.'

Barbara heard the front door close and lock, and Sarah's footsteps receded. She was alone and helpless once more. She sat tensely on the edge of her bed. The silence of the empty house excited and frightened her. She struggled briefly against the cords that bound her, but stopped when she had confirmed she couldn't get free unaided. There was no way to know how long she'd be tied up. Sarah hadn't said when she would be back.

Her complete helplessness and dependence on someone else excited her more than anything she could do on her own. Barbara knew she had to find a permanent partner to take care of her full time. The possibility of being held captive regularly was her goal. She didn't think she would ever be satisfied again with her solo efforts now that she had sampled the things Sarah had done to her.

Barbara looked at the clock, but it was turned face downward on the bureau. She hadn't done that, so it must have been Sarah, deciding that the game would be more exciting to the victim if there was no way to measure the passage of time. That was what Barbara did when she stopped the cuckoo clock from marking the hours. It must be a fairly common practice among the B&D set, and she was proud that she had hit upon it without being told. Only now Sarah was using it against her.

Barbara felt as if she had been sitting on the bed forever, but knew it couldn't have been more than an hour since Sarah had gone. She lifted her legs and rolled over until she could lie fully on the bed. Lying on her side was going to be uncomfortable with her arms bound as they were. She squirmed until her head was on the pillows, feeling the dildo moving inside her. The end bobbed in time with her struggles.

She rolled over onto her back, stretching her bound legs out straight. The external part of the shaft now stood upright between her legs. It was only possible now to lie on her back, or maybe sit up again with a great deal of effort. The stiff rod pointed at the ceiling, and she wished Sarah were there to bury it in her backside and ride her to a wild climax. Barbara realised with pleased surprise that it couldn't have been more than four or five hours since Sarah had done just that. It had to be one of the best ways to be woken up. She didn't know what she was going to do when Sarah went back to Glasgow and Elspeth.

Time passed slowly as it always did for her in her periods of enforced idleness. The shadows moved across the walls; the mail came; someone rang her door bell but walked away when there was no reply. The phone rang and Barbara heard Claire from the office leaving a message on the answering machine. The rest of the world was going about its business just a short distance from where she lay bound, gagged and penetrated in her disordered bed. She heard the central heating shut itself off on the timer, and knew it must be ten o'clock – the time it normally went off. The room gradually cooled off, and Barbara wished she had thought to tell Sarah to leave the heating on as she normally did whenever she had one of her solo B&D sessions.

As she grew colder, Barbara felt her feet and legs getting numb, due no doubt to the cords that impeded her circulation. Her fingers were numb too, but she couldn't decide if that were due to the chill or to the rope around her wrists. Since she had never been able to tie her hands, she didn't know the effects she could expect. She squirmed once again, trying this time to get under the duvet.

After what seemed like hours of struggle Barbara managed to get her feet and legs under the covers, but there was no way to work the covers over her upper body with her wrists and elbows bound as they were. Still, even this partial cover felt better. She felt proud of herself for managing even this much. And there was a definite warmth between her legs, where the dildo had shifted as she struggled with the bed clothes. The cords Sarah had bound around her breasts forced them into unnatural prominence and tightness, the nipples standing out stiff and shiny from the unaccustomed constriction. Her breasts felt unusually sensitive as well. Fringe benefits, she thought, moving her hips experimentally to see if she could help things along.

Barbara rolled partly onto her side so that the external part of her dildo pressed against the mattress, jerking her hips backward and forward and feeling the thing move with her. She realised she was actually fucking the bed. And then she felt herself start to come, and she stopped thinking of everything except the spasms that shook her. The gag choked back her cries, but she twisted and bucked and made herself come again. And then again. She was gasping for air but she kept on, revelling in her fantasy of the helpless captive being forced to come and come and come, driven wild by some vague tormentor. Finally she had to stop, exhausted by her exertions and the release of sexual tension. Her lungs were burning in her chest.

Gradually she caught her breath. Barbara was worn out but pleased with her efforts. A whole new dimension to DIY, but not one she would be telling anyone about. Barbara rolled onto her back again, the black shaft pointing at the ceiling. She had managed to keep her legs under the duvet, and she felt her feet getting warm again. She dozed.

And woke, still alone and helpless. She felt warmer, but she was also stiff from lying so long. It was like the last time she had used these cords on herself, but this time she wasn't going to be able to get loose. Barbara worked her legs from under the duvet and squirmed until she was able to sit up on the edge of the bed with her legs hanging down. She flexed her fingers and bent her legs to get the stiffness out of them.

It must be afternoon, she judged. The light no longer looked like morning light. And she could tell from the uncomfortably full sensation from her bladder that some considerable time had passed – enough for the morning's tea to work its way through the system and be ready to come out the other end. If Sarah didn't come back soon she was going to have a messy accident. Barbara decided that she had better try to get to the bathroom. At least the floor was tiled. She had a vague notion of getting into the bath tub so that she could turn on the water in case she pissed herself – though she had no idea of how she would manage that tied as tightly as she was. But first things first: get to the bathroom.

Barbara lost her balance as she slid off the bed, landing

on the floor with a bump that would have rattled her teeth if she had not been gagged. And there was still the small matter of moving herself from A to B without the aid of her hands and feet. Barbara discovered for perhaps the hundredth time that humans aren't well equipped for locomotion when their hands and feet were tied – but that was the idea, wasn't it? She rolled half onto her side and bent her knees, digging the spike heels of her shoes into the carpet as she pushed herself along the floor snake-fashion.

Her progress was necessarily slow, and the motion of her dildoes threatened to make her lose control of her bladder. She also found herself out of breath from the exertion and the excitement brought about by her situation. As she went through the doorway the shaft sticking out from between her legs struck the door frame, and Barbara felt herself leak at the shock. She almost lost control then, but she clamped down. Rolling over onto her other side to clear the obstruction, she continued her slow serpentine progress.

And then, like the cavalry riding to the rescue in the nick of time, help came. Barbara heard the sound of the key turning in her front door, and Sarah was there. 'Where are you off to?' she asked as she came in and set down her arm load of shopping.

'Ummmmmnnnnggg!' said Barbara.

'All right. From the urgency of the expression I guess you're about to piss yourself. The loo it shall be. Hold still while I untie your legs.' Sarah swiftly undid the cords that bound Barbara's ankles, knees and thighs.

Barbara groaned with the pain of returning circulation as Sarah helped her to her feet. She almost made it to the loo, but the sight of the goal so close was too much. Before she could sit down she felt a warm stream running down her legs, staining her tights and getting into her shoes. At least, she told herself, she was standing on a tile floor. When she was finished, she was also standing in the centre of a considerable puddle.

'Now look what you've gone and done,' Sarah said in mock anger. 'If it wasn't so much trouble to untie you I'd make you clean it up.' As she spoke she was unbuckling the ankle straps of Barbara's shoes and taking them off. Then she untied her wrists and stripped the wet tights down her legs, manoeuvring them past the black rod that projected jauntily from her bush. Sarah made no move to take that away, nor did she untie Barbara's elbows.

She did help Barbara to sit on the edge of the tub while she drew warm water for the clean-up. Sarah left her there to soak her feet while she fetched a mop and dried up the puddle on the floor. 'You need a litter tray,' she remarked with a smile. 'Even cats know enough to do their business in the right place.'

'Ummmnnngg,' Barbara said again.

Sarah let the water drain away and dried Barbara's feet and legs. Then she led Barbara into the front room, where she had lit the fire and laid out another pair of the new crotchless tights and a pair of shoes for her. 'Sit on the couch,' Sarah directed. This time she had to get Barbara into the tights and shoes unaided.

As she was being washed and dressed, Barbara realised with a shiver that she would have to be dressed and cared for by someone else every time she was tied up – as soon as she found her dream-lover.

Sarah finished with the tights and shoes, then retied Barbara's hands and feet. She used more of the cord from Barbara's collection, remarking that it was a good thing there was plenty around. When Barbara was once more packaged neatly Sarah sat on the couch beside her and took her friend in her arms. 'I enjoy looking at you all tied up. And I think you'll enjoy what comes next.'

Sarah began to stroke Barbara's tits, still constricted by the ropes she had tied round them in the morning. The unusual tightness of her breasts and the friction of Sarah's fingers through the sheer material of her bra set up disturbing currents in Barbara's belly and in her crotch. Sarah continued to tease her breasts until she was flushed and panting. Then she transferred her attention to the rubber shaft between Barbara's thighs, pulling on it, moving it in and out, side to side.

Barbara was on the verge of coming when Sarah stopped abruptly.

'That'll do for now,' she said decisively. She turned the TV on with the remote, continuing to hold Barbara and kissing her ears and eyes and throat from time to time as she watched the screen.

Barbara tried to twist in Sarah's arms in order to bring her tits or the rod into contact with something – preferably Sarah – so she could finish the job Sarah had started.

'Hold still!' Sarah said sharply, avoiding the attempted contact. 'I'm watching this programme.'

She didn't seem all that interested in the TV. Barbara guessed (correctly) that she was being teased, and she moved once more toward Sarah.

This time Sarah said, 'If you don't hold still I'll drag one of the kitchen chairs in here and leave you tied to it. That would keep you out of mischief. Would you like that – or will you hold still as you are?'

'Ummmnnnngg,' Barbara said.

'All right. Now just be patient,' Sarah ordered.

Barbara tried to relax and enjoy her fantasy. The warmth of the fire was comforting, and Sarah's presence was having a warming effect of another sort. So she held still, earning an approving nod from Sarah.

The programme ended, and Sarah turned once more to Barbara. She resumed where she had left off. Barbara was soon much warmer and heading for her first orgasm when Sarah stopped once again. Barbara was sweating and shaking but Sarah paid no attention to her. She got up to fetch one of the bags she had brought back from town. From it she took a large red bow made of silk ribbon.

'See, I didn't entirely forget you today,' she remarked as she tied it around the end of the black rubber shaft, being unnecessarily gentle in the process. Barbara wanted her to jerk it fiercely, and she tried to move her hips while Sarah was tying the bow on.

'Barbara,' Sarah said warningly, 'do you want to be tied to the kitchen chair?'

Barbara subsided reluctantly. She contemplated the incongruous decorative ribbon that adorned the end of her dildo.

Sarah seemed pleased with the effect. She settled herself once more on the sofa and took Barbara in her arms. She resumed kissing and fondling her breasts from time to time – just enough to keep her on the boil without going too far.

It looked like being a long evening. The TV was dull as it always is on a weekday evening, but even the best of programmes would have had serious competition for Barbara's attention. She was too busy watching Sarah and waiting for the next move in the game of tease-and-stop in which she was the victim.

Sarah seemed inordinately interested in the TV, but that may have been merely a pose she adopted to disconcert Barbara. She stroked her breasts idly, murmuring in her ear, 'My, what tight tits you have!' She patted the dildo near the red ribbon and asked, 'How's Black Rod now?'

'Ohhnnt opppp!' Barbara said.

But Sarah did, for an agonizingly long time. Eventually she decided it was time for the main event. She stood up and took off her clothes. Then she faced Barbara so that she could admire the effect.

Barbara sat tensely waiting for the next development.

Sarah sat down in Barbara's lap, facing her and forcing her heels behind her friend's back. Barbara obligingly slid forward to allow her more room. Sarah grasped the rod and untied the bow from the end. She applied hand cream to the shaft, then she lined herself up carefully and slid it into her anus, pausing to let her muscles relax so she could take more of it inside her. When she was fully penetrated, she leaned forward and began to caress Barbara's breasts with both hands. Her own somewhat more pointed breasts were poised invitingly in front of Barbara's face, but that meant nothing because she was gagged and could do nothing about them.

Sarah wriggled on the shaft that joined them, squeezing Barbara's nipples at the same time. She kept moving as she leaned forward to kiss Barbara on the mouth, over her gag.

Barbara closed her eyes and came almost at once. The

teasing earlier on had affected her perhaps more than Sarah intended. She whimpered and her hips jerked, introducing a different rhythm, more urgent than Sarah's slow steady one.

Sarah matched her. She seemed to want her to enjoy this as much as possible.

Barbara was becoming frantic, jerking against her bonds and bucking under Sarah's weight. The fingers on her breasts and nipples were sending urgent messages to her crotch, where the rubber dildo inside her was being driven by Sarah's movements. Her muscles clenched around the shaft as she came. She felt as if she was drawing it inside her. She moaned deep in her throat, bowing her head onto Sarah's shoulder.

Suddenly Sarah squealed, and then began to moan softly, with louder noises as she peaked. There were several more squeals before she was done.

Barbara was quite busy herself, but she was able to appreciate Sarah's enjoyment and to be glad that her friend was having a good time as well.

They lay joined for a long time after the last climax, coming slowly back to the present.

'Am I too heavy for you?' Sarah asked. Barbara shook her head. She didn't mind if Sarah stayed where she was, nor if she were left bound all night.

The ringing of the telephone interrupted that reverie. Sarah reached for the cordless phone that lay on the coffee table. She just managed to reach it without having to break their union.

It was Elspeth. Barbara knew that sooner or later she would call and ask how Sarah was doing and when she planned to come back. It was a reminder to both of them that Sarah was on borrowed time. From the tenor of the conversation Barbara gathered that her friend was wanted up North, but she sat quietly as Sarah chatted with her lover about things she was not a part of. The conversation made her feel acutely lonely.

Elspeth must have asked about Barbara, because Sarah said, 'She's tied up just now, but I can get her to the phone if you'd like.' As she spoke Sarah was using her free hand to untie Barbara's gag. She pulled the wad of tights from her mouth and offered her a sip of wine. Sarah continued the conversation with Elspeth while Barbara moistened the inside of her dry mouth. She had worn the gag for hours and she was quite dry. Finally Sarah said, 'Here she is,' and held the phone so Barbara could speak.

Elspeth seemed relaxed and easy over the phone. She didn't ask awkward questions about what she and Sarah were doing, as a jealous lover might. She seemed interested in Barbara's work and asked questions about the business of editing and publishing that showed a fair grasp of the profession. Barbara assumed she must have acquired her expertise in the course of marketing her own products.

Barbara was struck by how bizarre it was to be speaking on the phone to the lover of the woman who sat on her lap, joined to her by the double-ended dildo. And who squirmed mischievously from time to time during the conversation to remind her of that shared member. Sarah seemed to be trying to make Barbara lose track of what she was saying, causing several awkward pauses in the conversation by her movements. She was grinning as she moved, and her free hand was teasing Barbara's nipples, just to make things more difficult.

Barbara took advantage of one of Elspeth's longer remarks to mouth to Sarah, 'Stop it or I'll tell her about this.'

Sarah grinned even more widely. 'Go ahead.'

Barbara didn't intend to carry out her threat, but she was having trouble keeping her mind on the conversation. Elspeth ended with an invitation for her to come visit them. She sounded sincere. Then she asked to speak to Sarah again.

Barbara relaxed while Sarah chatted, enjoying the way her friend squirmed and jerked her hips from time to time, just to keep her interested while she talked. Suddenly she became aware that Sarah was describing the tableau in front of the TV.

Sarah described how Barbara was tied. She spoke of the

double-ended dildo and told Elspeth where each end was. And as she spoke Barbara realised that she was going to be made to come while Sarah and Elspeth chatted. Sarah was moving more determinedly in her lap, and the dildo was moving insistently inside her. Fleetingly she hoped that Sarah would come too. At least it would prove she had as little self-control as Barbara had.

But Sarah had the advantage of a free hand, which she used to tease and harden Barbara's nipples, and to caress her bound and sensitive breasts. The contest was one-sided, and Barbara was going to lose it. She could no more prevent herself from coming than she could stop Sarah from driving her over the edge.

And all the while Sarah was describing to Elspeth what she was doing. Barbara was mortified but Sarah seemed not to care. As Barbara began to gasp and moan with the onset of her climax, Sarah told Elspeth. 'Hold on, I'll just let you speak to her.' She held the mouthpiece of the telephone near Barbara's mouth. 'Say something to Elspeth,' she urged with another grin.

Barbara was not interested in making conversation. The best she could manage was a low moan, 'Ohhhh, God!' Her body was making the sounds it always made when she was coming, and then she came. Loudly and emphatically and often. She almost unseated Sarah as she bucked and heaved beneath her.

Sarah held on, remarking to Barbara (and incidentally to Elspeth) that it felt as if the couch were moving under her. 'Or maybe it's just the earth moving for you.' Then a look of surprise crossed her face and she stopped in mid-sentence. Sarah let out one of the squeals she made when she came. Her face was a picture.

Barbara was relieved to hear (through the telephone) that Elspeth was laughing. She began to laugh too, mainly in relief, but she saw the funny side of the situation as well. Finally Sarah joined them.

Barbara remarked that they had given a whole new meaning to the term telephone sex. Sarah repeated the remark to Elspeth, and they had another laugh. Finally

Sarah said, 'Yes. That's fine. See you late on Sunday evening – the train that gets into Queen Street around nine o'clock. Love you. Bye.' She put the phone down and hugged Barbara.

Barbara, unable to reciprocate, laid her head on Sarah's shoulder and kissed the side of her neck.

Sarah wriggled her bottom. 'Game for another?'

'I can't stop you,' Barbara replied.

They grinned at one another. Sarah got her legs under her and rose, the rubber shaft emerging from the tight sheath of her anus. She made a proper slow job of her withdrawal so that Barbara would know she wasn't being rejected. When she was free, she reached down to pat the shaft she had been sitting on.

'That's definitely the Best in Show. I should have bought a blue ribbon for it. By the way, Elspeth says you're invited to make a threesome any time you feel like it.'

Barbara was glad to know she hadn't caused any friction between Sarah and Elspeth. She thought she might just take up the invitation one day soon. She tugged at the cords on her wrists just to remind herself that she was still tied up, then relaxed and waited for the next development. It was wonderful not to have to make any decisions.

Sarah announced that she was starving. 'Sex makes me hungry.' She went to make sandwiches for them. When she came back with a platter of finger sandwiches, she brought a bottle of wine for them to share. She poured wine, then fed Barbara, eating between times herself.

'Let's have a slumber party tonight,' Sarah suggested. 'Do you have any more duvets?'

Barbara said that there were two more of them in the wardrobe in the bedroom. 'The covers are in the chest behind the door.'

'I plan to leave you tied up tonight just as you are,' Sarah said. She paused in case Barbara wanted to object. 'Motion carried,' she announced when Barbara said nothing. 'But I don't think I can carry you into the bedroom, so I thought we could bed down here if I use the duvets as a mattress and bring the pillows from the bed. We can use the duvet from the bed as a cover. It'll be just like camping out.'

Barbara said once again, 'I can't stop you.' Then she added with a grin, 'Even if I wanted to.'

'I take it you don't want to? Stop me, that is?' Sarah went to fetch the duvets and the pillows from the bedroom. When she came back, she moved the coffee table to one side and laid the quilts in the cleared space in front of the couch. She placed the pillows against the couch, using it as a headboard. Then she smoothed their impromptu bed and helped Barbara to slide from her seat on the couch down to the floor. There was only the slightest bump as she landed.

Barbara wriggled down until she was stretched out on her back. Sarah helped her get comfortable by arranging the pillows behind her head. Then she turned out all the lights and made sure the door was locked. The only light in the room came from the flickering TV screen as she came back to the bed. Sarah pulled the last duvet over them both and snuggled down against Barbara's side.

'Just you and me and Black Rod,' she said as she slid her hand under the harness and ruffled Barbara's pubic hair. 'He makes a nice tent pole. All this reminds me of my days in the Girl Guides. Were you one, Barbara?'

'No, Mother thought them too rowdy. Is that where you learned to tie knots?'

'Oddly enough, it was. We used to go to camps. You know, with little bell tents and cans of cold baked beans and stale sandwiches. And ants. There had to be ants to get into the food and crawl into your bed at night. That way you knew you were enjoying the great outdoors. Mother Nature and all that. It was fun for a while. All girls together and that sort of thing. But then as we got older sex reared its lovely head and everything changed.' Sarah paused as if reliving the memories.

'What, sex among the Girl Guides? Is nothing sacred any more?' Barbara asked. 'The ghost of Baden-Powell must be very uneasy nowadays.'

Sarah chuckled. 'I guess not. We were little hellions.

Your mother was probably right to keep you out of it. I had a chum – well, we all had chums in those halcyon days. She was cute and blonde and blue-eyed. Plump and rosy and aggressively healthy. A Shirley Temple kind of innocent. In fact, Shirley was her name. We joined up together while we were both schoolgirls, and we both stuck it out until we were nearly sixteen. I think she *was* sixteen. She was a month or so older than me. We were at the age when you have to quit Girl Guiding and do something terribly adult and boring like becoming a Brown Owl or some other sort of wise and worthy animal. You know, take charge of a troop of our own.

'The other girls always teased Shirley. I guess it had something to do with the way she looked, and maybe the way she acted. She never took part in the pranks the rest of us played, so she seemed like a goody-goody type. You must have had girls like that in the dormitory of your girls' school. Anyway, she always obeyed the rules and I always broke them whenever the chance came.

'She must have admired me for my outlaw mentality – wanting to be like me but afraid to. And I admired her for the way she took everything the others did and never cried. We were drawn to one another. We always shared a tent or a cabin at camp and we looked out for one another. We learned how to make awful coffee, and how to heat up a tin of baked beans over an open fire without getting ashes in the food. Basic cookery for when we Grew Up and Went Out Into The World. They thought in capital letters then. Or they wanted us to think that way.

'We were at our last camp of the summer. Which turned out to be our last camp ever, but we weren't to know that. It was also Girlhood's End, though we didn't know that either. Sounds Like an E. M. Forster novel, doesn't it? There must have been twenty other Guides at the camp, all younger than we two were. I guess maybe we represented Authority to them, because the adults tended to delegate things to Shirley and me. That may be why they resented us, even though we were Guides like them.

'It wasn't one of those glorious summers like the First

World War poets pretended the summer of 1914 was. It was a typical English summer – wet and chilly. We were shut up in our tents more often than we were running about in the woods doing the woodcrafty things we were supposed to do. One night toward the end of the camp the others ganged up on the two of us. They came to our tent well after dark, when the adults were fucking one another stupid, or down at the pub getting roaring drunk. We were on our own.

'They held us down and took all our clothes off. Amazing how early they begin to associate nudity with shame and hurt. Neither of us cried out for help. It just wasn't done. The other girls tied our hands behind our backs and manoeuvred us into the classic sixty-nine position, though none of us knew the term then. They spread our legs and tucked our heads between each other's thighs. Then they tied our ankles together. In order to keep us from pulling apart they tied a rope around my neck and tied the other end to Shirley's wrists. They did the same thing to her. Finally they rolled us into our blankets like a giant cocoon and tied them around us as well.

'It was dark and scary in there, and we couldn't get loose, and they were all laughing and rolling us about. Several of the more sadistic girls laid into us with rope-ends, trying to make us beg to be let loose, I suppose. Neither of us did. Eventually the others got tired and went away laughing in the darkness. We were alone and we couldn't get loose. We both tried until we were sweaty, but the others must have read the Girl Guide's Book of Knots before they did us up.

'Anyway, we were all hot and sweaty inside the blankets, trying to get free, when I noticed that Shirley smelled rather nice just *there*. I shifted a bit, and then kissed her damp little pubic mound. You would have thought I had jabbed her with a red-hot pin. She jumped and cried out, "Oh, Sarah, don't *do* that. You're . . . we're not . . . girls aren't supposed to do that with one another."

'I could have asked her if it was okay for two men to do that with one another, or if a man and a woman could do it, but I wasn't at the top of my mental form just then. I was at the tops of her thighs, though, and I kept going. Eventually she stopped fighting me and began to relax. Maybe she thought in for a penny, in for a pound. At any rate, she began to explore *my* sweaty cunt with her busy little mouth. After that there was no going back for either of us. We abandoned our attempts to get loose and concentrated on doing one another thoroughly.

'There must have been muffled shrieks and moans, and they must have come from us, since there was no one else nearby (that we knew of) in precisely our situation. But we had enough native caution to keep relatively quiet. What we were doing was Forbidden, and we didn't want to get caught at it. We weren't. It was a busy night, what with one thing and another. I suppose we slept during some parts of it, but we managed to wake one another up several times in rather startling ways.

'Although we didn't spend too much time trying to get loose after we discovered the things we could do to one another, we had luckily got some rather nasty marks on our wrists and ankles during the initial struggle. We were able to pass them off next morning as signs of our attempts to extricate ourselves from our Horrid Situation.

'Of course we were absent from roll call. No one knew where we were. It was an admirable example of not splitting on one another. It wasn't long afterwards that we were found – still tied hand and foot but prudently disengaged, mouthwise. Fortunately, there was no way to tell that we had been at one another all night. I mean, there were no obvious stains, and absolutely no one would admit to familiarity with whatever odour was detectable.

'We were suspected of Horrid Things of course, but we had been found tied up in a way that pointed suspiciously to Other Persons. It wasn't something even the most woodcrafty Girl Guide could have easily done to herself. So they couldn't pin anything on us, and *we* certainly weren't going to say anything. We were taken aside and questioned in the hope that one of us would crack without the other one knowing. It didn't work. We displayed our rope-marked wrists and adopted an air of injured innocence. The rest of the troop was questioned, singly and in groups. No one knew anything.

'Then they sat us all down and gave us the Number Two lecture on Unnatural Relationships (they make warts grow in places you're not supposed to admit you have). I wonder how many girls worried that night in private about blemishes in various places that were difficult of access. I know of at least one who didn't. For good measure they also warned us about Men (and Boys) and what they would Do To Us if we let them Become Familiar. If we had been gullible, we would have been terrified at the danger we were surrounded by. But you can't scare young people that easily.

'But that night was the end for Shirley and me. I never saw her again. Our parents were summoned and the News Was Broken to them – in the gentlest way possible. My mother had a fit, and she cross-examined me all the way home. But I kept quiet. I never learned what happened to Shirley. Maybe she decided to stay clear of Wicked Sarah and her busy mouth. And that was the end of my Girl Guiding too, but that wasn't so bad. I would have been kicked out – or upstairs – anyway, on account of my age. After That Night, though, out was more likely than upstairs. I was not an Influence For Good.

'And I've tried to stay that way ever since. Such are the influences of our formative years,' Sarah finished with a laugh. 'Did you do such things at school?'

'No. We were rather better behaved. Or more timid. Or maybe I went to the wrong school. I've been trying to make up for it ever since.'

'And not doing too badly, if you want my opinion.' Sarah gave a final tug at Barbara's shaft as they settled down for the night. Barbara slept fitfully.

In the morning Sarah untied her and Barbara made a bee-line for the loo. She felt better after that. It was Friday, and she had to go to the office that day. Sarah said she'd find something to amuse herself with.

Frank called Barbara at work and confirmed their meeting for Saturday. Barbara was almost sorry to be going out. She wanted to spend as much time as possible with Sarah. When she mentioned these reservations to Sarah that evening, Sarah told her not to worry. She reminded Barbara that she was going back to Glasgow on Sunday, and that their idyll was going to end shortly anyway.

'But if you come home at a reasonable hour on Saturday, I promise to have your ropes handy. And Black Rod. But don't pass up an opportunity to get yourself fucked stupid if the ambience is right.'

Barbara had been hoping they'd do something that night, but Sarah vetoed the idea. 'You'll need to be rested for tomorrow night. And besides, you don't want too many obvious marks around your wrists and ankles. The marks from last night are still visible for those who know what to look for.'

Barbara had to admit the justice of the observation. She hoped that no one at work had noticed the stigmata of her night in bondage.

When Frank came to pick up Barbara, she introduced him to Sarah. Frank did a double-take. So did Sarah. It was apparent from the way they spoke that they weren't complete strangers, but they said nothing and Barbara didn't want to pry into something that neither of them wanted to talk about.

Like most first dates, theirs was a bit stiff and awkward. They filled one another in on such things as family, job, friends and hobbies. Barbara didn't think it appropriate to mention her favourite pastime at the first meeting.

Barbara didn't like to make up her mind about a man after only one meeting unless he had obvious spiritual bad breath. Frank was not in that category. In fact she almost accepted his invitation to come to his place for a nightcap. And it would probably have turned into something more than a drink. But she refused, for reasons she couldn't exactly say even to herself. Perhaps, she thought, it was because Sarah was still there waiting for her. Frank was certainly attractive. And attracted to her, otherwise he would not have asked her about a mid-week meeting; was she free? They agreed to meet on Wednesday.

He dropped her off shortly after midnight. Sarah was waiting for her as promised, with the ropes all ready.

Barbara felt her stomach drop with her excitement. 'I was thinking of this all evening,' she confessed to Sarah.

'Was he such a disappointment, then? I thought he would be interesting. He certainly looked good.'

Barbara thought back to the moment when he and Sarah had seemed to recognise one another. 'Had you met him somewhere else?'

'Yes.' Sarah sounded hesitant.

'Well, tell me about it,' Barbara urged.

'I don't know him very well. You could say he was more of an acquaintance. I met him on the night of the dinner party when Elspeth and I eloped – or escaped, if you prefer – from my erstwhile mistress. He spent some time in conversation with her and they seemed to know one another from somewhere else. He seemed quite interested in her. In Phillipa, I mean. But I don't know any more about him. Or them,' Sarah said. 'You probably know more about him than I do. Tell me what you think.'

'Well, he's definitely interesting. I'll have to see him once or twice more before I make up my mind.'

'You mean, before you sleep with him?' Sarah asked. She was smiling, and Barbara was relieved to see that she wasn't jealous. Not that she had any excuse to be, but jealousy was a funny emotion.

'Well, yes, I suppose that's what I meant. But it's early days – or nights – yet. I'm seeing him again in the middle of the week – dinner at a restaurant he knows. I'll call you later and let you know how it goes.'

'Do that,' Sarah said. 'Don't lose touch again. I'm glad we got together again after so long.'

'So am I. And I'll call and write. Promise. After all, I have to redeem the compromising photos you took.'

'Oh, I'd forgotten all about them,' Sarah said unconvincingly. 'Thanks for reminding me. I'll hold them over you.' Changing the subject, she continued, 'I have to make an early start tomorrow, so we'd better make plans to go to bed soon. If you'll strip down to the essentials, I'll make you snug for the night.' Sarah indicated the rope she had laid out. 'Or would you prefer to be chained? That might be more comfortable.'

'What a choice to have to make!' Barbara said. 'You decide.'

'Let's keep it simple, then,' Sarah said. 'Take off all your clothes and come into the bedroom when you're ready.'

In the bedroom Barbara saw that the bed had been moved away from the wall as they had done before. Black Rod was lying on the duvet, and Sarah was running the rope through her fingers suggestively. Sarah helped her with the harness, sliding the dildo home for her. When Barbara was all buckled in and jutting out, Sarah pulled the bedding down.

Barbara stretched out as she had done before, pushing her hands and feet through the openings in the head and footboards of the bed. Sarah tied her wrists and ankles, ensuring that Barbara would not be able to move or roll over during the night. Then she added a refinement. With short lengths of cord Sarah tied Barbara's thumbs and big toes together. Barbara found this especially exciting. She wriggled and pulled against the cords while Sarah undressed and got into bed. As before, the duvet was held up by the black rubber shaft.

This time Barbara didn't wake up until Sarah had impaled herself fully on the dildo. It was a most pleasant way to wake up. They made slow love for what seemed like hours, each one trying to prolong it. When they were done Sarah pulled the duvet over them and they slept.

In the morning Sarah untied Barbara first thing. She had packed her things the night before while Barbara was out, not wishing to have to do it while she was there and so remind her of the impending departure. She made breakfast while Barbara used the toilet.

They ate in the kitchen. Both were glad that there was no strain. They had their separate lives to live. And they would keep in touch. It was the best they could do short of one or the other moving house. And Barbara knew that wouldn't work. Visiting was one thing, but if she lived nearby and remained unattached, Elspeth was bound to think of her as a rival. That would poison any relationship she might have with Sarah. And she was still hoping to find Mr (not Ms) Right.

Sarah planned to take a taxi to the railway station at about 10.00 a.m. That gave them something over an hour to say farewell. Sarah promised to call in the evening to let Barbara know she had arrived safely, and to check that Barbara was all right. For she also planned, as she had hinted, to leave Barbara bound and gagged before she left – a sort of parting gift. She left Barbara to finish her coffee while she made her own preparations.

When Barbara came back into the living room Sarah had arranged the duvets in front of the couch as she had done two nights ago. 'I'm afraid you'll have to make up the bed before you can sleep in it again, but I thought this would be more comfortable.' Sarah had also laid out Barbara's corselet and tights. And the rest of the dildo kit Barbara had bought from the sex shop. 'I decided to use Black Rod differently this time, in case you wanted to lie on your front or roll about as you struggle futilely to get free,' Sarah said with a smile.

Sarah helped Barbara with the dildoes, so that she was plugged front and back. She placed an oval rubber pad with 'fingers' on its inner (or Barbara) side inside the tights, just over Barbara's clitoris. She bound Barbara's breasts and helped her pull the top of the corselet into place and settle her breasts in the cups.

She gestured for Barbara to lie on the floor. When she did so, Sarah handcuffed her wrists behind her back. Then she tied Barbara's ankles, knees and thighs with the braided cord. She was careful with the knots.

'I'll be in Glasgow about nine o'clock tonight, so expect me to call about an hour later. I'll set this to give you about half an hour's lead to get loose.' She set the timer and dropped the keys to Barbara's handcuffs into the box and closed it. 'You're stuck now, little slavey. I hope you enjoy the experience.'

'I'll try,' Barbara replied. Her throat felt tight with anticipation. 'Thank you for a lovely week.'

'I managed to enjoy it too,' Sarah told her. 'You needn't

be too humbly grateful – unless you enjoy grovelling as well as B&D. Do you?'

'I hadn't thought about it. I just wanted you to know it was good for me.'

'Then you're welcome, love. And thanks for everything – bed and board and sex.' Sarah kissed Barbara on her mouth, an open-mouthed kiss that threatened to go on and on and threatened to escalate. The sound of the taxi's horn outside put an end to it. Sarah stood up and grabbed her case. 'Back in a moment,' she said.

Barbara felt lost as she waited for Sarah to return. It had been a lovely week, and she was sorry it was over. But there was no sense in going over that again.

Raindrops sparkled in Sarah's hair when she came back in. 'It's pissing down out there. Good job you're staying in. Will it be all right to leave the box here on the floor?'

Barbara nodded silently.

'Let's get you finished off then,' Sarah said as she inserted the plugs in Barbara's ears. She blindfolded her with masking tape, and before inserting the gag she bent down to kiss Barbara once more. 'Goodbye. We'll be in touch.' She stuffed the gag in and tied it in place. Finally she tested the handcuffs and cords to be sure they were secure. Sarah put her mouth against Barbara's ear and said, 'I'll lock the door and put the keys back through the letter-box. Don't forget to pick them up.' She kissed Barbara just below the ear and left without another word.

Barbara heard the door close and lock. Sarah's footsteps receded and Barbara was alone and helpless. She had planned to do this last Sunday. Only Sarah's welcome arrival had prevented her. Now it was a relief and a pleasure to have something to do on a rainy Sunday when she was alone once again.

3

FRANK

The affair with Frank developed quickly. Barbara went in to the office on Monday morning feeling at a loose end. With Sarah gone, she felt a sense of let-down, naturally enough after the sexual marathon of the last week. Even the Sunday had been a pleasure, and she had got loose in time to take Sarah's call. Both she and Elspeth repeated the invitation for her to visit them. Elspeth sounded eager to meet her. Barbara wondered what else Sarah had told her about the week in London.

As he had promised, Frank called her on Tuesday to set up their dinner meeting for the next evening. At the same time he suggested they plan on spending the weekend together. This evidence of his interest in her boosted her morale and helped Barbara get through the post-Sarah depression.

It was at this same time that Barbara began to feel that she was in a dead-end job. She wasn't going to get a chance to work on 'serious' books. She was too good at the job she was doing. She was beginning to think of a change of jobs. Maybe even a complete change of scene. Now Glasgow . . . Resolutely she put that thought aside. Maybe a change of scene, but not there, where the temptation to meddle would be too strong. She was beginning to acquire a talent for self-sacrifice worthy of a saint. It would help so much if Frank (or the next man, or the next) turned out to be *simpatico*.

On Wednesday Frank was more at ease when he came to pick her up for dinner. She thought he looked more like the man who had first caught her interest with his remark about lovely ladies who dined alone. She felt more relaxed with him as well. This might turn out all right after all.

They reached the stage of sexual appraisal and approval sometime during dinner. This time, knowing there was no one there, she invited him into her flat for a drink. And he accepted the invitation with none of the boorish licking of the chops which some men displayed at this stage. Things could still have gone either way. He didn't strike her as the type of man who would charge in and force her into bed against her inclinations. But she wouldn't mind a little seduction. Then she would know that he thought her attractive enough to make the effort.

Barbara showed him around the flat and he made the appropriate noises of approval, saying how comfortable the place was and how well she had furnished it. She left him looking over her tape collection when she went into the kitchen to make drinks. She heard *The Water Music* start up in the front room and she thought that at least they shared similar tastes in music.

Frank's hand touched hers as he took the drink she offered. He made the touch longer and more intimate than the situation called for. When she didn't draw away he took her hand and led her to the sofa. When they sat down he stretched out his arm and Barbara moved within its circle. She thought that felt good. She set down her drink and turned up her mouth to be kissed.

He kisses well, Barbara thought. The introductory fumbling and misunderstandings were the most embarrassing part of any new relationship, and she was glad to see that he was a good deal less awkward than many men she had met.

Then he too set his drink aside and used both arms to draw her closer.

Nothing loth, Barbara snuggled against him, thinking that the situation was developing into one straight out of the romances she was paid to edit. Things took a different course abruptly when he moved a hand onto the sexually unambiguous area of her bottom. Barbara knew that his hand hadn't missed her waist and strayed there. She knew that her waist, while not of super-model dimensions, was nevertheless unmissable. Ergo, the hand had arrived there on purpose. The ball was now in her court. She had to choose between the outraged maiden act or the experienced *demi-mondaine*. His hand felt rather good there.

And soon felt better in other, equally unambiguous places. She might have said that their kiss prolonged itself and grew hands. Hands that roamed over her erogenous zones, eliciting all the right responses. Or, she thought, if one wanted to be vulgar, one could say that she was being thoroughly felt up. She said 'ahhh' and 'ohhh' at what seemed appropriate places. He didn't need to be told what to do next. She thought that was another good sign. Frank was beginning to look like a man who knew what he wanted. Equally important, he knew what she wanted, which was more of the same but with fewer clothes.

Frank paid no attention (that she was aware of) to her carefully chosen lacy underwear, merely getting her out of it in record time. Barbara didn't mind. She was much too interested in the way his touch seemed to set her on fire. This situation occurred often in the romantic novels, usually before the protagonist said a reluctant but emphatic NO. Or just after the happy couple had been united in holy matrimony, in which case the response was a qualified and hesitant yes, before turning finally into, 'Not tonight. I have a headache.' Barbara's mother had taught her the routine, but she paid no attention to the advice. As a result she found herself in situations like this more often than not. Delicious situations, she thought, as her hand found his cock.

Frank too had levitated out of his clothes, and Barbara felt herself being drawn down onto a very emphatic erection. She didn't mind the almost complete lack of foreplay. It seemed she had been waiting for just this kind of masterful handling for a long time. She came almost as soon as he penetrated her, even before she had time to appreciate the hands which settled firmly onto her breasts and began to do pleasant things to her stiff nipples.

Frank had played the gentleman by letting her straddle him while he lay back on the couch. Or maybe he knew he could penetrate her more fully from that position (she certainly felt full). Or maybe he knew she wanted him to have his hands free to touch her breasts, her stomach, to worm their way between her legs and finger her clitoris. Barbara cried out as she came again. And still she rode him, rising and falling but always staying in contact with the cock inside her and the hands that stroked her. Suddenly she felt him tense and she knew he was going to come. She bit back a shriek as he came, thrusting deeply into her. Barbara came a moment later, gasping and moaning.

When she finally grew quiet, Frank said, 'I'm glad you had a good time.'

'Am I that obvious?'

'Fortunately, yes. It's not always that easy to tell from this end when a woman has come. And some of them are adept at hiding their reactions, or exaggerating them. I prefer the demonstrative type – like you.'

'Oh, and just how many women have you sampled?' Even as she asked the question Barbara was aware how silly and conventional it sounded, but he had raised the subject with his remarks. And besides, she was plain curious, as most women are, though they may not like the answer to that sort of question.

'You'll just have to count the notches on my cock when we're done.' As he spoke, Frank moved inside her.

Barbara gasped. Was he hard again? So soon? She felt vaguely flattered. No one had paid her this supreme tribute before. Shakily, she said, 'We don't have to find out just yet, do we?'

'Not at all.' Frank drew her down to lie atop him as he began to rock his hips up and down.

Barbara pressed her breasts against his chest and rode with the motion. This time it took longer for her to come, but the climb to the peaks was just as good. The urgency of the first time had been replaced by something gentler. She put her arms around his neck and pulled herself fiercely against him as she came, crying out softly this time. The first time had taken the edge off her desire. The second time was more like filling in the gaps. By the time she felt him come she felt thoroughly filled in.

They moved into the bedroom after that. Somehow the

question of Frank's staying overnight had been answered without being asked. Barbara snuggled against his back and wrapped her arm around him with her fingers just brushing his cock. Just to remind herself he was still there. She slept, if not the sleep of the just, then certainly the sleep of the thoroughly sated.

In the morning Barbara woke as Frank was easing himself inside her. This time he was on top. She didn't get this particular type of wake-up call every day. She parted her thighs and welcomed him in. When they were done there wasn't time for breakfast before they had to leave for work. Frank promised that the next time (Barbara was pleased to know he wanted a next time as much as she did) he would get up early and make breakfast – though she was not to take this for granted.

Barbara liked his assumption that they would be seeing a lot of each other. She also thought she had found a clever lover – just the right mixture of gentleness and assertiveness. Maybe this was it. But how to bring up the subject of B&D without (at best) seeming unappreciative of his technique or (at worst) frightening him off? She adopted the Scarlett O'Hara solution – 'I'll worry about that tomorrow.'

Before he left, Frank brought the mail into the bedroom. Barbara was at the stockings-and-suspenders stage of dressing, and he paused to admire. Among the usual bills and advertisements was a letter from Sarah. She knew Frank must have seen it but he said nothing. She forgot all about the mail when he reached from behind her to cup her breasts and kiss her behind the ear. Barbara leaned her head back against his chest.

But they both had things to do. Frank promised to call her later – either at work or at home. 'You're much too good to be left alone for long.'

The prospect of his call buoyed her spirits all day. Claire noticed her frequent smiles and relaxed manner at once. 'Have you been getting any lately?' she asked, jumping to the obvious conclusion.

'Whatever made you think that?'

'Oh, nothing except your general air of the woman who's

just had the cock and found the experience exhilarating,' Claire replied airily. 'Anyway, does he have any friends you could throw my way? I'm a growing girl and I need regular sex.'

'Don't know yet, but I'll keep it in mind. What sort do you like – dark or blonde?'

'Well-hung and randy. I'm not fussy.'

Frank didn't call until late afternoon. Would she be free the coming weekend – not just the Saturday evening but the whole time? He didn't say what he had in mind, but Barbara knew that sex was definitely on the agenda – hopefully one of the main items. She only realised how much she had been looking forward to his call by the feeling of let-down after it had come. But she brightened up as she thought of the weekend with him.

Claire, who had been eavesdropping shamelessly, said, 'Your eyes are the eyes of a woman in rut. Spare a thought for me while you're in ecstasy. I'll be reading spiritual books and living on bread and water in my solitary retreat the whole time you're enjoying the lustful embraces of your tame satyr.'

Frank had (he told her later) the use of a 'country cottage', as he called it. He didn't say whose, only that the place was in Sussex, near Pulborough, with an extensive view over the North Downs. 'Definitely a des. res.,' he told her. It looked as if there would be plenty of time – and space and privacy – for sex. Secluded country cottages had a way of lending themselves to the indoor sport. So did small townhouses, of course, as well as the back seats of cars and any wooded areas where the only witnesses were of the four-legged variety whose discretion could be relied on. But cottages were better, in Barbara's opinion. She spent a fair amount of time planning what to take with her. In the end she decided to emphasise things suitable for the bedroom rather than the great outdoors – more lacy lingerie than sturdy walking shoes and tweedy outfits.

Frank hadn't paid much attention to her underwear last time, being too intent on getting her out of it – with, she admitted, some help and encouragement from herself. But this time she imagined there would be more leisure for him to enjoy the aesthetic effects of a provocatively clad female bod of the Hilson variety. She didn't think the lily was any the worse for a bit of gilding. When she was packed, Barbara had managed to get everything into one small overnight case, not being one of those women who take along their entire wardrobe for a two-day holiday. At the last minute she packed the thumb-cuffs Sarah had bought for her. This might be the best opportunity to let Frank know which way she leaned. No matter what happened, it was going to be awkward for her to bring up the subject of B&D, but someone would have to grasp the bull by the horns at some point.

She was ready (in several senses) long before the weekend came around. On Saturday morning she was up with the postman, if not with the lark, and refused to allow herself to be put off by the usual collection of bills. She was going to have a good time. Frank arrived early as well, driving an ancient Land-Rover. Protective coloration, he called it. They wouldn't look so much like townies, and would attract less notice per square native.

'Are you eager or something?' Barbara asked. She was secretly flattered by his promptness and the thoroughness of his plans.

'Or something,' Frank replied. 'I promised you I'd make breakfast the next time, and I know of a great transport café that will help me keep my word.' He put Barbara's case into the back with his own. Holding the door for her, he said, 'Your carriage awaits, Milady.'

They made good time through the quiet streets and were soon bound south and west on the A24. Breakfast at the transport café outside Horsham was a success, partly because the rest of the clientèle consisted mainly of lorry drivers who did a lot of staring at Barbara. That didn't do her ego much damage, certainly not enough to make her decry the male chauvinist attitude her admirers displayed. She wondered if the most strident protests against ogling came from those women who didn't get that many admiring looks from men.

The cottage was indeed secluded, at the end of a muddy lane which in summer would be green and leafy but was now lined with bare trees and frozen-looking bushes. The house, however, more than made up for the dismal scenery of the early November day. It was a converted farmhouse which had been extended over the years since it had ceased to be the centre of an active farm. It looked like the kind of place that would be attractive to jaded City stockbrokers, to whom price was no object as they built their country retreats for the weekends that became increasingly fewer as the novelty wore off.

Although well cared for, the house had an unlived-in atmosphere; there was a damp smell inside. Frank opened the windows to let in the air and laid a fire in the huge fireplace in the sitting room. He lit it and they went upstairs to the bedroom. There Frank laid another fire. 'For later,' he said. 'For when we get laid.'

'Oh heavens,' Barbara said. 'I see you have brought me here under false pretences. I had thought we would sleep in separate bedrooms, rising with the lark to tramp over the fields in sensible outdoor clothing, then return to eat lunch, sated by the beauty of the countryside. I'm a lady of refined taste . . .'

'Who happens to enjoy fucking,' Frank interjected.

Barbara began to laugh and couldn't continue. She stopped laughing when Frank crossed the space between them and took her in his arms. She leaned against him as if she belonged there. There was a stirring in his trousers that reminded her why she had come here with this comparative stranger. Her knees felt weak when he kissed her. She thought of the things they would have time to do and shivered with excitement. That was the result of being alone with comparative strangers – one never knew quite what they were going to do.

Frank brought their cases upstairs and she did the domestic thing, putting their clothes away in drawers. He approved of her choice in underwear, saying he was looking forward to seeing her in it almost as much as he wanted to see her out of it.

Barbara was pleased by the implied compliment. Frank was clearly looking forward to having her in the very near future. This seemed like the moment to spring her surprise. As she was putting away the last of her things she managed to let the thumb-cuffs fall to the floor. The soft thud was audible to them both. Barbara hesitated just long enough to let Frank get there ahead of her. There was no going back now.

'Yours?' he asked unnecessarily. The question invited an explanation without demanding one.

Barbara nodded. 'Sarah bought them for me. You see, I'm rather into B&D.' She was feeling awkward already, but she forced herself to continue. 'My favourite sex fantasy involves being tied up and thorougly had.' This was harder than she had anticipated, even though Frank made no comment and showed no sign of fleeing incontinently. Barbara didn't know whether to take his silence as confusion or encouragement. But she was committed now, and she forced the words out. 'The classic female rape fantasy,' she said with a futile attempt at lightness. There was a tightness in her throat that had as much to do with embarrassment as with excitement. Was he going to force her to spell it all out in detail? Couldn't he see how awkward she was feeling?

Apparently he couldn't – or wouldn't. Red-faced, stumbling over the words, Barbara gave him an abbreviated version of her solo masturbation and bondage sessions, and of the week with Sarah. She caught herself just before asking whether he thought of her as a freak; it involved too much loss of face, and the answer might be worse.

At the end of the account Frank merely nodded. 'We'll have to drive into the local village for food and the usual last-minute things if we're to be cut off here for the next two days by sex.' Frank explained that one of his friends owned the house and asked only that anyone using it bring their own food and clean up after themselves.

Barbara was in limbo, but she felt relieved that she had managed to say her piece. His remark about being cut off by sex was encouraging. And he hadn't fled.

They bought mainly things that wouldn't require elaborate preparation – mostly sandwich and salad stuff and several bottles of medium-priced wine. Barbara suggested candles, thinking of adding a romantic touch to their meals. More promising, from Barbara's point of view, Frank bought a quantity of nylon rope. When Barbara asked him what he intended to do with it, he explained rather ambiguously that rope was always handy out in the country.

Back at the house Frank opened a bottle of wine and they put away the purchases. The fire in the sitting room had dissipated the dampness and warmed the room. It occurred to Barbara that it might be a good idea to light the fire upstairs ready for the time when they would retire to the bedroom. While Frank went to attend to it, she carried her glass of wine as she explored the ground floor of the house. There were several large rooms, mostly bare. That added to the impression of a house only sporadically occupied. Barbara became more conscious than ever of their seclusion. There were no near neighbours, and the empty house (to her heated imagination, at least) began to seem like the kind of place she had imagined in her fantasies – the ideal place for her demon-lover to imprison her.

Barbara went back into the front room when she heard Frank coming downstairs again.

'Hungry?' he asked her. 'I think I can manage a sandwich. Or if you prefer we can go for a walk in the countryside. Or there's a cinema in town.' Frank seemed to be deliberately talking around the subject which had brought them to this cottage in the (relative) wilds of Sussex. This might be his way of keeping Barbara on tenterhooks. Or he might be giving her an opportunity to retreat from her earlier admissions.

Barbara decided to cut through the fog. The sense of having to take charge when she wanted to be taken in charge was not to her taste. 'We're here to fuck, aren't we? Or did you really bring me here under false pretences? I could have been curled up with a good book at home if I thought you were really a closet environmentalist.'

'Well, I thought you might be having second thoughts about spending the weekend in a secluded cottage with an avowed sex fiend, and I wanted you to know there are alternatives in case you were getting cold feet – or cold anything else. I'm glad to know you're in agreement with the main plan. Indoor sports seem so much more attractive on dull wet days. But I'll put a brave face on it if you insist on going tramping about the muddy lanes.'

Indicating her high-heels, Barbara asked him, 'Do these look like the sort of shoes they recommend for walking holidays?'

'Well, no, now that you mention it. So I take it we can get down to the main business any time now?'

'Go and make the sandwiches and open another bottle of wine. Sex is always better on a full stomach. And leave your clothes in the kitchen before you come back here.'

Frank smiled ironically, bowed and left.

Barbara sat before the fire with her wine glass. She was rather looking forward to making love before the open fire.

When Frank re-entered with a platter of sandwiches he was nude, as directed, and erect, which was a pleasant addition to the scenario. Seeing her interest, Frank said, 'Damned thing kept bumping into things.'

'Well, so long as you didn't do yourself an injury. Come and sit here with me.'

'Don't you feel over-dressed? Part of the reason for this,' indicating his erection, 'was the thought of you nude on a bearskin rug in front of a roaring fire.'

'No bearskin rug,' Barbara pointed out practically. 'The rise of the animal rights movement has had certain adverse effects on secret trysts. But I wanted you to undress me a bit at a time. You're allowed to make appreciative noises as each bit comes off to reveal the classic beauty of my body. Start with my shoes.'

Frank sat on the floor and offered her a sandwich. 'Eat this while I get started. We'll make it a test to see whether you're more interested in food or sex. If you stop eating we'll both know the time has come.' He took a sandwich himself and used his free hand to stroke Barbara's leg.

She had worn stockings and suspenders especially for his benefit. He was about to discover how thoughtful she had been. And she was about to discover how he responded to her choice. His fingers on the smooth nylon were sending disturbing currents up her legs.

'Do you want me to tie you up now?' Frank asked abruptly.

This was his first direct approach to the subject of B&D, and Barbara had to make a real effort to keep her voice level as she replied. 'Maybe later,' she said, thinking to herself, why am I hesitating? Now that the right man had come along, she was strangely reluctant to proceed to the next stage. One part of her was insisting, this is IT! But some native caution urged her to put off the moment of truth.

Frank didn't press the point. He continued to stroke her, moving his hand further up her leg. He reached the tops of her stockings, where nylon ended and Barbara began. 'I'm glad you're the stockings-and-suspenders type. I grew up before tights became so popular, and I never got over my weakness for women who stuck to the old way.'

Still striving for calm, Barbara said, 'That's what I like, a cave-man attitude. When are you going to drag me off to your bed by the hair and have your wicked way with me?'

'Any time now. I just want to get you into the right frame of mind.' He stood up.

As he helped her to turn over on the couch Barbara saw that he was still erect. She heard the zipper in the back of her dress purr downward and she began to help him shuck her out of it. His hands on her shoulders turned her over onto her back. She lay back on the sofa in a half-slip, transparent bra and stockings, looking, she hoped, appealingly helpless and ready.

With a low growl which sounded genuine enough, Frank reached down and raised the hem of her slip to her waist and knelt between her parted thighs. He unsnapped her bra and as her breasts came free he cupped one in each hand and began to stroke them from base to nipples, as if he were trying to milk her.

Barbara was not lactating, so nothing came out. But her breasts sent an urgent signal to her sex: get ready to receive boarders. She didn't think she could have brought her legs together even if Frank hadn't been kneeling between them. It was like the first time all over again. Barbara skipped the foreplay and went right into the main sequence. She hitched herself forward until the tip of his cock was nudging her labia. Then she reached down to guide him in. She was wet and parted and she felt an immense pleasure as he slid into her fully in one long glide.

He continued to stroke her breasts as he moved in and out of her wet sheath. 'It feels so good,' he said.

'Likewise,' she managed to say just before her first orgasm shook her. 'Ohhhh! Ohhhhhhh!' she gasped. 'Deeper. Don't stop!'

Frank didn't say anything as he continued to thrust inside her as deeply as he could go.

Barbara came again and again. She clung to him as if afraid he'd pull out and leave her hanging. Her hands clasped his buttocks as they thrust together, her fingers digging into the bunched muscle frantically. She was having orgasms almost continuously. A tiny corner of her mind told her this was extraordinary. The rest of her body sent the same message, only not in words.

Barbara was caught up in the pleasure of being pinned inescapably against the sofa, unable to move away even if she had wanted to. Not that she wanted to. If anything she wanted to move forward, to take all of him inside her, to split herself on the magnificent cock between her straining thighs. She felt him thrust harder, as if he had the same thought, and she knew he was going to come. Barbara rose to meet him at the crest, her soft cries mingling with his low growls as he spurted inside her and she held him tightly against herself.

Afterwards Barbara realised she was still holding onto him. She felt as if she wanted to hold him inside forever. As good as the nights with Sarah (and Black Rod) had been, they couldn't compare to the feel of a live cock thrusting inside her, meeting her plunges with its own. The warmth of the fire and the after-effects of the love-making made her drowsy. Barbara felt Frank withdrawing, and she protested briefly.

'I'll be right here,' he told her. 'After you've recovered a bit I'm going to suck your toes.'

That sounded bizarre, but in her present mood Barbara was prepared to do or allow almost anything. She grunted sleepily and let the warmth of the fire put her to sleep. She felt as if she had been drugged, and her last thought was that sex was a wonderful way to relax. 'Must do this more often,' she mumbled.

'As often as we can manage,' Frank replied. His voice seemed to come from far away.

It was still daylight when Barbara woke up, so she knew she hadn't slept through into the next day. Sunday was still to come, which was a pleasant prospect. She gave a little shiver of delight. She was still lying on the couch before the fire, which had been made up recently. She was also covered by a blanket. Thoughtful of him. 'Frank,' she called, 'are you there?'

'No, I've abandoned you in a strange house without your clothes.' He came into the room from the kitchen, drying his hands. 'I've been tidying up while you slept. I hope you don't plan to make a habit of that.'

'You said something earlier about sucking my toes,' Barbara reminded him. 'I find them a bit dry and in need of moisture. And I find myself in need of some diversion with sexual overtones. Would you like to begin now?'

'Shrimping, it's called. The practice was made famous by a famous lady who is now suffering from a mild infamy. Can your reputation stand that? Would it help if you were tied up and couldn't resist?'

'I don't know if being tied up would help my reputation, but it would do wonders for my libido.' Barbara was now wide awake and she felt her heart begin to race at the prospect of finally realising her fantasy. Having to discuss the process beforehand made it less spontaneous, but she supposed that was unavoidable in the earlier stages while they were still discovering one another's preferences.

He lifted the blanket off her and Barbara removed her stockings and suspenders while Frank went to collect the rope he had bought earlier. Then Barbara sat expectantly on the couch trying to catch her breath. Her nipples were erect in the cool air and the light from the fire painted her a rosy colour. When he came back she was still breathless with excitement.

Wordlessly he bound her wrists behind her back. Barbara didn't resist. 'At this stage I need your legs free, but be patient. I promise – or threaten, if you prefer – to tie you so you are completely helpless.' Frank assisted Barbara to sit down once more. He sat on the floor with her feet in his lap. Lifting one foot, he began to lick the undersides of her toes.

It tickled slightly, but the overall effect was relaxing. She lay back against the cushions and closed her eyes. Barbara gasped as his tongue darted between her toes, moistening the soft skin there. Then he began to suck gently on her toes, one after the other. It was not something she would have thought erotic, but it was. That may have been because almost anything he did would have been erotic to her, given the situation. But whatever the reason Barbara found herself thinking of soft tongues and lips all over her body, licking and kissing her. She thought how nice it would be if he gave her a tongue bath, paying particular attention to her crotch and labia.

But Frank confined his attention to her toes, doing first one foot and then the other. The air was cool on the soles of her feet and around her toes when he finished one foot and turned to do its mate. Frank worked over both feet thoroughly, sucking her toes and licking the bottoms of her arches. He planted a row of kisses over her insteps and around her ankles.

Barbara moaned softly. Frank was a *very* clever lover.

'Sexy feet,' he said. 'Like the rest of you.' He held her feet and considered each one carefully.

Barbara twisted on the couch, gasping and red-faced. The things he was doing to her feet were having unexpected results between her legs. Suddenly she wanted him inside her. She tried to move so that Frank could enter her. But he held onto her feet and she couldn't do anything with her hands tied behind her. Barbara lay back on the sofa finally, letting him have his way with her. She savoured the Victorian overtones of the phrase. And the sensations radiating from her feet and collecting in her belly. Her nipples stood out stiffly and her breasts felt heavy, engorged. Occasionally she moaned softly.

Barbara became aware that his mouth was moving up her legs. Frank was kissing her knees, her thighs, finally nuzzling her labia and hovering tantalisingly over her clitoris. She cried out, 'Oh God, Frank, take me now!'

'Patience,' he said, with a maddening patience of his own. 'There's no hurry. I plan to drive you wild with desire, if you'll forgive the purple prose.' He resumed kissing her parted labia. His tongue made a long, slow, maddening traverse of her, from top to bottom, darting inside to taste the salty wetness of her. Then, even more maddening, he returned to her feet and sucked her toes again.

Barbara was moaning loudly and continuously now, writhing on the couch. Frank switched his attention to her breasts and nipples, neglected until this moment. He used both hands to cup her breasts while his tongue slid once more inside her. when he nipped at her clitoris, Barbara came at once, surprising both of them. 'Come inside now, please!' she begged, surprising herself by the urgency in her voice.

This time Frank obeyed. He lay down on the carpet while Barbara struggled to her feet. She straddled him and he drew her down onto his erection.

She received him eagerly, spreading herself to let him probe the full depth of her. Barbara heard his groan as he felt the heat of her surrounding him. She began to thrust with her knees at once, sliding up and down his shaft. Once she moved too violently, crying out as she lost him. With her hands tied she couldn't guide him back in.

Frank did that himself, seeming as eager to be there as she was to have him.

Barbara plunged back to work gratefully, being careful

only not to lose him again. She came again, feeling herself grow wetter and more slippery. And, if possible, even hotter. She could feel her own internal heat, a new sensation for her.

With one hand Frank reached up to tease her nipples in turn. He wormed the other between her legs so that Barbara's clitoris came down on it when she reached the bottom of her stroke.

She gasped each time she came down onto his fingers, and what he was doing to her breasts at the same time drove her over the edge. Barbara shuddered again and again as she came, thrashing wildly. Her head was thrown back and the taut lines of her straining throat stood out in the firelight. She bit back a scream as she felt him come. His orgasm seemed to last a long time, Barbara clenching herself around him as he spurted. His hands tightened on her straining body.

Somehow she managed to remain sitting up after her last orgasm, though her body was streaming with sweat and her muscles were quivering from the after-effects of their love-making. She wanted to do nothing more than lie down, but she knew she'd never get up if she did.

Frank's arms supported her as she came back down to earth. She felt him soften slowly inside her with a mixture of regret and relief. When she opened her eyes she looked down at him with a weak smile. 'Do you do this with everybody?'

'No,' he answered at once. 'We do seem to work well together.' Changing the subject abruptly, he asked, 'Do you want me to untie your hands now?'

'It's up to you. Do what you want.' She felt content as she uttered these words of surrender. Frank was beginning to look like the lover she had been dreaming of.

He reached behind her back and caressed her arms and wrists, toying with the rope. 'All right. You'll stay as you are for now. We'll see how things turn out. Can you stand?'

Barbara nodded dubiously and tried to rise. Her knees refused to obey her, and she said weakly, 'You'll have to help me.' After her string of orgasms she felt a great lassitude. She wondered if Frank felt weak too, but he showed no sign of it as he rolled over onto his side and disengaged from her. He slid out from underneath and got to his feet, leaving Barbara kneeling before him. She looked down at the floor, not wanting to meet his glance for some reason.

She kept her eyes on the floor as Frank reached down and helped her to her feet. Barbara felt his fingers under her chin, forcing her head up. She opened her mouth to speak but before she could form the words, his mouth covered hers. Her knees went weak again as the kiss went on and on. Finally he drew back and lowered her to the couch, where she lay drawing in deep, shuddery breaths. Frank went into the kitchen and she could hear him making drinks. Barbara was glad for the respite. There was no etiquette book that covered this situation, and she was grateful that he was creating a ritual for them both: first sex, then submission and finally drinks. Then what? Wait and see, she told herself, with the feeling that she was on the brink of an entire new way of life.

Barbara drank the wine slowly from the glass Frank held to her lips. He rested his hand on her thigh and caressed the bare flesh. She found the touch soothing, almost hypnotic. If he kept it up long enough she knew that he would have a wild woman on his hands again. Even so she couldn't tell him to stop. Such an act of will was beyond her.

It was Frank who broke the spell as he sat down beside her. He drew her down until she lay with her head in his lap. He drew the blankets up over them and continued to caress her from time to time in an absent-minded fashion.

Barbara turned until she could kiss his stomach just above the pubic hair. She could smell their mingled odours on him and abruptly she remembered when she had kissed Sarah in just the same way. But this was so much better. She dozed, waking from time to time to enjoy the feel of his arms around her or the touch of his hands on her body. It grew dark outside, the shadows deepening in the room. Barbara was glad he didn't turn on the lights.

Awkwardly because of her bound hands, Barbara turned

in his embrace until she could take his cock into her mouth. It grew hard as she used her tongue and lips and teeth on him. She took pleasure in knowing that she was arousing him for a change. Usually it was he who took the active role. This time his hands merely stroked her hair and her neck as she worked on him. His breath became shallow and rapid and his cock swelled in her mouth. They were past the point of no return before Barbara was aware of it. He came in her mouth in jerks and spurts and she had to swallow the slightly musky fluid quickly.

They lay quietly in the dark room until Frank moved to get up. He helped Barbara to sit, and offered her a glass of wine to sip. 'Time for bed,' he announced when she was finished. When they reached the stairs he took her elbow to help her climb. The gesture made Barbara feel cared-for. Not many women were adept at climbing stairs with their hands bound, and his attention made her feel safe.

The fire in the bedroom was a nice touch. It made her feel romantic. Or randy, as she phrased it sardonically to herself. But she had never considered randy a dirty word, nor the condition unladylike. 'How many of your lady friends have you brought here? Or am I the first?' Barbara was fishing for the kind of information that would tell her how she stood with him.

Frank didn't rise to the bait, merely smiling in a way that made her stomach turn over with sudden desire. She thought she had come as often as she could and would need time to recover. But now she realised she had not yet reached her limits. Frank looked like the man who would take her there. There was something in the intense way he set about pleasuring her, a certain ruthlessness that thrilled her at the same time as it frightened her.

Barbara was thinking like the little slavey Sarah had called her, but she didn't care. She must be among the most unliberated of women, revelling as she did in her subjection to a man, wanting to feel him inside her, liking the way he made her come and come. She liked the feel of the ropes around her wrists, reminding her that she was a captive and that she was facing (if that was the proper word) more intense sexual stimulation very soon. Sexual stimulation that had stirred her more deeply than she had ever been moved by a man. Deeper even than Sarah had affected her, she realised.

Frank went downstairs to lock up. Barbara moved over to the window and looked out over the darkened land. There were no other houses in sight. They might as well have been the only people for miles around. She was alone in a secluded house with her hands tied, waiting for her captor to return. It was like a fairy-tale, one she had dreamed of for a long time. Now that it looked like becoming real, she felt a touch of apprehension. Be careful what you ask for, she told herself. You might get it.

'Firelight becomes you.'

Barbara jumped. She hadn't heard Frank come up the stairs. He set a small covered dish on the mantel shelf and took her in his arms. He led her to the bed and drew back the covers to let her climb in. Then he got in beside her, arranging her so that she was lying half on top of him. He covered them and took Barbara once more in his arms. He didn't untie her hands. 'Good night,' he said.

Barbara was going to have to make the best of her position. She didn't want to ask to be untied; it would feel too much like breaking a spell that she wanted to last for as long as possible. She tried to compose herself for sleep, but for a long time she lay awake, tugging now and again at the ropes that held her to remind herself that all this was real.

The level sunlight shone through the window and Barbara woke with the light on her face. Frank was awake. Naked and unable to cover herself, she felt herself flush under his gaze. This is stupid, she told herself, after what we did yesterday. In order to cover her confusion Barbara said lightly, 'Will I pass?'

'You'll do, but only just,' Frank said as he got up to get the covered dish he had set on the mantel shelf last night before they went to bed.

Barbara saw that it contained butter, slightly melted in the heat from the fire overnight. Sarah had used honey, but

Frank apparently prefers me buttered, she thought. Doesn't anyone like the natural flavour? But she said nothing, waiting for the next move, which necessarily had to be his. And she tingled as she waited, unobtrusively she hoped.

Frank turned Barbara over onto her back, arranging the pillows under her so that they took some of the weight off her bound hands. When she was comfortable, he spread her legs and tied her ankles to opposite corners of the footboard. Then he used a scarf to blindfold her.

Barbara liked being handled, treated like an object. It was much more satisfactory than having to ask and direct someone else. And infinitely better than the best she had been able to contrive on her own. Who'd be a liberated female? she thought as he tied the blindfold behind her head. Barbara waited in the darkness for him to do whatever he wished to her.

The bed sagged as he sat on the mattress beside her. His fingers trailed down her belly, massaging her muscles and sending little sparks of excitement down her legs. She felt his lips follow the same route, planting kisses on her stomach, her pubic mound, the tops of her thighs. He seemed to be in no hurry, and she had lost the edge of urgency too. This slow and steady arousal had its own appeal.

There was a pause. Barbara heard the soft clink of china as Frank moved the butter dish. When he touched her breasts, his fingers were slippery on her flesh. He applied butter to her nipples and areolae, working the butter into her skin as if it were moisturising cream. Under this slippery massage her nipples grew erect and her breasts felt as if they were slowly filling with molten lead, growing warm and heavy as she became excited. The slow massage, the slippery feeling of his fingers on her, was bringing her to the brink of orgasm. Unable to see, she was forced to concentrate on what she could feel. Then Frank bent to lick the butter from her engorged nipples. Barbara moaned and her body began to twitch involuntarily, her legs jerking against the ropes that held them.

Frank stopped abruptly, letting her subside. Barbara

wanted to cry out, to urge him to go on. With difficulty she kept silent. She wasn't in any position to give orders. If this was the fantasy she had longed for, there was no point in protesting now against her inability to direct its course.

Fortunately for her, Frank knew what he was about. He applied more butter to her nipples and breasts, his fingers touching her lightly and expertly. Barbara began to breathe rapidly once more as her nipples became taut with excitement. Then he licked her clean slowly, breaking off whenever her whimpers became too urgent.

Next he shifted his attention to her crotch, rubbing the butter into her labia, beginning at the bottom of her cunt and working steadily toward the critical area of her clitoris. Once again he stopped before she could come.

Barbara felt slick and warm all over. She twisted her body, pulling against the cords on her ankles, trying to bring her heated skin against his hands. But either he was out of range, or avoiding her deliberately. Was he enjoying the spectacle of a bound woman on heat? She was certainly enjoying the experience. This was what she had wanted to happen, but she hadn't been able to imagine all the details. Frank was doing that for her, and he seemed particularly good at his job.

The blindfold heightened her excitement. Since she couldn't see anything, Barbara could only imagine what he was going to do next. The cool air seemed to caress her heated body. Her breasts and thighs and crotch were all slick with butter. She was ready for sex. And still Frank did nothing. He had to be aware of what he was doing to her, had to know she wanted him to go on and finish her.

Eventually he did. There wasn't much else he could do short of walking out and leaving her there. He was still and silent for so long that Barbara thought he might have done just that. Then his hands and mouth returned to explore her body. He licked the butter from her pubic mound, then he cleaned her labia. His tongue found her clitoris first try. Full marks for accuracy. Barbara gasped and jerked as the tongue slid inside her labia and touched the small slippery grape at the apex of her thighs. His mouth covered her and she felt his teeth nipping gently at her sex. Barbara felt herself losing control.

She whimpered as she fought to prolong the arousal. Frank didn't pause this time. She groaned and thrashed as she came, lifting her hips clear of the mattress and forcing herself against his face on the up stroke. With his hands on her slippery breasts at the same time, she was lost. Barbara couldn't stop herself from coming. Her cries filled the room and, for all she knew or cared, the house and yard and fields.

Finally she heard someone gasping, 'No more! Please! You'll kill me.' She realised in surprise that it was her own voice. She had never before asked for quarter. Frank and the butter and the ropes had driven her to exhaustion. When he stopped, Barbara was limp. Despite the cool air in the room, sweat was running down her ribs and between her thighs. Barbara hoped he didn't mind women who became sweaty in heat.

Apparently he didn't, asking merely, 'Enjoy yourself?'

'Wasn't that obvious? But there were some bad moments when you left me hanging.' Barbara spoke in a tone of mock severity.

'That's what I intended,' was the unexpected reply. 'Testing the depth of your interest in B&D, you could say. We both have to know your tolerances and reactions if we're going to go on.'

Barbara had never considered that they wouldn't. Or more exactly, she had assumed that it would be she who called a halt if anyone did. That Frank might be the one to make the decision gave her pause. Even further, Barbara realised that her dream of being dominated and helpless depended ultimately on the willingness of the dominant partner to see things her way, to accept her desires as the controlling limits of their partnership. But logically, the submissive partner depended on the other for everything. The dominant one must decide how far to go, how often they would indulge their mutual fantasy, where and even if. Really hundreds of decisions were involved, and none of them were going to be hers. Even the matter of respecting her limits was in Frank's hands. He might really hurt her, and she would be unable to stop him.

That was the dark and difficult side of her fantasy. Did she really mean to put herself wholly in someone else's hands, someone who could do literally anything with her that he wished? Because that was the decision she had to make. If she said yes (and she knew she wouldn't say no), then all other decisions would be his.

Frank didn't press the matter any further. He began to untie her from the bed. When her legs were free, he helped her sit up and untied her hands. The light was dazzling when he removed her blindfold.

Subconsciously Barbara had expected Frank to call her on Monday, if only to say hello. When he didn't, she wondered why. She didn't want to call him. When he didn't call the day after that either, Barbara considered calling him. It was then she realised she didn't have his phone number, or his address. There was no way she could get in touch with him. At the same time she began to wonder if this state of affairs might be deliberate. Was this his way of telling her that she was the slave and he the master?

When he didn't call on the Wednesday, Barbara began to worry that he had abandoned her. He would vanish from her life as suddenly as he had entered it, leaving her exiled from her fantasy paradise. It can't be that, she told herself. This is all part of the dominance game. He wants me to sweat a bit, get anxious and worried, before he calls and sweeps me right off my feet and into the tightest, most restricting strait-jacket in the sex shop. By Thursday Barbara was frantic. Yes, that was the word, she decided, as she found herself reading the manuscript before her and losing track before she could finish the page. Friday was, if anything, worse.

But when she got home that Friday evening there was a note, hand-delivered like the one she had received earlier. As she stared at the plain brown envelope Barbara felt her heart hammering. He's not vanished after all. He still wants me. Or this is his way of saying farewell. She set the unopened envelope on the table, forcing herself to put away the shopping and make herself a proper meal when she really wanted to rip the letter open. Only when she had eaten and cleared up the kitchen did she sit down to read it. Like dessert, she told herself, opening the envelope carefully. She didn't know who this show of firmness was meant to impress.

The brief note it contained hardly seemed worth the elaborate care she had taken. On a single sheet of paper he had written, 'Meet me for lunch at the usual restaurant. Be there at 11:30. Wear nothing but high-heeled knee boots with stockings and suspenders under the shortest coat you have.' At the bottom he had added, 'If I'm not there by 12:00, ask the bartender if there's a message.'

Barbara knew she would go. Frank had told his slave what to do. From her wardrobe she selected a leather coat that ended just at her knees. It had been a favourite of hers, but she hadn't worn it for years because it was out of fashion. Still she had kept it, hoping fashions would change. She found a pair of black leather boots with four-inch heels and laces up the front. They too had been favourites at one time, and like the coat were now unfashionable. She laid them out on the bed with the stockings and suspenders. Her heart was hammering and there was a choking sensation she couldn't fight off when she imagined what Frank would do with her.

Barbara slept fitfully, waking early and thinking she still had ages to go. She forced herself to eat breakfast. Then she took a shower and fixed her hair. She decided on a French twist to go with the coat and boots. Like them, it was unfashionable, and would make her stand out. She guessed that Frank had had something like that in mind when he told her what to wear. As she did her make-up, Barbara thought 'I hardly know him and I'm letting him tell me how to dress'. But she never thought of disobeying.

She left in plenty of time, intending to take a bus to the restaurant. She felt conspicuous in her coat, attracting the interested stares of several male passengers. Barbara imagined they all knew she was naked under the coat. She pulled it down as far as it would go. This must have been how the with it girls had felt the first time they wore a miniskirt. She herself had just missed that era, and she often wished she had lived through it (though without the inconvenience of making herself ten years older thereby).

Barbara got off in the centre of town, feeling as if she were surrounded by comic-strip heroes with X-ray vision. As she had half-expected, Frank was not at the restaurant. This must be another part of her training in the humiliation/obedience that went hand in hand with B&D. She felt conspicuous both for her clothing and for the fact that she was the only unescorted woman in a place otherwise filled with couples. Frank must have taken that into consideration as well.

She ordered a cup of coffee and studied the menu. It was as absorbing as the label on a bottle of tomato sauce, but she had to do something to avoid looking as if she had been stood up. Frank didn't come by 12:00. Somehow she had known he wouldn't. Barbara waited until 12:15, then gathered her courage and went to speak to the bartender. 'Did a Mr Richards call for Barbara Hilson?' she asked, feeling herself go red.

The bartender said there had been no calls, but Mr Richards had been in earlier and left a note. He handed Barbara an envelope exactly like the one she had received at home. He had never intended to be here, she told herself bitterly. This might be his idea of a test, or a joke, but it was wearing thin quickly. Barbara took the envelope back to the table with another cup of coffee, feeling more conspicuous than ever. But she would have felt even more conspicuous standing on the corner reading a letter.

The second note was as terse as the first. 'Go to the Baltimore Hotel in the Cromwell Road and ask for the key to room 553. Look in the top drawer of the table by the window for further instructions.'

Barbara thought the whole affair resembled one of those run-around chases so dear to the writers of spy novels. But she knew she would do as she had been told. There was no point in balking now after coming so far. She took a taxi this time, getting an appraising stare from the driver. She got another one from the desk clerk when she asked for the key. By this time Barbara was beginning to imagine there was a sign on her back saying she was here on a dirty weekend. The hotel was one of those that had been made by knocking three or four houses into one, but it was still pleasant, even genteel, not seedy as many of them were in this area. Barbara gave Frank good marks for taste.

The place was a warren, with passages and side halls everywhere. Barbara had to ask directions from one of the chambermaids. She blushed guiltily, imagining that by now everyone could tell she was naked under her coat, and that she was hurrying to an assignation with her kinky lover. The woman seemed to wear a knowing smirk as she gave directions.

Barbara made her way to Room 553 and let herself in. She expected the décor to be International Hotel Anonymous but was agreeably surprised. The bed was old-fashioned, with head and footboards and four sturdy posts. Exactly the kind needed if one were into B&D. There were two comfortable armchairs and even a two-seater couch, all facing the ubiquitous TV set. There was a small kitchenette and a spacious bath and shower ensuite. Not a cheap room.

In the bureau by the window Barbara found the note from Frank. She also found two pairs of handcuffs and a roll of masking tape in the drawer. It wasn't hard to figure out what Frank had in mind. She read the note, and discovered that he had thought up another novel scenario for her. The note said, 'Take off your coat and hang it in the closet. Then use the tape to gag and blindfold yourself. When you have done that, you are to kneel in front of the clothes-horse with your back to it. Use the handcuffs to chain your wrists and ankles around it. Then wait. Someone will come for you.'

As she hung up her coat, Barbara wondered about the 'someone'. If it wasn't Frank, it could be anyone. Any stranger could walk in on her. And do anything to her. She shivered with the by now familiar mixture of apprehension and anticipation. She considered leaving, but rejected the idea almost at once. This was what she had been dreaming of, wasn't it? And she had come this far. Someone with a different viewpoint might have thought it silly to go on past this point, no matter how far one had come. She examined the clothes-horse. It was only intended to keep clothing from creasing, but it was quite sturdy. And because this was a hotel, it was bolted firmly to the floor to discourage theft.

Just right for leaving one chained to, Barbara thought. She wondered how many other women he had brought here. Frank had to have been here before to know how the room was furnished. And it was foolish to imagine he had been alone. But then, she told herself comfortingly, he can't have found too many women who would go along with this elaborate domination and humiliation ritual.

She stood in the centre of the room wearing nothing but her boots, stockings and suspenders. And she was excited. Her nipples were all crinkly and her stomach felt tight. Barbara glanced out the window at the hotel across the street. She saw a man looking back at her. He didn't move or change expression. Barbara moved hurriedly out of the line of sight, her heart pounding. The idea of having someone spy on her at just this point was worrying. The man could have no idea of what she was about to do, but a guilty conscience makes one jump at the silliest things. And it was always possible that he would cross the street and find her in the room. Fortunately the clothes-horse was far away from the window.

Barbara went to the loo, reasoning that she might not have another opportunity for some time. And also because her excitement made her want to pee. She took her time exploring the bathroom, wanting to prolong the prelude to her captivity. Next she looked over the kitchen, noting that the fridge was well stocked. There was enough drink for a small party. All this pointed to a prolonged stay in the room. She shivered slightly and her breath became ragged.

But finally there was nothing else to do and no reason for putting off the inevitable any longer. Being careful to avoid the window, Barbara sat down at the dressing table and glanced at herself in the mirror. An attractive woman looked back at her, even if she did say it herself. Full body; heavy rounded breasts (no sag there); generous hips and thighs, long legs. Nice waistline. You'll do for a few more years, she told her reflection. Barbara picked up the roll of masking tape Frank had provided and tore off several long strips. She closed her mouth and sealed her lips with the tape, using enough to ensure that it wouldn't come unstuck. She lifted her hair out of the way and wound several strips completely around the lower half of her face, around under her hair behind her head. Now the attractive woman in the mirror wore a gag. She let the long dark hair fall again to her shoulders.

Before she taped her eyes shut, Barbara made sure of the location of the clothes-horse so she could find it when she was blindfolded. Just before she taped her eyes, Barbara had another thought; would the handcuffs close around her ankles? She had never tried that particular variation. She picked up one pair and tried the fit. They wouldn't go around her boots. She unlaced the boots and laid them aside. When she tried again the cuff closed around her ankle. It was a snug fit. She didn't try the other one just then. Frank hadn't left the keys for her, and she still had to make her way across the room to the clothes-horse.

Barbara used the tape on her eyes, then groped for the second pair of handcuffs. When she found them, she felt her way to the wooden frame, the open cuff dragging from her ankle. Barbara lowered herself to the floor in front of the frame. She knelt with her back to it, the vertical part between her calves. She reached down and fitted the open cuff around her free ankle. Another tight fit, but she got it closed. The steel bands around her ankles would make themselves felt for a long time.

Finally Barbara straightened up with her back against the vertical part of the frame. She locked one cuff around her left wrist, brought her arms behind her and around the frame, and locked the open cuff around her right wrist. Now she was left on her knees with her wrists and ankles locked together around the wooden frame. She tugged experimentally against it, without result. She was helpless. She felt an added tingle when she thought of what she had done to herself on the orders of her master. She hoped he would like the result.

It wasn't very long before Barbara discovered that kneeling could be uncomfortable. Her knees began to hurt, and she tried to find a more comfortable position. Unfortunately, her options were limited. After some squirming, she found that she could spread her knees and sink back with her bottom resting on her calves and with her back against the vertical part of the frame to which she was chained. Barbara remembered reading somewhere that this was the usual posture adopted by slaves in order to show submission. In her mind's eye she saw herself as another might – legs spread so that her sex was openly displayed, breasts thrust out prominently because her hands and arms were held behind her back. The only thing necessary to complete the image of the captive slave girl was to bow her head. She did so. She hoped someone would come before too long.

Nothing happened for what seemed like a very long time, and Barbara had to shift her position several times as various parts of her anatomy became numb or cramped. She was beginning to doubt the wisdom of putting herself into this position, but she was helpless to alter it now. Nor could she summon help with her mouth taped. When she tried, the only sound she could make was an explosive grunt which wouldn't attract the attention of anyone outside the room.

The sudden ringing of the telephone was loud in the silent room, startling her. Her heart pounded and she struggled futilely in her chains. After what seemed like ages the phone went silent and Barbara slowly caught her breath. It was terribly silent both inside and outside the room. She might easily have been in a deserted house – as they had been last weekend. It seemed incredible that all that had happened a few days ago. It felt as if it had taken place in another lifetime as she waited in this room for someone to arrive. And suppose no one came? How long would it be before the hotel staff came to investigate?

She was, she realised, deliberately frightening herself. What was the point of having a woman chain herself to the furniture if no one came to take advantage of her condition? Unless, of course, Frank enjoyed the idea of her waiting, and waiting, growing hungry and thirsty, maybe wetting herself, struggling vainly to get free or attract help? And what if no one ever came? Stop it, she told herself firmly. But she couldn't.

When finally she heard the sound of the door opening Barbara was frantic, tugging at her chains and making choked-back noises of panic behind her gag. She was hyperventilating and thought she would pass out. The door closed. Frank. It had to be Frank, come to rescue her.

But her visitor said nothing. Barbara became even more frantic. Footsteps on the floor, coming nearer. 'Nnnnnkkk?' Gagged as she was, that was as close as she could come to uttering his name. Still he said nothing. Was her visitor a man? Might it be a woman? There was no way to tell anything except that she was alone and helpless with someone who wouldn't speak to her. The silence itself became menacing.

The darkness that surrounded her grew hands, hands that found her breasts. There was a disturbing unfamiliarity about them as they pulled and twisted her nipples, sometimes painfully, but always making the sensitive flesh stand out more stiffly, and sending definite signals to her crotch. Barbara realised that her captor was wearing close-fitting rubber gloves, probably of surgical latex. The fingers felt uncannily smooth on her breasts, cupping her and pulling at her nipples.

Barbara became more frantic, but now she was thrusting herself as far as her chains allowed, trying to offer herself to the hands that touched her with such frightening expertise. She had not forgotten her fears, but they were being submerged in the tide of her arousal.

'Nnnnkkk?' she tried again. There was no reply. By now her mental state was scarcely to be described. The sensations flooding in on her made her so agitated that she didn't know if her struggles were aimed at freeing herself or at getting closer to those smooth rubber-clad hands that now touched her everywhere; her breasts, her labia, sliding into her sex, driving her wild with pain and pleasure and uncertainty.

This was another aspect of her fantasy, and like the others she had encountered, it was not something she had thought about when dreaming of being forced to submit to someone else. She was in the position of the slave being handled by her master, who never explained anything no matter how much she might demand. But Barbara didn't have enough time to think through this new aspect. Too many things were happening to her, things she couldn't prevent, things she didn't want to prevent.

Suddenly the hands went away, and she twisted her body, trying to make contact with them again. She was teetering on the edge of orgasm and wanted more of the terror and excitement to drive her over. But the room was silent. She knew her tormentor was still there, watching her, waiting for the right moment. But the right moment to do what? She felt dizzy as she thought of the things that could yet be done to her, things she was powerless to prevent or influence.

Smooth under their rubber gloves, the hands returned to trace the line of her waist, the flare of her hips, the length of her legs. The sensation of the smooth rubber through her sheer stockings was simultaneously disturbing and exciting, as all good erotic plays should be. Then the hands returned to her breasts, twisting the nipples so abruptly that Barbara moaned with the pain. Then she was being cupped and teased again, so that she forgot the pain, dismissing it as an accidental thing, a small crime of passion.

One hand insinuated itself between her parted thighs, finding her sex wet and parted and waiting. A latex-clad finger probed her, the touch at once impersonal and terribly intimate. It was as if her tormentor was insulating himself (herself?) from his (her?) victim by wearing these gloves. But of course Barbara could feel every movement through the thin covering between her and the hands that touched her everywhere. No part of her body was protected from them, and she was unable to influence where or how she was touched, felt, weighed, probed.

And it was delicious. Barbara was awash in the sense of her vulnerability. She was perilously close to orgasm once more, shuddering uncontrollably and moaning through her gag. Once again she was twisting and squirming, offering herself to her tormentor. Take me! she screamed silently. Make me come and come and come! I can't stand any more suspense!

As if her tormentor had heard this silent plea and wanted to be deliberately perverse, the hands withdrew. There was nothing now except her own burning need to be touched, penetrated, ravished. But there was no way for her to realise her desire unaided. And she wasn't aided.

Gradually Barbara retreated from the brink, unsatisfied. She was trembling and felt as if she was burning with fever. Her skin felt warm all over, as if she were seated near a fire. She tried to recall the fire in the cottage she and Frank had shared, tried to recall what he had done to her and how he had made her come. Maybe, she hoped, that would make her come now, relieve the awful need she felt. But it didn't.

After an eternity the hands returned. This time they didn't go straight to her breasts or her open sex. This time they manipulated something cold and rigid between her legs from behind her. When her tormentor leaned close to her to move the thing into position, Barbara smelled faint traces of perfume, so faint they might have been the traces that lingered on a man's clothing after he had been with a woman. When the clothing touched her, it felt like cotton, which told her nothing about the sex of the person who had come to her. The androgynous anonymity was carefully preserved.

'Nnnnkkk?' she grunted again. There was no reply. She knew there would never be a reply; she could be being used by a complete stranger, but if this was Frank, that was obviously his intention. Barbara remembered that in the erotic fantasies she had read, slaves were often loaned or given to others. And she was a slave. Even Sarah had recognised that, and had called her 'little slavey'.

In the meantime her tormentor had finished the adjustments to the thing between her legs. It didn't take a genius to figure out that it was some sort of sexual apparatus. You didn't go to the trouble of luring a woman into this situation merely to try out body-building devices on her. Barbara felt something long and rounded being moved into place against her shins. She could tell it was a pipe or rod from the feel of it as it was set cross-wise against her lower legs. She was sure it was a rod when the thing was rotated and one of those latex-covered hands on her shoulder urged her down onto it. The other hand held the rod and guided it into her anus. The ease with which it slid into her told her that it had been lubricated. Her tormentor appeared to have thought of everything.

She was held down on the spike while her captor did something behind her back to the handcuffs. There was a snap as something was fastened to the short chain between her wrists. She felt her ankles being lifted slightly, the steel bands biting into her flesh. There was another snap, and the hands went away again. When she tried to move again, Barbara discovered that her hands had been joined to her ankle cuffs by some sort of hook or chain. She could no longer kneel upright. Her body – especially the part of it which was penetrated by the rod – was held down close to the floor. She couldn't escape that anal penetration.

But there was some movement possible, a carefully calculated distance she could shift herself. As she straightened to the limits of her chains, Barbara felt the bar under her legs come into contact with her shins. The spike inside her slid out until she could rise no further. When she sank down again, she was impaled fully. She realised then what had been done to her. She could now fuck herself with the rod if she moved up and down. Clever, but her captor wasn't finished with her yet. There was the sound of tape being unwound and torn. The bar under her legs was being taped to her shins. By the feel of it there was a lot of tape being wound round and round her calves.

When the job was done, Barbara was left impaled with just enough slack in everything to slide herself up and down the rod inside her anus without being able to slide off it. The bar taped to her legs prevented everything from shifting. She felt a fluttering excitement in her stomach. Barbara wondered if some similar arrangement could be made for her cunt. But no. She was left unplugged there. She could only hope that that would be remedied later in some fashion. Barbara had forgotten her earlier fears. Just tie me up and give me something to screw myself on, she thought wryly, and I'll soon work myself into a lather. Sarah had been right. She was a natural sex slave.

Her captor was not finished with her, however. One hand returned to tease her nipples and to trace slow maddening circles around her breasts. The other hand went between her thighs and toyed with her labia before sliding inside to find her clitoris. Barbara found the combination of anal penetration and frontal stimulation highly agreeable, as no doubt had been intended. She began to heave and pant and show all the usual signs of orgasm, rising and falling frantically on the rod in her anus.

This time when the hands went away she had something else with which to amuse herself, and she made full use of it. She was interrupted by a sharp stinging pain across her breasts. It was followed by another, and yet another. Barbara was so surprised that she held herself rigid. She realised that she was being lashed by her captor, who appeared to be using a leather strap of some sort. The blows descended to her stomach and to the tops of her thighs. Barbara was trying to cry out but the cries were strangled by her gag. She flung herself about frantically to the limit of her chains as she tried to escape the stinging blows that landed on every exposed part of her body, but with particular emphasis on her breasts and belly.

Unable to rise off the rod in her anus, Barbara slowly became aware that she was caught between the pleasure from that penetration and the pain being inflicted on her. And then her nervous system seemed to overload from the conflicting stimuli. Or it may be that she had been searching for just this particular combination of pain and pleasure and helplessness. At any rate, she surprised herself completely when she felt an orgasm begin to build between her straining thighs. It swept through her and she cried out. Once started, she couldn't stop. The spasms came one after another and she lost control, shuddering and moaning as she flung herself about.

This torment was a new experience for her. When she thought about it afterwards, Barbara concluded that like many submissives she harboured a streak of masochism. She thought then that she was more fortunate than most other people because she was able to transmute pain into pleasure. Like doubling your fun for a very small price.

But she didn't think so when the lash landed on her sex, by accident or design she couldn't say. If she could have screamed, she would have done so then. The muscles in her throat were straining as she tried to cry out, but the strangled noises she made would hardly have been heard in the next room. The shock was unbelievable. She had never been struck there, and she almost fainted from the pain.

Abruptly the blows stopped. Barbara felt as if the entire front of her body, from breasts to knees, was on fire. She was shaking and sobbing, struggling against her chains without realising that she had already tried vainly to escape. But when the pain subsided there was still the effect of the rod up her backside. Each frantic jerk and heave reminded her of her impalement and her helplessness. And that sent a definite message to her sex. Barbara couldn't believe the trick her body was playing on her as she began another long series of orgasms that left her shaken and sweaty some eternity later. At some point Barbara realised that her tormentor had joined in by sliding one of those disturbingly smooth fingers into her vagina and was massaging her swollen clitoris in time with her rhythmic rise and fall on the rod inside her anus.

Her cries now were more frantic but much less distressed. The sounds of pain and passion were almost identical. And in her own case the sensations were disturbingly similar. At the height of it Barbara passed out, like the heroine of a romantic novel, though this heroine was more intent on pleasure than in preserving any virtue she may have had left.

Later, when she recovered consciousness, Barbara realised that she had experienced what the French call *la petite mort.* Not too many people experience the sexual intensity that produces that effect. Too bad for them, she thought when she understood what had happened to her.

She also realised that she was no longer chained to the clothes-horse, though she was still gagged and blindfolded. She was lying in the bed on her back and her wrists were handcuffed to the bed posts. Her ankles seemed to be tied to the footboard of the bed, as she discovered when she tried to move her legs. The steel rod was still inside her, but it was no longer taped to her legs. She was lying on it, and her weight kept it in place.

So it seemed that there was more sex play in store. Barbara had pleasant memories of being tied to the bed during the last weekend. But this time there was the possibility that she would be beaten again. There was no way to guess what would happen next, but at least this was more comfortable than being chained to the clothes-horse. And there was something she could do to amuse herself while she waited for the next development. She squirmed experimentally and felt the rod shift inside her anus. Interesting side effects were also felt in an area not a million miles away.

As if he (she?) had been waiting for some sign that Barbara was awake again, her captor approached the bed. Barbara heard the footsteps and lay still, but it was too late. She had been seen. And the lash fell again. This time the entire front of her body was treated to a series of stinging blows. Barbara writhed and twisted but there was no escape. This was worse than before. Then she had been aroused before she was beaten. Now she was being beaten first.

But as she shifted and squirmed on the bed, the rod inside her made itself felt. She concentrated on the slidings and jabs and found herself becoming excited. The pain and the pleasure began working together again. And her imagination was at work too. In her mind's eye Barbara saw the image of a woman bound to a bed, writhing and twisting as she was beaten. The image of the suffering woman became her own image, and the stirrings of arousal in her belly and the tops of her thighs became stronger.

This time her tormentor must have been alert for the signs of arousal, because the blows stopped when they became obvious. The bed sagged beneath the weight of another person, and this time Barbara knew beyond doubt that her captor was male. His scent was different. And there was a most emphatic cock thrusting itself into her sex. She sighed as it slid home. Spread like a starfish and penetrated back and front, Barbara came almost at once, moaning deep in her throat. This was what she had dreamed of; bound helplessly, she was being had by a strange male. It was the classic submissive fantasy, the woman helpless to prevent her arousal and so free to enjoy it without guilt.

The anonymous stranger rode with her, helping her to reach one peak after another. When she felt him tighten inside her she knew he was about to come. She clenched her vaginal muscles to help him, and felt him come inside her. Even after he was done she went on, shaking and moaning while he held her tightly. When she was done he withdrew. He lay beside her and she dozed.

The rest of the weekend passed in a haze of lust, as Barbara later described it to herself. She was never allowed to remove the tape from her eyes, so she never saw her captor. At times it seemed there were two people, for there were different odours at different times. But she couldn't be sure. Frank might have been one of them, but she didn't think so. She believed she had been loaned out to someone else, just as the women she had read about had been loaned out to teach them that the master could do as he wished with his slave.

From time to time her captor untied her to let her use the bathroom. He fed and bathed her, but mostly she remembered the times he took her back to the bed for more of that mind-numbing sex that shook Barbara to the core.

They never left the room, and he never spoke to her. He prepared food from the supplies in the kitchen or sent out for champagne from room service. She was never out of his sight, and never far from the hands that touched and probed her body. Her willing body, to be more accurate.

When it was time for him to go, he handcuffed her to the bedpost. Barbara was still blindfolded, and she was gagged once more. He kissed her on the cheek and put a key into her hand. She knew without being told that she wasn't intended to unlock her handcuffs until he had gone. Obediently she waited until his footsteps had faded down the hall before she fumbled the key into the lock.

Even after her hands were free Barbara made no attempt to remove the tape from her eyes or her mouth. She was reluctant to admit that it had ended, though she was exhausted. But eventually she peeled the tape from her eyes, wincing slightly as it clung to her skin. It was getting dark outside. Sunday evening. She had lost track of time. Her blindfold and the pattern of arousal and climax had combined to distort her sense of time. She peeled the tape from her mouth and went into the kitchen for a glass of wine. Her captor had left nothing by which she might guess his identity or imagine what kind of person he was.

Barbara took the glass of wine back into the bedroom, lingering over it, not wanting to go back to her empty flat which was bound to seem emptier after this weekend's encounter. In the mirror she looked at her body. There were faint red marks where she had been lashed, but they would fade. There was no broken skin or blood, and the blows Barbara remembered had stung more than anything else. Except for that one slash between her legs. There was a dull residual ache but no external damage.

She still wore her stockings, now with snags and other signs of wear, but still not laddered. Her boots lay beside the bureau where she had left them. As Barbara put them on, she saw an envelope addressed to her. 'Barbara Hilson' was written on it in strange handwriting. This weekend had begun and ended with notes and instructions. She had spoken to no one since she had entered Room 553.

'Dear Barbara,' the note said, 'Thank you for a memorable weekend. I hope you enjoyed it as much as I did. I hope we'll meet again. The man at reception has instructions to call a cab for you.' It was signed, 'An admirer.' The trite phrases were the only indication he had enjoyed her. There was a fifty-pound note in the envelope, which was either his estimate of her worth, or was intended to pay for the taxi and several new pairs of stockings.

Barbara took her coat from the closet and put it on over her nakedness. As she was about to leave she remembered the handcuffs she had worn for most of the weekend. It might not be a good idea to leave them there for the hotel staff to find. She put both pairs in her handbag. If no one asked for them, she would add them to her collection.

The receptionist caught her eye as she came down in the lift. Barbara flushed as he smiled at her. Really, she told herself, I'll have to get rid of these silly feelings of guilt. He stepped to the door with her, summoning a taxi and helping her into it without comment. Barbara thought he must know what she had been doing, but he said nothing. At least he's polite, she thought gratefully. But then hotel receptionists were paid to be polite.

In her empty flat there was too much silence and too much time to think. To avoid that, Barbara called Sarah. They chatted about the recent visit, but when Sarah asked about Frank, Barbara found herself strangely ambivalent about the relationship. She didn't reveal any details about the interlude in the hotel room either. She hadn't had time to think about it yet, and she felt vaguely ashamed, as if she had done something wrong. She knew that was due to the way she had been taught to think of sex and sexual pleasure, but couldn't bring herself to discuss it even with the one person she knew would understand. And after the call she felt badly because she had been evasive with Sarah. Sarah deserved something better than that. But the conversation had at least cheered her up.

After she had hung up, Barbara was still disturbed by the encounter with the stranger(s), and vaguely resentful about how casually she had been loaned out. She got out her journal and tried to set down her thoughts on this past weekend and the one before that. After the weekend in the country, she had been convinced that her dreams were coming true. Now she was not so sure. But she had to add, in all honesty, that she had enjoyed the encounter with the stranger most of the time. And she was learning some of the less obvious aspects of her desire to be dominated. It was early days yet, she told herself, temporising.

But that sounded as if she couldn't make up her mind, as if she had no will-power, or as if she were afraid to set down clearly how deeply she had been shaken by her discovery of the masochistic streak in herself. But then it *was* early days – too soon to make a firm decision about letting Frank teach her the finer nuances of B&D with humiliation. The intensity of her response had been overpowering. Even now she remembered the two weekends with a shiver of delight. She wondered what a week or a month of that would be like.

Barbara knew she would never have the time to find out. The rich and the independent could join sex clubs which were open to them because of their money and independence. They could afford to spend as much time as they liked exploring their fantasies, with as many different partners as they liked. She was in a different class, as were most of the people she knew. Their sexual explorations would have to be done piecemeal, as the rest of their obligations allowed.

In a fantasy, the phone only rings to summon you to the ecstasy of another assignation. The postman doesn't even knock once. No one interrupts the dream by choosing the wrong moment for a visit – unless they are fellow devotees, come by invitation to join the fun. You don't have to shop or cook or clean or pick up the kids or take the car to the garage. The dog, if you have one, joins in the fun on command and never whines to be fed or taken for a walk when you're at it. Every moment is charged with sexual excitement. No let downs except as necessary to add piquancy to the highs. And time. All the time you need. And of course, there is your fantasy mate, the demon-lover who knows exactly what you want.

For most of us the fantasy has to find space between the visits and the phone calls and the shopping trips. Sexual pleasure is something stolen from the million other things that must be done. It is always subject to interruption by persons from Porlock with (they believe) prior claims on your time. So sexual adventure (Barbara rationalised) is not something to be discarded lightly. Seen this way, Barbara's intention to continue with Frank was almost a duty. She must see where this extraordinary adventure led.

There was another note from Frank waiting when she went into the office on Monday morning. This too had been hand-delivered. Didn't he trust the Royal Mail? Or maybe he simply wanted to be sure the notes came at the proper time. Barbara felt a momentary flash of resentment at his ability to touch her life with these notes and commands and his infrequent phone calls while she had no way to contact him. At the same time his hold over her imagination (and her body, she added) was growing stronger. She calmed herself with the thought that she was the submissive one, the slave. She shouldn't expect to be able to influence him.

Barbara read the note: 'I hope you enjoyed the weekend. Please meet me for lunch on Wednesday. No tricks or notes this time, I promise. You can even wear something more substantial under your coat if you like, though I'll be imagining you naked under it all.' It was signed simply, 'Frank'. As she decided to keep the rendezvous Barbara imagined she could hear Sarah's mocking voice calling her 'little slavey'. She was determined to be a good slave.

4

PHILLIPA

Frank was waiting for her when she got to the restaurant. He was smiling, and as darkly handsome as ever. Barbara felt her heart thump as she remembered their weekend in the country. Was he going to propose another tryst like that? She found herself thinking of ways to accept gracefully without seeming too eager. The day was warm for November, and she wore only a light trench coat. He helped her take it off and hung it up for her, the perfect gentleman looking after his lady.

'I see you decided to wear something more substantial under the coat.'

'Did you think I'd be able to go into the office dressed as I was last weekend?' Barbara asked with some asperity. 'Or did you imagine I'd duck into the ladies' room to shed my clothes just before coming to meet you?' She was baiting him and enjoying the experience. He needed to be told that she wasn't quite the casual possession he took her for.

Frank didn't rise to the bait. 'One can hope,' he said with another of those smiles she found irresistible. 'And anyway, I'll bet you're naked under your clothes. I'll have to content myself with that thought.'

As before, he ordered for them both. Barbara found herself talking easily with him, as if last weekend hadn't happened. When she thought about it, she realised she had forgiven him without thinking. He had that effect on her. As well as several others which were equally pleasant.

But he seemed not to be concerned with matters of forgiving and forgetting. Frank was . . . well, Frank. He assumed command of her and the situation naturally. She found this casual assumption both exciting and frightening, something it would be perilous to question. She was in danger of being dominated completely by this man who didn't make any outward show of his dominance. There was only the casual assumption that she would do as he asked. And she responded by doing it.

Before she even realised what she was doing, Barbara found herself agreeing to spend the next weekend with him. He didn't tell her where they were going. He acted as if that were no concern of hers. And because she thought she had a fair idea of what they would be doing, she was content to leave the where to him. And the uncertainty excited her too.

Back at the office Barbara went through her work with a happy glow. They were going to steal some time from the dreary round of everyday routine. And they were going to do . . . What they were going to do brought another happy smile to her face.

Claire noticed her sunny mood at once. 'Surely you didn't manage to have it away during lunch, did you?'

'Is that all you think of?' Barbara retorted, but without malice.

'Is there anything else?'

In order to shut off the speculation, Barbara said, 'Let's talk about your sex life for a change.'

Undaunted, Claire shot back, 'Where shall I begin?'

'Sometimes I think you'd be better off editing pornography than this romantic stuff. You seem to have the mind for it.'

'I'd love that,' Claire said. 'I could be horny all day, and maybe I'd meet a hunk who could make me honk all night. Do you know if people who write pornography are at all well hung? And do they practise what they preach? Utter bliss! Ah just know Ah'd swoon with desiah,' she finished in her Southern Belle voice. 'Do you know of any jobs like that going?'

'If I did, do you think I'd still be here?' Barbara said. She was glad the conversation had moved off the subject of her own sexual adventures. Whenever she was not with him, Barbara still felt ambivalent about Frank. When they were together, he kept her too occupied to worry about worrying about him. She wasn't ready to tell Claire (or even Sarah, who was the closer friend) that she was living out something like the scenarios found in some of the pornographic books they were talking about. Don't want to talk it away, as Hemingway once said. Don't want to let others into the good news either, as she herself often said.

The rest of the week seemed an eternity, as it had when she was a schoolgirl impatient for the weekend and freedom. She went home on Friday evening feeling buoyant. No more waiting. Just time to do the shopping for Monday and to pack some of her more daring gear to please Frank. As an afterthought she packed the thumb-cuffs Sarah had bought for her. They might come in handy. She went to bed early.

And woke up early. This was the day! She found herself humming as she made final preparations. This time Frank picked her up in a conventional saloon car. Apparently they weren't going back to the country cottage. In fact they merely drove to Knightsbridge, stopping outside an impressive block of townhouses.

'Is this where you live?'

Frank shook his head. 'Can't quite afford this kind of house yet. Give me a few more years and things may be different. Just now I wanted to introduce you to a friend before we begin the weekend's frolic.'

'The same friend I met last weekend?'

'No. Someone else. Come along.' This last was said almost impatiently, as if Barbara was being entirely too inquisitive. He helped her out of the car and led the way up the front steps of a well-kept building with a mock-Georgian facade. Frank went through the lobby as if he knew the place well. They went up one floor in the carefully restored wrought iron lift and entered a long hall with expensive looking carpet and fresh paintwork. Frank knocked at the door of one of the two apartments.

It was opened by a woman who could only be described as daunting. At least that was how Barbara saw her. She was tall and erect, her posture almost stiff. Her blonde hair was braided and coiled atop her head, making her seem even taller than she was. She reminded Barbara of an illustration she had seen for *Die Valküre*. She was definitely the Valkyrie type. She had a direct, challenging gaze, and her blue-grey eyes seemed to change colour with her mood. Her mouth was generous and severe at the same time. When she spoke, her voice was clear and assertive.

'Ah, Frank, I see you brought your little friend along.' To Barbara she said, 'How good to see you, my dear. You're every bit as lovely as Frank said you were.'

She extended her hand and Barbara noticed how long her fingers were. She didn't take it immediately, feeling resentful at being styled Frank's 'little friend'. The 'little' was almost a synonym for inconsequential. And her resentment was increased by the familiarity between Frank and this woman. The jealousy she had felt earlier woke again. Were they lovers? When she finally took the proffered hand, Barbara's impression of strength was confirmed by the firm grip.

Frank was either unaware of the tension or chose to ignore it. He was performing the introductions as if it were the most natural thing to bring potential rivals together. 'Barbara Hilson . . . Phillipa Kennedy,' he was saying as the blonde woman stepped aside to let them enter. Frank closed the door behind them.

When Barbara entered the front room she had the faintest sense of *déjà-vu*, even though she knew she had never seen the place before this day.

'Frank tells me that we have a mutual friend,' Phillipa was saying as she preceded them into the lounge. She gestured for them to sit.

Barbara and Frank sat on the couch. That made her feel a bit better, as if he were taking sides with her. Phillipa sat in the armchair opposite. She crossed her long legs with negligent ease, as if she knew well enough what effect that would have on a man. Barbara felt her anger flare again.

'I was thinking of Sarah,' Phillipa continued.

The penny dropped. This was Sarah's ex-lover, the lesbian who had beaten and humiliated her. Barbara now knew why the place looked so uncannily familiar. Sarah's description of the house in which she had been kept naked and in chains fitted this room, this place. She looked around instinctively for some sign of her friend's presence. Of course there was none. The room had the look of having been newly redecorated, but the newel post to which Sarah had been tied when she was beaten was there. The bedroom door was where Sarah had said it was. Yes, this was the place, and this was the woman who had enslaved Sarah. Barbara understood now Frank's double-take when he had met Sarah. The woman seemed even more threatening now. Why had Frank brought her here?

'How is Sarah these days?' Phillipa asked. 'I rather lost track of her some time ago. There was some unpleasantness between us then, but I'm over it now.' Phillipa sounded as if she were forgiving a penitent for a minor error.

Barbara remembered Sarah's description of how she and Elspeth had left this woman spread-eagled on her bed, bound and naked and with a large sausage stuffed in each of her entrances. Barbara felt anger once again at the negligent, almost lazy demeanour. In an attempt to penetrate the facade, she asked, 'Did you enjoy the salami, then? And what did the friendly cops say when they burst in and found you?'

Phillipa coloured instantly, two spots of deep red suffusing her cheeks, and Barbara was gratified to see that her shot had gone home.

Phillipa didn't reply to her. Instead she turned to Frank. 'Your little friend is impertinent. I thought you said she was well trained.'

'No, what I said was that she was coming along nicely,' Frank replied with a hint of nervousness.

Barbara couldn't believe they were discussing her, dissecting her, as if she weren't there. And obviously Frank had discussed their relationship with Phillipa. She felt as if she had been violated. Which in a way she had been, but she could see how it all fitted in with the casual humiliation Frank had inflicted on her. And in which she had participated. This was nothing more than an extension of something she had tacitly agreed to already. She hadn't objected or refused or even complained. Rather she had connived at her own subjugation. It was part of her initiation into the world of B&D she had dreamed about. Nevertheless she found herself on her feet and moving toward the door.

Frank sat silently, observing the conflict between the two women.

It was Phillipa who spoke first. 'Sit down, you little fool!' she hissed.

The force of her anger stopped Barbara in her tracks. This was the side of her personality which had moved Phillipa to humiliate and torture Sarah.

'I said, "sit down". I don't like to repeat myself. Frank, would you see that she obeys.'

Frank said, 'Sit down, Barbara.' He patted the couch next to him.

He didn't appear angry, but there was more colour in his face than before. Barbara suddenly realised that her behaviour might be embarrassing to him. She had no way of knowing what he had told Phillipa about her, but obviously he had described her as being in training. And now she was showing the other woman that she had not been subdued – that Frank had not yet broken her to his will.

He was speaking to Phillipa again, as if he knew that Barbara would return, like a dog ordered to heel. 'She has great potential, but it will take some time to develop. She takes to bondage beautifully. The rest will follow.' He was doing his best not to sound defensive about her. And he did sound more matter-of-fact than otherwise.

Barbara had to admire his control. Still seething, she sat down. But by returning she knew she had crossed another line and that there was no retreat.

Finally Frank turned to her and spoke directly. 'We three are going to spend the weekend seeing how well you have learned submission. Phillipa will give the orders, and you will obey them.' There was the faintest overtone of menace in his voice. He didn't say what his own role would be.

Barbara felt a stab of fear. This was an aspect of her dream-lover she had not seen. Until now, he had seemed the smiling and relaxed man of her dreams. The glimpse of steel beneath the surface unnerved her. But the urge to leave had left her. She knew that if she did, Frank would never call her again. And in that case she would be lost. In a very short time Frank had become a major influence on her. And that was not wholly due to his own manner. Her consent had been necessary. And she had given it.

Now Phillipa turned to her with a smile. 'I'm sorry for the misunderstanding. Let's see if we can become better acquainted in the next few days. I think we'll get on well together. And I'm sure we'll all enjoy the experience.'

To Barbara the smile had all the kindliness of a basilisk's, but she thought she would lose too much face if she turned and ran now. The opportunity had passed. The best course now, she told herself, was to go ahead and show them both that she could take whatever they could do. And she was seduced by the vision of being driven once more to ecstasy by the man of her dreams, who still bore an uncanny resemblance to Frank.

'I'll go and fetch her bag from the car,' he said. 'You two can get better acquainted in the meantime.'

There was an uncomfortable silence between the two women after he had gone. Barbara still feared and distrusted this self-assured and dauntingly beautiful blonde. She felt as if she now had a dangerous rival in the battle for Frank's attention. She didn't want to say love, partly because it sounded so conventional, and partly because she wasn't sure it was the right word to describe her feelings. Fascination might be more accurate, she thought, wondering at the same time why that word was so much less satisfying than the other. That was probably because she, like almost all other women, had been taught that 'love' was the goal they were all seeking, the fulfilment of every woman's dream. What she and Frank had at the moment was more like lust, which she had been taught was BAD, utterly beyond the pale. As she had learned earlier, shaking off one's early moral training wasn't easy. But she kept trying. She liked to think she could at least take credit for that.

Phillipa meanwhile seemed to decide on a more conciliatory approach. 'Would you like coffee or tea? Or something stronger? The sun's near enough to the yard-arm.'

The jollity seemed forced to Barbara, but there was nothing to gain by being hostile. She had already made up her mind to see this through. 'Coffee would be fine, if you're having some.'

'Shan't be a tick,' Phillipa said, rising to her feet in one smooth sinuous motion. She seemed to flow rather than to walk. 'You look around the place while I make coffee.'

Barbara had no desire to 'look around' the apartment. She would know soon enough what it was like. Instead she put in the time wondering why she was finding the long-sought fantasy so strangely unsettling. She had been dreaming of being the captive of a man who would bind her and have his way with her and look after her. The reality only partly resembled the dream. She liked the bondage, and the sex was terrific. And Frank was handsome and dominant and self-assured. But what were these other people doing in her dream?

Frank came back with her bag and set it down near the bedroom door. He came and sat beside Barbara once more.

'Phillipa's making coffee,' she explained in response to his faintly questioning look. She felt better with him beside her. And when he leaned over to kiss her softly under the ear she felt herself melt. It was going to be all right. And she refused to examine her motives further. The unexamined life was a lot quieter than the other sort. Barbara was just turning toward Frank so he could kiss her properly when Phillipa came back with the coffee. They both froze, like teenagers caught by their parents.

'Don't let me interrupt anything,' Phillipa said as she set the tray down on the coffee table. She looked curiously at them, as if waiting for them to continue. When they didn't, she shrugged and poured coffee for them all.

The mood of a few moments ago was broken. The third person, especially this third person, made intimacy with Frank impossible. And what she wanted just now, Barbara decided, was a bit of intimacy with him. Something to restore her sense of being important to him. She tried to tell herself that Phillipa wasn't a serious rival, despite her undeniable beauty. After all, she was a lesbian, wasn't she? But Barbara knew that, lesbian or not, she had all the necessary equipment. It was only the inclination that was lacking – if indeed it was. She might be bisexual.

When she had finished her coffee, Phillipa took off the velvet gloves. She stood up and said abruptly, 'Let's begin.'

Barbara was accustomed to more in the way of preliminaries, but clearly her wishes counted for very little with Phillipa. She turned to Frank for support. He smiled encouragingly and began to unbutton her blouse. She reached up and covered his hands with her own, urging *him* to undress her. In this way she was saying to the other woman, I'm doing this for Frank, not for you.

Beyond a slight smile, Phillipa paid no attention to the scene being enacted before her.

Frank had meanwhile finished with the buttons and he was pulling the blouse free from the waistband of Barbara's skirt. He slid it down her arms and carefully laid it on the back of the couch. He stood and took her arms, urging her to stand as well. When she did, he removed her skirt. This time he paused to admire Barbara's choice of underwear.

She stood before him striving to ignore Phillipa's presence and her ironic smile. The sheer flesh-coloured bra she wore supported and shaped her breasts but did nothing to conceal them. Her nipples (damn them! she thought) were erect beneath the transparent material and betrayed her excitement. If she had been alone with Frank, she would have been glad for him to see her arousal.

Frank removed her half-slip, pulling it down slowly until it lay at her feet.

Barbara stepped out of it and stood before them in her bra and her crotchless tights. She had decided against wearing pants, liking the idea that she was open to Frank under her clothes. It made her feel owned and vulnerable and desired at the same time.

He stepped back to admire her, and Barbara flushed a bright red that started in her face and neck and spread quickly to her breasts and torso.

Phillipa broke the spell suddenly. 'Very pretty, no doubt, but I wonder if you two love birds could get on with it. Frank, I'm surprised at you. I thought you'd already have told her not to wear tights. She needs to be open to anyone who cares to touch her. Stockings and suspenders if your male fantasies demand it, but no tights.'

Frank smiled slightly, as one does when he catches someone like Phillipa out. He beckoned her over and showed her the open crotch of Barbara's tights, with the labia poking out.

Phillipa rudely parted Barbara's thighs for a closer look, at the same time thrusting a finger into the opening and, incidentally, into Barbara.

Barbara tried to stand still as she was penetrated, to show no sign of her humiliation or her arousal. But Phillipa's finger had found her clitoris, and she gasped when it was first prodded, and then stroked. She couldn't hide the sudden heat and wetness inside her. Her breathing also became more ragged, another dead giveaway. She was being examined like a prize cow by a woman who frightened her, and still she felt weak with desire. She remembered Claire's remark about swooning with desire. That might yet happen to her, though she fought against it, not wanting to show how completely she responded to the situation and to the woman whose finger was still stroking her intimately.

When she heard herself moan, Barbara knew that her body was going to betray her. It had an agenda of its own. There was something like a wire running directly from her clitoris to her brain, and it was carrying all the right signals. She tried to keep herself from shuddering, and almost succeeded until Frank joined Phillipa. He stood behind her, and somehow his clothes had evaporated. She could feel his cock pressing against her bottom. He reached around from behind and cupped her breasts, so that he had the whole weight of them in his hands.

He took her nipples in his fingers and they grew stiff and crinkly and very sensitive. Barbara said, 'Ohhh,' then again, this time with a startled note in her voice: 'Ohhhh!' She came, a small shudder between her thighs and in her lower belly. Then she came again. Nothing small about that one. Barbara threw her head back and moaned aloud as the spasms shook her. Her knees buckled, and it was only Frank's hands on her breasts and his arms around her that kept her from falling.

She was too far gone to get angry at Phillipa's disparaging remark, 'You were right. She *is* a hot little number. Something may be made of her yet.'

Frank didn't answer. He seemed to be too busy supporting Barbara and arousing her further.

Despite her remarks, Phillipa didn't stop what she was doing either. Her fingers on Barbara's clitoris stroked and pinched. They slid in and out of her slick heated flesh.

This was another first for Barbara. She had never engaged in sex with more than one person at a time. This threesome was beyond her wildest dreams, and her response startled her. She came again, crying out, 'Oh God, oh God, oh God!' And she came very near to swooning with desire, as Claire had jokingly described it.

But she didn't. Frank and Phillipa decided that she had had enough for the moment. Between them they carried her to the sofa and laid her down. Phillipa went to the kitchen and came back with a bottle of champagne and three glasses.

Barbara drank the bubbly wine in quick little gulps. Frank smiled at her and she felt reassured. She smiled back. If he was satisfied, she must be doing well. Gradually she caught her breath and became quieter.

Phillipa was as cool as ever, hardly a hair out of place, and the only one still wearing her clothes. By Barbara's Rule, that made her the dominant one in the trio. By the same rule, she was the junior member, since she had lost her clothes (and her cool) first. Frank was somewhere in between, which was unsettling. She had been thinking of him as the one in control. Now he was deferring to Phillipa.

'I like your crotchless tights,' Phillipa said. 'And I like that transparent bra. I must think of getting one for myself.' She brought Barbara's overnight bag over and set it on the coffee table. 'Let's see what else you've brought along to surprise us with.' She didn't ask Barbara's permission to open it. That might not seem necessary to her.

Barbara was angry, as if she were being violated once more by Phillipa's casual assumption that she could paw through her clothing. 'I'd rather you didn't do that, Phillipa,' she said in a tight voice.

Phillipa looked up in faint surprise, then she stood erect and moved to the couch where Barbara lay. Her face was inscrutable, but Barbara was alarmed. She tried to rise.

Phillipa reached her first. She bent down and struck Barbara twice across the face, open-handed, first the palm and then the back of her hand. Barbara's head rang and she tasted blood inside her mouth where her teeth had cut the inside of her cheek. She was stunned, both from the force of the blows and from the casual manner in which they had been dealt.

There was no anger in Phillipa's expression, and when she spoke her tone was normal. 'I will decide what I want to do. Your wishes count for less than nothing here. The sooner you learn that the better you will be treated. If you want to spare yourself needless pain you will remember who is in charge. And don't call me "Phillipa". Address me as "Mistress", and don't say anything unless I tell you to speak. If I ask you a question I expect you to answer it. Otherwise you'd best keep quiet.' She returned to her inspection of Barbara's case.

She found the thumb-cuffs, and held them up for Frank to see. 'Look what she's carrying about with her. Do you think she'd like to model them for us?' Without waiting for his reply she strode over to Barbara and commanded, 'Hold out your hands.'

Barbara didn't move. She was stunned by the events of the last few minutes, first the blows and then the casual laying down of rules. And now this – Phillipa holding Sarah's gift and casually ordering her to submit to being cuffed.

Once again her head rang as Phillipa struck her across the face.

'I've already said that I don't like to repeat myself. From now on I will simply strike you whenever you are slow to obey me. And I will use whatever I have in my hand at the moment. You can consider yourself lucky I happened to be empty-handed just now. Your hands. Now.'

Barbara held out her hands and Phillipa locked the thumb-cuffs on her. She pocketed the key. 'Do you have anything else like those?'

'Not here,' Barbara replied.

Phillipa struck her again. 'The correct reply is, "not here, *Mistress*". Let me hear the capital letter on "Mistress". Where are the things?'

'At home. In the bureau in my bedroom, Mistress.' With flaming cheeks and ringing ears she heard Phillipa tell Frank to get dressed and go and have a look through Barbara's collection.

'Bring back anything that looks interesting,' she said as she dug into Barbara's handbag and tossed her keys to Frank. When he had gone, Phillipa relaxed somewhat. 'It's sometimes a strain to maintain the proper manner in public. Now we can relax a bit. What will he find, I wonder?'

When Barbara didn't reply, Phillipa asked, 'Cat got your tongue?' Her tone was menacing. 'I have ways to make you talk, as the old joke goes. I'd like to be civilised about this, but the choice is yours.'

Dazedly Barbara looked up at this impressive woman who was now her captor.

Phillipa looked back at her expectantly.

In a low voice Barbara began to describe her collection. When she mentioned the ropes, Phillipa stopped her.

'How do you use rope when you're alone? I'm something of an expert in the art of human bondage, but I know of no way for someone to tie their hands unaided. Do tell.'

Barbara described how she used the rope and handcuffs in combination. She told Phillipa how she put the keys in the lock box with the timer. At the last moment she remembered to end the recitation with 'Mistress'.

Phillipa listened intently. 'Ingenious,' she commented at the end of the tale. 'And those thumb-cuffs? How do you get in and out of them when you're alone?'

'I can't, Mistress. They were a gift from a friend who warned me not to use them when I was alone.'

'Good advice. I assume your friend comes to visit you from time to time so that you can use the gift. Will he come this weekend? And does Frank know about him? You're a dark horse, Barbara, full of hidden depths.'

'I don't see her very often,' Barbara said hesitantly, hurriedly adding 'Mistress' when she saw Phillipa's face darken. 'She doesn't live in London.'

'She, is it?' Phillipa paused, then laughed. 'It wouldn't be Sarah, by any chance? Not little Sarah who ran away from me? Yes, I see it is. How nice. I may just keep the thumb-cuffs here, so you'll be reminded of her whenever you come to see me.'

Phillipa seemed to relish the situation, and Barbara guessed that she harboured more than a little ill-will towards Sarah. Barbara wanted to ask about her relationship with Sarah and Frank but couldn't bring herself to speak for fear of what she might learn. And there was always the chance that Phillipa would get angry if she got too inquisitive. She didn't want to be struck again, or worse, now that she was cuffed and vulnerable. Even if her hands had been free, Barbara didn't think she'd be a physical match for Phillipa. It had taken both Sarah and Elspeth plus a drugged drink to enable Sarah to escape from her. She found Phillipa both fascinating and repellent.

The silence became uncomfortable once more. Even if she had had something safe to talk about, Barbara knew that she mustn't speak unless invited to. Phillipa remained silent, even when she poured more champagne for them. Barbara held her glass awkwardly in both hands.

The silence lengthened. Obviously they had very little in

common. Phillipa appeared to reach a decision. She rose abruptly and went into the bedroom. She returned with a pair of leg-irons. Wordlessly she locked one around Barbara's ankle. The other she locked around the leg of the coffee table. She flung on a coat and left, locking the door behind her. There was an air of ill-concealed impatience about her.

Barbara saw that the champagne bottle had been left within her reach. But there was danger there too. Was it a trap? A test to see how far she would presume? And what would Phillipa do to her if she succumbed? Barbara knew that Phillipa wouldn't hesitate to beat her, and that the beating mightn't be as gentle or as arousing as the one she had received in the hotel room with the stranger. She sat alone in the quiet house, feeling a bit anxious about what Phillipa might do when she returned.

Frank got back first. He was empty-handed. 'Did Phillipa say where she was going?' he asked as he took in Barbara's thumb-cuffs and the chain on her ankle.

'No. She just left. In a huff, seemingly.'

'Good. I wanted a chance to talk to you alone after you'd met her, so I didn't go to your place. I waited until I saw her leave. I intend to tell her there was nothing interesting there. But the question is, do you want to stay? If it's too much for you, we can go now.'

From the tone of voice Barbara guessed he wanted her to stay. She was ambivalent about the situation. There was too much room for jealousy. But there was a part of her that responded to the idea that anything could happen to her. She could not deny the excitement brought on simply by the uncertainty of what might happen. And there was the undeniable fact that between them Frank and Phillipa had almost made her pass out with the pleasure they had brought her. Balanced against that was the possibility that Phillipa might beat her as she had beaten Sarah. She felt perversely excited by that thought.

Barbara moved her leg and the chain clinked softly. 'Were you planning on taking the coffee table as well? It might make the neighbours talk. And Phillipa is sure to miss it. She might not be amused. I'll have to stay.'

Frank seemed relieved. He came to sit beside her. Without speaking he took Barbara in his arms and began to kiss her fiercely, forcing her mouth open with his tongue. His hand went between her legs and his fingers touched her labia.

Barbara felt a surge of desire. When she parted her legs his fingers slipped inside and found her clitoris. 'I want you inside me, Frank. Please. Now.' She forced the words past the tightness in her throat.

Still without speaking he stood up and undressed. He drew her to her knees on the carpet and lay on his back beside her.

His cock was erect, and Barbara was glad to know she had this effect on him. She was wet and parted and eager. Awkwardly, hampered by her thumb-cuffs, Barbara straddled him and lowered herself until she was fully penetrated. 'Oh God, Frank, that feels so good!' The quick slide of their coupling and the feel of his cock hard inside her excited her tremendously as she tightened herself around him. At the same time she was reassured that he wanted her, even in Phillipa's house.

Frank reached up to take her nipples with his fingers, making them grow hard as he slowly teased and pinched them. He didn't move, making her wait when she wanted to be fucked hard and fast.

'Slowly. Slowly this time,' he said.

'I can't wait, Frank. Please. It feels so good. Come. Come with me. I want to feel you come inside me.' She tightened herself around his cock.

He dug his heels into the carpet and ground his hips against her pelvis. He groaned, a deep animal sound of satisfaction as he spent himself hotly inside her.

Barbara had her hands braced against his chest, supporting her upper body. Her head was thrown back and she was gasping wildly as she came again and again. Waves of heat spread from her straining crotch. When she finished, she collapsed slowly forward until she lay fully on top of him, her breasts crushed flat against his chest. Her joined hands were stretched above his head as if she were strung up by her wrists.

They lay for a long time. Barbara was content to lie atop him forever. She tightened herself to hold him inside her, and was surprised and pleased to feel him getting hard again.

Frank shifted until he could reach her breast with his mouth. He took the nipple between his lips and began to suck gently on it. From time to time he used his tongue and teeth to flick it or nip gently. With his hand he cupped her other breast.

Barbara moaned softly. Incredibly, she felt herself responding again. She had thought she was spent, worn out. But the familiar signs were there. She moved her hips, liking the slide of him inside the tight sheath of her sex. This time she took charge, moving against him, thrusting herself down against him then rising until she almost lost him before swooping down once again. She was wet again, loving the hardness inside her as she moved. 'Ohhh! Ohhhhh! Oh, Frank! Ahhhh!' She was inarticulate as she came once, then again, before she felt him lose control too. Barbara ground her hips as he came, moaning as her body shook with her own orgasm.

Once again they lay quietly. Barbara began to wonder how long Phillipa would be gone, and what she would do if she walked in while they were still coupled. If nothing else, it would show the bossy blonde that Frank enjoyed her company. It would also be a challenge to Phillipa – who might well retaliate violently.

Barbara managed to slide her joined hands until she could lift herself off Frank's chest and sit more or less upright astride him. From there she rose to her feet. She felt a momentary regret as she felt him slide out of her, but on the whole she didn't want Phillipa to find them in a vulnerable position. And it was hard to get any more vulnerable (in several senses) than during and just after violent and satisfying sex, even if she had not been chained.

Barbara sat on the couch. She wished there was something she could use to dry herself. There were telltale smears and wet patches on her tights as well, and there was no way to get them off short of washing them out and letting them dry. There wouldn't be time for that before Phillipa came back. But she could do something about her body.

'Frank, could you please get up and get me a towel from the bathroom? I'd go myself but . . .' she indicated the chain around her ankle. 'And for heaven's sake get that silly satisfied grin off your face before she gets back.'

Frank stirred and got up. When he returned with the towel, he asked, 'Am I suitably solemn now?'

Barbara felt herself grinning, then he saw her and grinned himself. They both burst out laughing, like a pair of children after a particularly daring prank.

Frank took the towel and dried himself as well. He replaced it in the bathroom and poured more champagne for them.

It had gone flat but Barbara was too thirsty to care. He sat down beside her and began to tease her breast idly as she drank. Then he took her in his arms and laid down on the couch. Barbara lay atop him, and in that position they fell into a doze.

The sound of the door opening woke Barbara. She started up, waking Frank. Of course it was Phillipa. She didn't seem angry at having caught them in almost-*flagrante*. With both of them nude it wasn't too hard to guess what they had been doing. 'Did I miss anything good?' she asked. 'You two look almost indecently sated. I hope you enjoyed yourselves.'

She might as well have added, 'Because now the fun is over.' Barbara felt a distinct chill in the atmosphere, merely because Phillipa had come back. Some people had that effect on her regardless of what they subsequently did (or didn't do). It was the equivalent of spiritual bad breath.

Phillipa drew a sheer transparent bra from her shopping bag and showed it to them. 'I thought I'd just nip out and treat myself to this before I changed my mind. And I thought you two might need some time to kiss and make up, though from the look of you there was a good deal more than kissing involved.'

Barbara was on guard, but Phillipa did nothing more

menacing than step over to the couch and remove the thumb-cuffs. She laid them on the table and fished another key from her handbag. She stooped to unlock Barbara's chain from the coffee table. She locked it around her free ankle and put the key back in her pocket.

'I thought you might like to use the loo. You positively reek of raw sex, and in any case you'll be more use to everyone if you're mobile. When you come back you can start by opening this.' She drew another bottle of champagne from her bag and set it on the table. 'And bring clean glasses from the kitchen.'

Barbara went to the loo to freshen up, though there was not much to work with. She washed her face and took a sponge bath, dabbing at the stains on her tights as well. Then she went to the kitchen to carry out Phillipa's orders. When she came back, clinking softly, Frank was sitting up on the couch, but the relevant part of him wasn't standing up. She allowed herself a small smile of satisfaction. She had been enough to keep him from showing any interest in Phillipa.

Phillipa may have noticed the smile, or it may have been Frank's lack of reaction that caught her eye. She was sitting directly opposite him with her legs crossed and a lot of very shapely thigh on show. Barbara had thought (from Sarah's description) that Phillipa was much older and much less attractive than she was. Even though she disliked the woman, Barbara had to admit that she had a lot of body to flaunt – as she was doing now.

Whatever the reason, Phillipa got up and announced to no one in particular, 'I might as well get undressed too. No sense in letting you two have all the fun.'

Her idea of 'getting undressed' was considerably different from what Barbara had expected. She shed her pale blue-grey dress and laid it carefully on the armchair. Unlike Barbara, Phillipa wore a full-length slip. She took this off as well, and stood before them with the air of one who expects to be admired.

Admiration may not have been the correct word. What Barbara felt was a kind of awe. Beneath her street clothes

Phillipa wore a tight-fitting panty corselet of polished black leather. It fitted her like skin, and was so smooth it gave off dull highlights. That explained why she appeared to be so stiff in her movements. In addition to this remarkable garment she wore a pair of gunmetal-grey tights which clung to her long legs, emphasising their shape. Like her corselet, the tights gave off highlights as she turned in a slow circle before them. Her high-heeled shoes caused her to shift her weight as she moved, the muscles and curves of her legs moving and changing.

If Barbara was impressed, Frank was more outspoken. He gave an appreciative whistle, and Phillipa rewarded him with a small smile.

'I found a divine leather worker last month who made this for me. I thought laces would be more eye-catching, but he persuaded me to have a zipper up the back. He pointed out that I could zip myself up, but that I'd have to have help with the laces. Still, one day,' and here her voice became almost wistful, 'I'll have one with laces – when I have some more reliable help.'

Barbara thought that Phillipa might have even more trouble with the servant problem than most people, being what she was. But there was always the possibility of her finding another Sarah. Or even a Barbara, she thought. Maybe that was what Phillipa meant by becoming 'better acquainted'.

While this fashion show had been going on, Barbara had been standing by with the glasses and the newly-opened bottle of champagne. She set the glasses down and poured for them all.

And while Barbara was pouring, Phillipa moved casually to the couch and sat down next to Frank, who was by now standing up. Phillipa's costume had had an amazing effect on him.

Barbara was chagrined but couldn't do anything without losing face – and quite possibly suffering in some more painful ways. She moved reluctantly to the chair Phillipa had vacated.

Idly, as if unaware of what she was doing, Phillipa laid

her left arm along the back of the couch and stroked the back of Frank's neck in a familiar way. More familiarly, she grasped his erect cock with the other hand and massaged him gently but purposefully, moving her clenched fist up and down the shaft.

Barbara couldn't imagine what she hoped to accomplish beyond making her watch while she fondled Frank. Encased in her tight leather corselet, Phillipa might as well have been wearing a chastity belt. There was no access to her vagina or breasts or anus short of peeling the garment off her. So she must have wanted to see Barbara's reaction to her casual handling of the man Barbara thought of as *her* lover. She may even have expected Barbara to get angry and make an issue of it. She had expected correctly.

In a tight, choked voice that quivered with anger, Barbara said, 'Get your hands off him.' Even as she spoke, she knew that she was breaking several of the other woman's 'rules' at once, but she was too angry to care.

Phillipa looked up at Barbara without stopping her slow manipulation of Frank's cock. Her expression was complex. She seemed to be striving for surprise and anger, as if Barbara's reaction had been completely unexpected. And there was a hint of triumph in her expression as well, as if she had been looking for a way to show Barbara who was in charge of Frank. She succeeded marvellously in both endeavours. But she adopted her affronted mistress look and voice as she said icily, 'What did you say, little girl? Have you already forgotten what I told you?'

Barbara knew she had crossed the line that Phillipa had drawn just for the purpose of having it flouted. But she repeated, 'Get your hands off him,' in a voice that still shook. She didn't know who she was more angry with – Phillipa for baiting her, or Frank for letting Phillipa handle him so casually. The adage about stiff pricks having no consciences was true, she thought bitterly. At the same time she was angry at herself for having walked into Phillipa's trap.

Phillipa flowed to her feet in the way that reminded Barbara of a cat's movements. The leather garment creaked gently in the frozen silence of the room. She went into the bedroom without a word.

Barbara looked accusingly at Frank, who sat on the couch with an erection out to *here* and a slightly (but only slightly) embarrassed look on his face.

Before she could think of anything to say that wasn't blindingly obvious (What do you think you're doing? Answer: Letting Phillipa stroke my cock) or downright silly (How could you? Answer: Quite easily. In fact, I like it), Phillipa returned with a riding crop and a silk scarf. She moved purposefully in Barbara's direction.

There was no mistaking her intentions, but Barbara held her ground. A part of her was saying she couldn't back down now, and another part of her was telling her to get the hell out of here – she's a madwoman. Still another part of her said, how far do you think you'll get when you're naked and in leg-irons?

Phillipa's grip on her arm made her wince. Barbara felt powerless to resist as her arm was twisted behind her back and the thumb-cuffs locked onto her. She made only a feeble resistance as Phillipa pulled her free arm behind her and fastened her thumbs together. Phillipa twisted the scarf until it resembled a thin rope. 'Open your mouth,' she ordered. She struck Barbara sharply across the bottom when she refused. The crack of leather was loud in the room.

Barbara's cry of pain and surprise was louder, but it had the effect of making her open her mouth. Quick as a striking snake, Phillipa was on her, pulling the scarf between her teeth and deeply into the corners of her mouth. She knotted the ends tightly behind Barbara's neck. A sudden hard push between her shoulders sent Barbara stumbling towards the couch. The chain between her ankles came taut and she fell heavily to the floor.

'Hold her, Frank,' Phillipa ordered.

To her dismay Barbara felt his hands on her shoulders, pinning her to the carpet. His whispered, 'Don't fight it, love' was less than reassuring. She felt tears in her eyes and angrily tried to blink them away.

The first blow landed heavily across her bottom. It felt

as if someone had drawn a line of fire in her flesh. The crack registered dully in her ears. The main impression was the unbelievable pain. This was nothing like the erotic beating she had received last weekend in the hotel room. This was the real thing. If she hadn't been gagged, Barbara's scream would have brought the neighbours running. As it was, her breath was driven from her body in an explosive grunt, 'Unnnnhhh!' She bucked wildly in Frank's grip, trying to twist away from the next blow. But he held her as another line of fire was drawn in her flesh where her legs met her bottom.

When she had fantasised about being beaten by her dream lover, Barbara had imagined a series of gentle taps, just enough to arouse her to fever pitch while letting her know there was more pain if she resisted. And in her fantasy, she had resisted only enough to call down the next gentle blow. She had imagined herself writhing as she was gently lashed, and coming again and again under the stimulus of the erotic pain. Her fantasy had not included the full-armed swings of a riding crop in the hands of a powerful woman who wasn't interested in making her come.

The object here was pain and terror. Phillipa continued to rain down the blows, a criss-cross pattern of pain that covered Barbara's squirming body from the knees to the small of her back. But perversely Barbara felt the first stirrings of desire, even as she sought to escape the blows that landed on the backs of her legs. Her body was playing a trick on her once more, transmuting the pain into a fierce sexual pleasure that surged through her like fire. This was another unexpected twist to her fantasy.

Phillipa seemed to recognise that Barbara was not responding as she had intended. She stopped abruptly and left her hanging near orgasm. Doubtless, since punishment was her object, she felt she could accomplish her objective by preventing her victim from enjoying the experience. There was a fierce, almost demented look on her face as she looked down at her helpless victim. Then abruptly she smiled and lowered the crop. Forcing Barbara's thighs apart with her foot, she thrust the handle of the crop up inside Barbara's sex. 'I do hope this has been instructive, Barbara.'

'Mmmmmmmnnnngg!' she grunted through her gag.

'Were you trying to say, "Yes, Mistress"?'

Barbara nodded her head, trying to convey to Phillipa that she was close to coming and wanted to be pushed over the edge. She struggled to turn onto her side so as to present her sex to the other woman – or to Frank. Phillipa helped her turn over, placing the toe of her shoe against Barbara's hip and pushing her over onto her side. Then she seemed to forget all about her. Phillipa asked Frank to pour her some champagne for them, and they sat talking as if Barbara wasn't there.

She closed her eyes and fell into a doze. Her dreams were of more pain and humiliation and sexual pleasure. She woke when she was lifted in Frank's arms and carried upstairs to the guest room. He stood her on her feet and untied the knotted scarf that gagged her before preparing the bed for her. In the full-length mirror she caught sight of her back and bottom. Her tights were ruined where the lash had cut through them. There were red stripes on her bottom and legs. She shuddered in recollection of the beating but wished Phillipa had carried on long enough to provide the release she craved.

She felt too weak to stand any longer, but she didn't dare sit down on her sore bottom. 'Frank, help me,' she said weakly. She was swaying on her feet. She felt the riding crop slide out of her and fall to the floor. Dully, she stared at it.

He eased her down onto the bed and helped her to lie on her stomach. 'I'll be right back,' he promised. He came back with a basin and a sponge and a pair of scissors. With them he cut the ruined tights from her legs. He laid the rags to one side and began to sponge her bottom with warm water.

Barbara was glad he was there with her, and being so gentle, but he was still the one who had brought her to this house. He had held her while Phillipa did this to her. It was only her sense of fairness that prevented her from taking him to task for the part he had played in her humiliation.

She had agreed to stay, tempting fate, daring to find out what she could endure, and what she might enjoy.

Barbara groaned when he touched the worst bits, and he stopped to let her recover. He was rubbing some sort of ointment into her cuts and weals when Phillipa came into the room.

'How is she, Frank?'

'She hurts,' Barbara answered for him. Something in her forced her to resist being treated like a child who was supposed to keep silent no matter what was done to her.

Phillipa came closer to look at her handiwork. With a cool finger she traced one long weal that stretched across Barbara's bottom. Her touch was surprisingly gentle, as if she regretted having to do all this.

Barbara shuddered at the touch, but the shudder wasn't all revulsion. She responded to the gentleness as well.

Phillipa surprised her by kneeling beside the bed and stroking her face, pushing back the sweat-dampened hair where it had strayed into her eyes. She kissed the corners of Barbara's eyes, licking away the traces of her tears. Her mouth moved to the side of Barbara's neck, kissing the pulse that throbbed beneath the skin just there. She nuzzled Barbara's ear, licking and kissing the delicate whorls while her hand stroked her head like a mother soothing a fevered child.

Barbara found this sudden gentleness even more disturbing when she realised she was responding to its erotic overtones. This was the same woman who had beaten her unmercifully not more than an hour ago. But as she planted her soft kisses on eyes and ears Barbara was aware of a familiar warmth spreading in her belly. Her body was once again confusing the pain and pleasure signals, mixing them to produce a rising excitement that Barbara was powerless to control.

She turned her head to get a better view of Phillipa. Barbara was not surprised to see that she was still wearing her corselet and tights. But she was surprised by Phillipa's next act. When Barbara turned her head, Phillipa kissed her fully on the mouth, darting her tongue inside and opening Barbara's lips wide.

This time Barbara's groan had very little to do with pain. The pain was still there, a dull background, but what Phillipa was doing had the opposite effect. There were hungry spasms from between her legs, as if, having been made to suffer, her treacherous body now demanded an equivalent pleasure.

Phillipa held the kiss, probing Barbara's mouth with her tongue, their breath mingling. Her hand was on Barbara's hip, urging her to roll over. Frank's hand was helping, steadying her when she was in danger of rolling over onto her back. He continued to attend to her hurts while Phillipa attended to her arousal. Their efforts were curiously complementary.

Barbara no longer wondered or resisted. When Phillipa's finger pushed into her sex, she opened her thighs obligingly to let her have full access. The finger was joined by a thumb, and the resulting 'carrot' penetrated deeper while the knuckle bumped gently against her clitoris. Phillipa's free hand found her breast, cupping and caressing it. Barbara had no resistance left. Her groan was one of surrender and acquiescence.

This was more like something from her fantasy. She lay on a bed in a strange house, helpless in her thumb-cuffs and leg-irons, while her dream-lover did gentle things to her lacerations and the woman who had beaten her now seemed intent on making her come.

And Barbara did. The first one was small, tentative, as if her body was not yet ready to accept the pleasure hard on the heels of the pain. But Phillipa's hands and mouth continued her slow arousal, and Barbara's low moans became more frequent. Without conscious control she bent one leg and straightened the other so that her sex was opened more fully. She twisted her shoulders so that her breasts were presented more fully to Phillipa's fingers and, before too long, to her lips and tongue and teeth.

The next spasm was stronger, and Barbara whimpered as it rippled through her. Phillipa was relentless. She extracted another orgasm from her captive. And then another. Soon they were so frequent that they need not be drawn from her. It became more a matter of timing them, so that Barbara could derive full pleasure from each one. Her arousal was being drawn out to the point of torture, prolonged, encouraged, allowed to subside, and then encouraged again.

Barbara's body was burning again, but not from pain. She shuddered as her orgasms took her, moaning almost continuously as she came, and rested, and came again. When Phillipa finally withdrew, she fell almost at once into an exhausted sleep.

When she woke it was dark ouside, the street lights still lit but the sky lightening in the east. She had to pee, and she was stiff and sore all over her back and legs. It hurt to move, and she cried out softly when she moved too suddenly. Barbara discovered that her hands were free, but she was chained to one of the bedposts by her ankle. Apparently Phillipa was afraid she might escape.

There was a chamber pot beside the bed, and Barbara felt better after she had used it. But she still hurt from the beating, and the sex that had followed it had tired her out even more. She lay down on her stomach and went back to sleep.

When next she woke it was bright day outside. No one had come to waken her. Perhaps Frank and Phillipa had decided she needed the rest. For a moment she thought she was alone in the house, but then she heard noises from downstairs. Her back and bottom had stiffened overnight, so each movement cost her a certain amount of pain. She had to go to the toilet again, and when she got carefully out of bed she discovered that the chamber pot had been emptied. Room service, she thought sardonically. Her ankle was still chained to the bed post.

Almost before she had finished peeing Phillipa came into the room. She looked softer this morning, less stiff, and her hair was tousled with sleep – or maybe she and Frank had been at it while she slept alone. The probability that they had done something more than just sleep didn't make Barbara as angry as it had the previous day. She wondered if that was because she no longer saw Frank as the ideal lover. She wasn't ready yet to give him up, but now she knew about several of his less-than-ideal characteristics. And it may have been that he had brought her here to teach her that she didn't own him, as she had begun to let herself believe.

And maybe she had learned that lesson. It hadn't been necessary for Phillipa to beat her to drive it home. The sadistic part of her character must have taken control yesterday, just as it had with Sarah. And as it might well do again at any moment. Even without Sarah's cautionary tale (which she had discounted), yesterday's beating would have shown her that Phillipa was dangerous. The fact that Frank hadn't done anything to prevent it – had even helped hold her at Phillipa's order – was more evidence of his own dark side. If she wanted to go on seeing Frank, it would be on his terms. And possibly Phillipa's. His terms might include her toleration of the proverbial 'other woman'.

Phillipa showed no remorse for yesterday. But she did stop to examine Barbara's back. She touched the raised weals gently with her fingertips. 'Lie down,' she directed. 'I'll be right back with something for those.' She didn't ask if it hurt. She knew how much she had put into the lashing, and must know how it felt to be on the other end.

When Phillipa came back she carried a jar of ointment. She sat on the bed next to Barbara and began to spread the faintly scented salve over her back and legs. The soft touch of her fingers on the sore flesh was soothing, and Barbara wondered again how she could be so fierce one moment and gentle the next. The pain lessened as the ointment did its work, but Barbara knew she would take some time to heal. She wouldn't be able to sit for a day or so, and work on Monday was probably out of the question. She'd have to call in sick, plead some excuse to stay at home. Phillipa's fingers were soothing the pain, and under their touch Barbara drifted back to sleep.

This time it was late afternoon when she woke. While she had slept, someone – Phillipa, most likely, since she had the keys – had unlocked her from the bed. Her ankles were once more joined by the leg-irons. From this Barbara concluded that she might go downstairs if she wished. With some difficulty she negotiated the stairs to find Phillipa alone in the front room.

She was more casually dressed in a loose housecoat, but her hair had been carefully rearranged as it had been yesterday. It made her look severe again. 'Frank is away for a while,' she said in answer to the unspoken question. She didn't say where he was, nor how long 'a while' might be. And she carefully left unanswered the question of whether his absence was on account of his wishes, or her own. Barbara had of course not been consulted, since her wishes counted for nothing here.

Phillipa had been sitting on the couch. She got up and patted the seat. 'Come lie down here,' she said as she moved to the armchair.

Barbara saw that she was wearing her sheer grey tights once more, and assumed that Phillipa had donned her leather corselet as well. Her movements were stiff as they had been the day before.

'Please, Mistress, could I have something to eat. I haven't had anything since . . . since,' she hesitated, then went on in a rush, 'since I got here.'

Phillipa smiled at her, apparently pleased that Barbara had remembered the proper form of address. 'Of course. I've been thoughtless.'

Barbara thought she had been somewhat more than thoughtless. 'Remorseless', or 'relentless', might have been more accurate. 'Sadistic' might also apply. And she was naked and in chains, alone in the house with this unpredictable and dangerous woman.

Phillipa rose and led the way into the kitchen. Her leather garment creaked faintly as she moved. Together they prepared a meal of sandwiches and salad. Barbara was beginning to associate sandwiches with sexual encounters. At those times she was in a hurry to get to the good bits and didn't want to take the time to prepare a proper meal. This time she was again too hungry to bother, but she promised herself that just once she would do a proper meal with wine and candlelight and soft music – if she ever found herself in a settled relationship. Her mother was fond of quoting the old saw about the way to a man's heart. Barbara was often tempted to retort that her own heart could be reached by the same route, but no food was involved.

Phillipa opened a bottle of wine and they carried the food through into the front room. Barbara lay on the couch and they ate in something resembling companionable silence with overtones of menace. Phillipa even poured more wine for Barbara when she saw how much pain the effort to help herself cost her. Even the devil takes a holiday sometimes, Barbara thought. This particular devil could be pleasant enough if she made the effort.

It was getting late when they finished. There was no sign of Frank, and Barbara was beginning to think of getting home. 'Please, Mistress,' she began. Phillipa looked up with another of her smiles. Her smile transformed her usually severe face. Barbara thought she should smile more often. She plucked up her courage and continued, 'I need to get back home. I have to go to work tomorrow, and I need . . .'

'Nonsense,' Phillipa said, not unkindly. 'You shouldn't be left alone in your condition.' She said nothing about who was responsible for that 'condition'. 'And as for work,' she went on, 'do you think you'll be able to go into an office in the morning and sit at a desk? It's likely to be several days before your sit-upon is in any condition to be sat upon. I know all about that from my own experience.' There was something almost soft about her expression as she said this, as if she were remembering a distant but pleasant time.

She had a point. Barbara had been thinking of staying on her feet all day – literally. The prospect hadn't been appealing. Phillipa's last remark had sounded strange coming from her. Who would have the strength or the temerity to use a whip on this daunting female? And how had she let herself get into a situation where she was the whipped rather than the whipper? But Phillipa said no more about her experience, and Barbara knew enough by now not to ask.

'And how did you plan to get home?' Phillipa continued. 'Riding the bus wearing nothing but a pair of leg-irons and a new set of stripes is almost certain to get you noticed. You'll stay here tonight. Tomorrow we'll see how you feel, and I'll decide when you can go home.' She paused, and when she went on she was smiling engagingly again. 'Don't look so woebegone. I don't beat my visitors every day, despite what Sarah may have told you about me. Nor do I eat delicious young girls like yourself – you needn't be modest with me – like you for dinner. Though I might be persuaded to taste certain parts of them now and then,' she said with a wicked grin.

Despite the memory of yesterday's beating, and the pain she was still feeling, Barbara felt her stomach contract in the old familiar way whenever sex reared its lovely head. It didn't seem to matter what form the sex took, nor with whom it was enjoyed. Her tastes, she thought wryly, were becoming more catholic.

Phillipa said no more, and the silence showed signs of stretching out. Barbara knew nothing about Phillipa, so she had nothing to use as conversational material. And there was the injunction not to speak unless spoken to. So far as she knew, it was still in force, and she lacked the courage to test it. If things continued like this, it would be a long and awkward evening. Barbara had slept late and didn't need any more rest.

The pain in her back and legs had settled into a dull ache which was bearable so long as she didn't move too much. So it was with some relief that Barbara thought of clearing up the remains of their meal. It would give her something to do, and would no doubt please her captor to see her making herself useful without being told. She got up from the couch, keeping her back as straight as she could, and began collecting the plates and glasses. Phillipa gave her a small smile of approval as she went into the kitchen with them. Barbara lingered over the tidying up as long as she could. When she finally went back into the living room, she was relieved to see that Phillipa was watching TV. Conversation would not be required.

They watched TV for an hour or so, then Phillipa got up and beckoned Barbara to follow her into the downstairs bedroom. More sex? she wondered as she followed the blonde woman. This must be the room in which Sarah and Elspeth had left her bound, gagged and stuffed artistically, but Phillipa said nothing. She brought out the jar of ointment and Barbara lay face-down on the bed without being told. It was medication time again.

Phillipa's fingers were gentle as before, and some of the pain eased as the balm did its work. Barbara relaxed under the soothing touch. After the salve had been worked into the sore spots, Phillipa moved higher, massaging the muscles of Barbara's upper back and shoulders. It was surprising how tense they had been. As the fingers unknotted her muscles Barbara began to feel warm and loose. Phillipa went to work on her arms next, kneading the tight muscles and smoothing them out. Next the lower legs, from ankles to calves, received and same treatment.

Barbara felt relaxed and drowsy afterwards, and she wasn't surprised when Phillipa lay down beside her on the bed. It seemed the most natural thing in the world when she was turned half on her side and Phillipa began to trace slow circles around her breasts with her fingers. They smelled of the salve that had been rubbed into her back, a faint perfume, not at all medicinal or disagreeable.

From there they progressed to the open-mouthed kissing stage, Barbara sighing softly as her body warmed slowly. She felt the long length of Phillipa's body against her own. Their legs became entangled, and a knee found its way into her crotch, moving softly, pressing her labia. The sheer nylon slid smoothly against her, reminding her of the gloved hands that had touched her last weekend. Could that have been Phillipa? Barbara wondered. But by then Phillipa was sucking and licking at her nipples, and she didn't pursue the thought. The other woman's tongue and breath were hot against her breasts.

Barbara moved her hand to Phillipa's stomach, intending to slide it between her legs and help arouse her. She encountered the tight smooth leather, an impassable barrier. She could feel the muscles moving beneath this second skin as the knee in her crotch slid maddeningly against her cunt, but there was no way to reach Phillipa's own sex. Barbara went lower and stroked the leg that was thrust between her own, the nylon of Phillipa's tights smooth beneath her hand. There was a damp patch on the sheer material, and Barbara realised it had come from her. She was wet between the legs, ready for sex. On a sudden inspiration she stroked the wet patch, covering her hand. Then she put her wet palm against Phillipa's nose so she could smell the evidence of her arousal.

Phillipa's breath caught as she smelled Barbara's wet hand. She inhaled deeply, then licked the hand, taking the aroma and the taste into her mouth. That seemed to be the trigger for her. She sat up abruptly and pulled off her housecoat. She stood before Barbara wearing the corselet and tights, the wet patch dark on her thigh.

'Help me,' she said, turning her back so that Barbara could reach the zipper that ran up the back of the smooth garment.

As she tugged the zipper downward, Barbara wondered about what sort of effort had been required to utter those two words. Then her own breath caught as she helped Phillipa out of the constricting leather. The woman's back was criss-crossed by fine white lines of scar tissue. Some of the scars were raised, smooth ridges in the fine grain of her flesh, but most of them were merely lines, like the finest of surgical incisions. More and more of the fine spidery lines were revealed as Barbara tugged the corselet from Phillipa's back and worked it down to her hips.

She raised herself until she could stand behind Phillipa. With her finger she traced the lines slowly, knowing now something of what they represented in the way of pain. On impulse, Barbara put her arms around Phillipa, holding her breasts as she bent to kiss the scars on her back.

Phillipa raised her own hands, holding Barbara's tightly against her breasts. She sighed as Barbara kissed her back, bowing her head. Momentarily this domineering woman was undone by the display of tenderness from the woman she had beaten so unmercifully.

Barbara herself couldn't have unravelled her feelings at that moment. She hadn't forgotten – couldn't forget – her own pain, and she wondered if she would bear scars like Phillipa's. But she felt still an odd sympathy for the other woman. Releasing her, Barbara tugged the stiff garment down over Phillipa's hips and bottom, her mouth following its slow progress, kissing and licking at the scars. Phillipa stood rigidly.

At some point the tenderness became fierce desire. Phillipa stepped out of the corselet, letting it fall to the floor unheeded. She reached down to the waistband of her tights and began to peel them off. Barbara squeezed her breasts once more and then said in a harsh whisper, 'Let me.' She turned Phillipa to face her and slid her fingers under the sheer nylon, working the tights down off Phillipa's long legs. She knelt so that she could get them off her feet.

Barbara took her hips in both hands and drew her close. She burrowed her face into the crisp blonde hair, kissing the plump mound of Phillipa's sex. Hands clasped her head, stroking her hair and pressing her face deeper into the warm fragrant cleft between her legs.

Then the legs parted and Barbara caught a whiff of Phillipa's own wet fragrance as she pushed her mouth against the pink labia nestled in her crotch. She licked and sucked at the lips until she could part them and slide her tongue inside. Phillipa gasped with delight as Barbara licked her from bottom to top, lingering over the hard button of her clitoris. The pressure of the hands on her hair, holding her there, told Barbara that she was doing what pleasured the tall woman. And she was glad to be able to do it.

Then Phillipa was raising her to her feet. She lay on the bed and held her arms up to Barbara. 'Come to me,' she invited. Her breathing was rapid, her breasts rising and falling with now and then a shudder.

Barbara got slowly onto the bed, being careful not to move her sore parts any more than necessary.

'You get on top,' Phillipa told her. 'I don't want you to try to lie on your back. Hold still while I move.' Phillipa arranged them in the sixty-nine position and drew Barbara slowly down until her knees touched the tops of her shoulders. She reached up beneath the younger woman and cupped her hanging breasts. Without waiting for Barbara to position herself, Phillipa fastened her mouth over Barbara's sex and began to lick and suck her.

It didn't take much to set Barbara off. She was shaking with her own excitement. She cried out almost as soon as she felt the mouth on her cunt, coming in short intense spasms. Between orgasms she found Phillipa's sex with her mouth and fastened onto it hungrily.

The two women stayed locked together for what seemed like forever, each striving to give pleasure to the other with hands and lips and tongues and teeth. Their soft cries were drawn from deep inside them. It was gentler, slower than sex with a man, and it had its own flavour. Barbara understood why Sarah had stayed with Phillipa in the hope that she would do this again. When finally it stopped neither moved. Gradually pulse and breathing slowed. Muscles tense in orgasm loosened and their bodies melted together in repose.

Barbara moved first, the chain between her ankles clinking softly. She turned so that she could lie beside Phillipa. She felt arms close around her. The blonde woman seemed exhausted by her orgasms. Barbara's own exhaustion came from the sex, of course, but in her case there had been several sessions. Not to mention the beating, which had taken a lot out of her. She was surprised to see Phillipa so languorous.

At length she spoke. 'Thank you. No one ever kissed my scars. They seemed not to want to look at them, and so I always felt defensive about them.'

'There was no need. You have a beautiful body, and those lines on your back have the effect of beauty spots. Or so I think,' Barbara replied.

'Out of the mouths of babes . . .' Phillipa said with a smile. 'Sleep now if you can.'

In the morning Barbara found that she could move more freely, but work was out of the question. She called in sick from the phone in Phillipa's bedroom. She wore nothing but her leg-irons and a faint blush as the other woman watched her lazily from the bed. When she had made her excuses Phillipa patted the bed and Barbara went over and lay down. Once again the gentle fingers spread the salve on her weals and bruises.

As she had once before, Phillipa went out without saying anything about where she was going or when she would be back. She got dressed while Barbara was washing up after their breakfast. When Barbara came back into the living room she was sitting on the couch applying lipstick. There was no trace of the softness of the night before. The scars were covered up and seemingly forgotten. A pair of handcuffs lay on the coffee table. The old Phillipa was back on duty.

Barbara didn't like the change. It frightened her to see how completely different this woman could be from one moment to the next. But she said nothing, not wishing to reveal her uneasiness. She wondered what would happen to her now.

When Phillipa finished her make-up, she summoned Barbara over to the couch. As Barbara approached she stood up, handcuffs dangling. Wordlessly, Barbara turned her back and brought her hands behind her, but Phillipa turned her with a hand on her shoulder.

'I don't think you'd be very comfortable with your hands behind your back. You'd find the handcuffs painful against those stripes.' She cuffed Barbara's hands together in front of her. 'Make yourself at home while I'm away.' And she was gone.

Barbara heard the door lock behind her. Although she knew what she would find, she nevertheless went to the door to examine the locks. The door itself was heavy, and there was a deadbolt in addition to the mortice lock. No way to get out without the keys. And no question of trying. Nude women wearing handcuffs and leg-irons were not all that common in these parts. Someone was sure to notice if she got out into the street. This must have been what Sarah had faced during the time she was with Phillipa.

Barbara walked slowly through the ground floor, just to

pass the time. She already knew all she needed to know about the kitchen, loo and living room, though she made a mental note to explore the bookshelves along one wall if she had the time. She touched the newel post, imagining Sarah tied to it and being beaten by Phillipa in a frenzy. She went into the bedroom they had shared the previous night. The bed was still unmade, and Barbara made it up. That would no doubt please Phillipa when she got back. But that was really a delaying tactic Barbara used to put off what she knew she was going to do. The best way to understand a person who says nothing about herself was to search for information among their private things. Barbara was going to see what she could learn, hoping only that Phillipa would not return while she was doing so.

To her surprise, nothing was locked, though locks were fitted to the drawers and cupboards. Maybe this was Phillipa's way of saying, look around as much as you like. And maybe it was a trap to see how far Barbara would pry without specific permission. But if it was a trap, Barbara was going to walk into it.

The dressing table yielded nothing more than the usual assortment of cosmetics and lingerie, though there was a surprising amount of dainty, lacy things for a woman who leaned toward other women. Barbara would have said that Phillipa's choice of underwear was calculated to be attractive to a man, but that may have been only her own preference making itself felt. For all she knew, there might be thousands of women of Phillipa's persuasion who were attracted by lacy things.

She turned to the closets. Phillipa had a large wardrobe, so she must have a fair income, or at least private means. Barbara found nothing remarkable until she came to the drawers built into one side of the closet. They contained Phillipa's collection of B&D gear. From the size and variety of the collection, Barbara knew she had been a long time assembling it. Those kinds of things couldn't be bought in job lots and sent around by a delivery service.

The handcuffs and shackles were very much like those Barbara owned, though there were more of them. Phillipa kept some rope around, but she appeared to be mainly into chains. There were no keys, so Barbara wasn't going to be able to get loose that way. Phillipa didn't look like the type to leave them lying around. If she had been that careless, Sarah would have been able to escape unaided. Barbara was just as glad there were none. The excitement and pleasure of being left in chains lay in the inability to escape, so keys would have a disappointment. Still, one had to look, if only to be sure there were none.

In the whip department Phillipa was well equipped, even though only a few would be really necessary. Her tastes ran to riding crops and leather straps, with a paddle and a wooden ruler (for 'naughty schoolboys'?) for good measure. Barbara wondered which of the riding crops had been used on her, but there was no way to tell. Even as she turned away with a shudder, she felt a small shiver of excitement. There was a tightness in her stomach as well. Getting to be a proper little masochist, she told herself.

But the real excitement lay in Phillipa's collection of exotic clothing and 'restraint' items. Some of the things were obviously meant for their owner. The black leather corselet was carefully laid out, as if waiting for Phillipa to don it. So she didn't wear it every day, or whenever she went out. Or maybe she had two. There was a rubber suit which looked as if it were tailored as well. Barbara wondered what it would feel like to be inside that for hours at a time. Hot, she imagined, in several senses of the word.

The things that caught Barbara's eye (and that made her breath catch as well) were the ones designed to be used on other people. There were leather harnesses with straps that buckled and locked; a leather and a canvas strait-jacket; gags of several sorts that Barbara had never dreamed of, including one that was inflated after it was in the mouth.

Most of these things required another person to lace or buckle the wearer into them, so although Barbara would like to have something similar, she realised it would be a waste unless she found someone to help her. And therein lay part of the urge to stay with Frank (and possibly Phillipa, regardless of the risk). If no one was perfect, as the philosophers insisted, then she should expect imperfections in them as well – if 'imperfections' included the way they had treated her the other day.

She picked up and examined a leather helmet which was designed to cover the wearer's head completely. There were holes in the nose-piece to let air in, but the eye and mouth areas were closed. It had adjustable straps that buckled behind the head and under the jaw. Barbara imagined herself strapped inside the helmet, with a gag and ear plugs, unable to see or hear or speak. She shivered with excitement at the idea. The tightness in her stomach spread to her chest, making her breathing shallow and thin, as if suddenly there were not enough air in the room. She brought her manacled hands down to touch her labia. Her fingers came away wet.

What, she wondered, could she do to induce Phillipa (or Frank – mustn't forget him) to use it on her? Asking directly would reveal that she had snooped, even though that had been implicit in Phillipa's leaving her here alone but not immobilised. And asking would reveal too much about her own deep need to be dominated and helpless. Such secrets were meant to be extracted a bit at a time, she believed, lest she lose too much face. And asking would be in bad taste according to the protocols of the B&D game she was playing. On the other hand, she had read fictionalised accounts of slaves who had been taught to beg for punishment or bondage. So – what to do? The etiquette books were silent on this point as well.

Barbara's solitary fantasies were broken by a noise outside the door. Her heart thudded against her ribs. If snooping was bad manners, then being caught at it was much worse. With great relief she realised it was only the postman, but the mood was broken. She put the things back as she had found them and reluctantly closed the door on Phillipa's hoard. She went back into the living room, intending to inspect the more neutral territory of the bookshelves.

The books were arranged according to no particular system. They ranged from contemporary fiction through to the classics and included books on music and several collections of poetry. Phillipa was a well-read person – not just a moron with sadistic tendencies who also happened to be beautiful and wealthy. But, being what she was, Barbara found herself drawn to the erotica in the collection. Here Phillipa's tastes were more evident. The titles dealt mainly with lesbian relationships and with sadism and masochism – S&M to the initiates. Barbara's own interests were also fairly well represented.

Barbara would have liked to pass the time by reading what others had written about her kind of person, but her bottom was still too sore to allow her to sit comfortably. Instead, she tidied the kitchen and prepared a meal which she could heat up when Phillipa got back. She did this mainly to have something to do. Barbara thought it would be terribly dull to have to do this every day, as so many women had to. She was glad she had a job – a good excuse to avoid housework for the most part. This time there was the spice of novelty and menace. Not many women she knew did their cooking while wearing handcuffs and leg-irons. But even that might become dull if she had to do it every day. Better still to avoid becoming a housewife.

Phillipa didn't come back until almost tea time. As before, she offered no explanations. She did, however, look closely at Barbara's back before she sniffed appreciatively at the food that was keeping warm in the oven. 'You'd make someone a good housewife,' she said. 'Let's eat, and then I'll put some more ointment on your back. I think you'll be able to go to work tomorrow if you want to, so long as you avoid sitting too much. You'll stay here tonight, and you can make your way to the office in the morning.' Phillipa opened a fresh bottle of wine for them.

After they had eaten, Phillipa applied more salve to Barbara's back. And as before, one thing led to another, and that led to sex. Barbara thought wryly that almost anything lately led to sex. Not that she was complaining. She had intended to ask Phillipa if she would have scars from the beating, but the occasion never seemed to arise. She slept that night in her chains. Phillipa made no move to unlock them until it was time for her to get ready for work in the morning.

'You can come back after work for your things, and then we'll see what develops. Anything special you'd like to eat tonight?' Phillipa asked.

This is getting all cosy and domestic, Barbara thought. She wasn't ready to start living at Phillipa's place, as she seemed to be planning. She valued her private life, and of course there was the small matter of what had happened to Sarah and, just recently, to herself. And Phillipa was not equipped to satisfy Barbara's most basic need: to be dominated by a man. She wanted to feel a cock inside her while he was doing it. It was a matter of plumbing that didn't connect as well as predilections that didn't match.

And the business of saying 'mistress' and not speaking except when spoken to was all too ritualistic. Some people might like that sort of thing, but to Barbara it was irrelevant at best and awkward at all times. The rituals of slave and master took too much time from the main agenda.

Now that she was dressed and going out of the door, Barbara found it easier to say no to Phillipa's offer. Amazing what a few bits of cloth did for one's self-assertion. 'I need to go home for a while,' she said as she picked up her bag. 'I want to think over what happened this weekend.'

Phillipa merely nodded. It was that easy.

5

ABDUCTION

At work Claire noticed her careful movements, and ascribed them immediately to the wrong cause. 'Sex makes *you* stiff too? You must have been at it all weekend. It must have been really something if. you couldn't tear yourself away until today.'

Her remarks invited Barbara to describe what she had done all weekend. She was tempted to lift her skirt and show Claire her now-fading stripes, but that would have involved endless explanations and descriptions. And the matter would have been all over the office by the end of the day. So she allowed Claire to believe that she had had wild, abandoned non-stop sex. It seemed to make her co-worker happy to imagine that someone she knew was getting it regularly.

During the rest of the week Barbara's stripes healed, and to her relief there seemed to be no sign of scarring. She decided that she didn't want or need another set, which meant that she would not be going back to Phillipa's house. It was clear that the woman had a dangerous violent streak that might emerge at any time without warning. And the elaborate rituals of slavery which Phillipa seemed to enjoy so much were not at all to Barbara's taste. They did not satisfy her desire to have sex while bound, and indeed took time from that activity. And she was afraid she might grow to like the whip too much. She already leaned too far in that direction for her own comfort. Phillipa might not stop the next time.

That left the matter of Frank; was he detachable from Phillipa? And if not, was she prepared to share him with Phillipa? And was he worth sharing after the way he had abandoned her to the mercies of the blonde Valkyrie with the gentle hands? The only way to decide the matter was to see him again and ask him what he intended to do. Barbara would have to ask him if he was interested in a long-term relationship with her. Marriage was not important, but the matter of what they both wanted and expected from the other was. Barbara knew (or thought she did) what she wanted. She didn't know if he knew, or if he was prepared to fall in with her desires. And maybe he didn't know what he wanted himself. So she knew that the next time he called (if he ever did) she would have to bring all this up and find out what (if anything) the future held for them.

During the week there were two calls from Phillipa which she didn't return. She wanted to avoid a confrontation with her; in fact she didn't want to talk to her at all. She thought Phillipa might get the message if her calls went unanswered. But she did make one call which she considered important. She called Sarah and they decided she would spend the Christmas break in Scotland. Barbara learned also that Colin was back, and had said he would like to meet her. He planned to be in London the week before Christmas on business of his own, and he would call Barbara. Sarah said she would be along as well – to introduce them properly and act as chaperone. If things worked out all right, they could all travel back to Glasgow together and get better acquainted over the holiday. Barbara promised to leave a door key and an explanatory note with the neighbours in case she wasn't home when they arrived.

Barbara intended to settle things with Frank one way or another and then go to Scotland for a break. It was nice to know that even if things went badly with him – as well they might – she still had the prospect of meeting another man in the next week or so who might be congenial. The fact that Colin was a friend of Sarah's was a point in his favour. The office would soon be closing down for the holidays, and she was looking forward to getting away and meeting Colin.

So it was with less trepidation than heretofore that she found another of Frank's notes waiting for her at the office on the Friday morning. She was bidden to another weekend in the country. He had, he said, begged the use of the cottage they had used the last time. He said nothing about Phillipa, nor did he comment on his part in Barbara's beating at her hands. The memory of that earlier weekend was pleasant. Barbara had tried to reconstruct that time in her journal, describing where they went, the isolation of the house, the things they had done. She had been both excited and disturbed as she set down her thoughts. Yet this same man had turned her over to a stranger in a hotel room, and had introduced her to Phillipa shortly thereafter. So she had to sort things out with him.

But she decided to put off the confrontation until she was almost ready to go to Scotland. It could go badly, and she wanted to be able to escape over the holidays if it did. There was no way to contact Frank to tell him that she didn't want to go to the country that weekend. She supposed she could call Phillipa and have her pass the message on, but that was distasteful, especially as she was avoiding contact with her too. In the end she made a point of being out early on Saturday morning so as to avoid him. If she had been thinking straight, she would have realised the significance of her decision to avoid him – you don't avoid someone you really care about. He was more like a bad habit than she cared to admit.

There was another note on the mat when she got home late in the afternoon. She stood it on the mantelshelf unopened. It was a test, she told herself. If he really cares, he'll come again, or leave another note. If he didn't do either, that was the end of it. It was her way of demonstrating to herself that she didn't have to do everything he told her to do. The note challenged her all weekend: open me. But she didn't.

Another note came for her at work. This one she stuffed into a drawer in her desk. She told herself it was easy to guess what it said. Either it was another invitation to meet him, or it was a good-bye note. She'd open it later, after Colin and Sarah had arrived. She might be glad of their company.

That year Christmas fell on a Tuesday, and she knew

Sarah and Colin would be there by Saturday at the latest. The office party took place on the Friday, so Barbara got home earlier than usual. There was a message from Sarah on her answering machine. They would see her at noon on Saturday, and she was threatened with a real haggis. 'Have a cage ready for it,' Sarah said before hanging up. Barbara was glad to know her friend was in good spirits. She was looking forward to seeing her again.

Barbara needed to slip out for some shopping early the next evening, so she took the precaution of writing a note for the neighbours next door. She slipped it and the door key into an envelope and went down the hall to push it through the letter box.

Back in her own apartment, Barbara was making a cup of coffee when there was a knock at the door. When she opened it she was face to face with Phillipa. She was doing her impression of a Valkyrie once again; hair braided and coiled atop her head. This Valkyrie, however, wore a severely tailored grey pin-stripe suit and dark grey stockings. Her shoes were a light blue-grey, and she wore a pearl choker that gave her the air of a society art patroness. Barbara could tell from the way she held herself that she was wearing her leather corselet underneath it all.

'Surprised to see me?' she asked. 'I don't take refusals very well. May I come in?' She moved as she spoke.

Barbara found herself giving way, backing into her own front room before the advance of this determined woman. Phillipa herself closed the door. Barbara watched fascinated as she removed her dark grey leather gloves and put them in her handbag. There was an implacability about the woman that defied Barbara to resist her.

'Nice,' Phillipa commented, looking around the room. 'Cosy,' she added, somehow suggesting cramped. 'But I really came to wish you a happy Christmas and invite you to a party this evening. You can come as you are. Ready to go?'

Barbara was taken aback by Phillipa's self-assurance. She seemed never to have considered that her invitation would be refused. 'I have other plans,' Barbara said.

'Cancel them, and come with me.' That sounded more like an order than a renewed invitation. As she spoke, Phillipa reached into her handbag. When her hand emerged, she held what looked like a pistol. It was pointed at Barbara. 'I can be very persuasive when I have to be,' Phillipa said easily. 'It will be so much easier on you if you come willingly.'

Barbara said, 'You're mad. You can't go around threatening people with a gun.'

'Why can't I? I have a gun. You don't. And as our American cousins say, I have the drop on you.' She must have seen the determination on Barbara's face, for she raised the gun and pointed it at Barbara.

Barbara stood very still. This couldn't be happening to her. All she wanted was to avoid further entanglement with this woman. But in some part of her that she didn't understand fully even yet, there was an urge to go with her, to see what she had in mind. Something like a horrible fascination. There was something in Phillipa's nature that appealed to Barbara's submissive side. Being forced to obey under threat was also appealing. That freed her from all responsibility for her actions. And maybe Phillipa wasn't really a monster.

Still she hesitated. She heard a soft 'Phffft!' and a soft 'thunk' as something struck the armchair beside her. She looked down and saw a small dart-like projectile embedded in the fabric. She stared at it uncomprehendingly for a moment, then reached over to pluck it out. When she looked up again Phillipa had reloaded the gun and was once more pointing it at her.

'The next one won't miss,' Phillipa said with a tight smile. 'The dart is loaded with a tranquillising drug.' When Barbara looked at her in alarm, she continued, 'Oh, don't worry. It won't harm you. It's just a little something to make you drowsy and cooperative. Think of it as one of those tranquillising darts they use to sedate wild animals whenever it's necessary to handle them. It's suitably altered for use on wild women such as you might otherwise become. You should consider this a compliment. It shows how much I want you to come along with me. You know how much I dislike having to repeat my orders, so I brought along a little persuasion in order to avoid that unpleasantness.'

Barbara felt herself flush with something like excitement. This *was* happening. It looked as if she would have to go with Phillipa one way or another. The room seemed to close in on her, trapping her and this woman in a bizarre world where one gave the orders and the other must submit. Barbara looked around wildly for some avenue of escape. But there was none. She felt her knees going weak, and she knew she had to sit down before she fell. She collapsed onto the settee and waited for the next move. Barbara felt that almost any movement was too much effort.

Phillipa watched her for a minute or two in silence, then she crossed the room and sat next to Barbara. She plucked the dart from the fabric and laid it on the coffee table. 'Relax and try to enjoy it,' she said. The dart gun was pointed negligently at Barbara. 'Frank told me how much you like playing the slave's role, and in this case you don't have any choice. Think of it as another adventure.'

Phillipa was speaking softly, persuasively, not in her usual manner. Barbara found herself wanting to cooperate with her, to follow her orders. Resistance was too much of an effort. Part of her was saying she should flee, but another part of her urged her to go with the blonde woman, see what she had in mind. Maybe she was going to be pleasant this time. Maybe being her slave wasn't such a bad idea. She listened to the hypnotic voice urging her to come away.

The blonde woman was speaking again. 'Just this once I'll break my rule about proper conduct. By rights you should be helping me, but these are special circumstances. You sit quietly and let me get your coat.' Phillipa moved to the closet as she spoke, soothingly and softly as if to a child. She returned with the garment and extended her hand to help Barbara stand up. 'Let's get this on you,' she urged. 'It's cold outside.'

She sounded considerate, concerned for Barbara's comfort. This was most unlike the Phillipa Barbara was trying to avoid. She felt an urge to please her, a desire to seem obedient, to do anything Phillipa wanted. Barbara took her hand and rose shakily to her feet. Once again the room seemed to waver, and she was glad of the support.

Phillipa helped her into the coat and did up the buttons for her when Barbara's fingers fumbled at them. 'There you are,' she said as the last one was done. 'Now you're almost ready to come with me for a nice ride in the country.' She sounded like a mother persuading a reluctant child. As she spoke she produced a roll of wide surgical tape from her handbag. She began to tear off several long strips, saying in a conversational tone, 'This is just something to keep you from making a fuss. We don't want to be noticed, do we? This can be just our little secret.'

Barbara stood still while Phillipa taped her mouth, pressing the tape firmly into place. She wrapped several long strips completely around Barbara's face, behind her head and under her hair, which she lifted carefully out of the way. Barbara remembered how Sarah had gagged her on the day she left, but this was entirely different. Sarah had been thorough but playful. She had wanted Barbara to enjoy the experience. She thought that Phillipa might have other intentions.

'Now for a scarf,' Phillipa said as she wound it around Barbara's face and covered her hair, as if she were muffled against the cold. The scarf hid the tape that gagged her. 'Now, this is what we'll do. You'll take my arm as if we were old friends. We'll go out to my car and get in. If we meet anyone, let me do all the talking. No attempts to attract attention, please. We wouldn't like others to know about this. And I promise you you'll like what I've arranged at our destination.'

Barbara nodded. She had no will to resist. The idea sounded bizarre and sensible at the same time. And seductive. Weakly Barbara followed Phillipa to the door, leaning heavily on the supporting arm. They met no one in the hall or in the lift. In a part of her mind Barbara was hoping that they would meet someone she knew, who would see that she was in distress. As they walked through the lobby Phillipa nodded pleasantly at a couple entering the building, other tenants apparently but unknown to Barbara. They nodded back and paid no further attention. Barbara wanted to signal wildly for help, but the desire to obey this strange woman was stronger.

Phillipa's hand on her arm urged her down the steps and across the street toward a Ford saloon. It didn't look like the kind of car Phillipa would own, and as they came closer Barbara noticed that it was a hire car – anonymous, ordinary, indistinguishable from thousands of others. The perfect vehicle for an abduction, which this was.

Phillipa opened the door on the driver's side. She told Barbara to get in and slide across to the passenger seat. Barbara got in and seated herself where directed. Phillipa got in behind her, locking the doors. 'That should discourage the casual purse snatcher,' she said conversationally. 'It's a rather long ride, but try to relax and think of what we'll do when we get to our destination. I think you'll recognise it when we get there. You've already been there once, and you might have gone there again if you hadn't had your little fit of independence. You might have enjoyed it, and it would have saved me the trouble of having to come collect you like this.'

She spoke chidingly, but the steel wasn't far from the surface. Barbara realised then that Frank's invitation had been calculated to draw her into Phillipa's hands. And she knew that he was Phillipa's puppet. He had been on the look-out for a suitable victim for her when he had found Barbara. And that meant he wouldn't be riding in like the cavalry to rescue her from the clutches of the wicked witch. Indeed, he might be waiting at the cottage to have his own turn when Phillipa was done with her.

Phillipa rummaged in her handbag once again. When she came up with two pairs of handcuffs, Barbara thought of Pandora's box.

'One pair for your ankles, if you don't mind. I'd rather not have you kicking about and causing trouble. And these might make the ride more interesting for you.'

As if in a dream Barbara locked the cuffs around her ankles and reached for the other pair which dangled from Phillipa's hand. She hitched herself forward in the seat and was bringing her arms behind her when Phillipa stopped her.

'In front, I think. It will be more comfortable – and less conspicuous,' she said.

Barbara locked the cuffs onto her wrists and sat with her hands in her lap.

'There's just this,' Phillipa said almost apologetically as she brought a short length of chain from her capacious handbag. It had a snap hook at each end. She fastened one end to the chain between Barbara's ankles and drew her legs up until the chain almost reached her handcuffs. 'Bring your wrists down a bit, there's a good girl.' She snapped the other hook to Barbara's handcuffs.

Barbara was left sitting with her legs drawn up and her wrists drawn down almost to her knees. There was no slack in the chain that connected her wrists and ankles. Phillipa knew a good deal about transporting captives. It was equally obvious that she had planned this abduction with some care. She didn't seem to have missed anything. This conclusion was reinforced when Phillipa reached across Barbara to buckle her seat belt. It came down across her arms, pinning them to her sides. Phillipa pulled it as tightly as she could manage, and Barbara was helpless in her seat. In spite of the danger in her situation Barbara found herself responding to the chains. There was just the trace of excitement in her tight stomach muscles and a faint stirring between her legs.

'Don't want to be stopped by the coppers for not wearing our belt, do we?' Phillipa said gaily. She drove off through the darkened streets. No one paid any attention to the car with the two women in it as it made its way through the light traffic of the evening.

As they drove, Barbara thought of one of her fantasies. In it, she had imagined herself being driven through crowded streets as a prisoner, bound and gagged and unable to attract the attention of anyone to help her. Of course, in the dream she hadn't really wanted to escape because her captor was a handsome man who was taking her to some secret but delightful destination where he would have her again and again as she struggled first to get free, and then later to please him as he drove her wild with desire. She was keenly aware of her tendency to dream in purple prose.

It was ironic that some of the aspects of this actual abduction fitted her fantasy. She didn't like to dwell on the uncomfortable differences. What she already knew of Phillipa was worrying enough. There was no way to say what she might do when she had Barbara helpless and completely safe from discovery at the cottage. Barbara thought of the imminent arrival of Colin and Sarah. Would they be able to track her down and rescue her? And how long would that take? She might be in Phillipa's power for some time before her friends could find her. But she clung to the belief that they would come for her.

And immediately she began to imagine herself being rescued from her captor by Colin, who would carry her off to his own secret place and make her come and come as he . . . She was amazed by her ability to create sex and bondage fantasies while in the midst of what could easily become a nightmare. Uneasily Barbara shifted in her seat, aware of the steel bands on her wrists and ankles. Under the gag her mouth was dry. She swallowed, trying to work some saliva around with her tongue.

Phillipa drove speedily and with a certain flair, ignoring the rest of the traffic. Soon they were on the open road, out of the city, heading inexorably for the cottage and whatever Phillipa had planned for her.

Hypnotised by the motion, Barbara found herself drowsing as they sped through the dark countryside. She woke up as the car bumped over the cattle guard at the entrance to the farmyard. There were lights in the house, shining through the trees in what under normal circumstances would be a welcoming and cheery manner. She remembered the first visit to this house with Frank as a scene from another life. She had come a very long way from that in a very short time. Tonight she was being brought here as the captive of a dangerous and unpredictable woman.

And she was uncomfortable. The handcuffs were digging into her wrists and ankles and she was cramped from sitting so long in one position. But she could do nothing about these discomforts herself. She was entirely in Phillipa's power and could see no escape.

'Back among the living, then?' Phillipa observed as she saw Barbara stir in her seat. 'We're here, and now you can look forward to a bath and a chance to get out of those wrinkled clothes. But I seem to have forgotten to bring anything else for you to wear. Thoughtless of me. The only bright spot is that you will feel less eager to escape if you haven't anything to wear. And, who knows? You may even come to like it here. You'll have plenty of time to get used to the regime. No one will miss you over the holidays, so we have days and days to bring you around to our way of thinking.'

Now that they were away from everyone else Phillipa's remarks seemed more menacing than persuasive. She was reverting to type, Barbara thought. To her mind there came the dark premonition of another beating, perhaps several. She shrank from that prospect. Out here in this isolated house, Phillipa could do anything she wanted without attracting attention from anyone else. And only weeks ago Barbara had thought of this same isolation as an advantage. Would Sarah and Colin even be able to find her here? But she pushed that doubt firmly aside. She had to endure until someone came for her.

Phillipa drew up outside the front door and honked the horn. She switched off the motor and got out. As she opened the door on Barbara's side, the front door of the house opened as well. Frank stepped out and gave Phillipa a welcome-home kiss. To Barbara it seemed to go on for a long time.

Finally they stood apart and Phillipa said, 'I've brought your reluctant playmate along. Help me get her inside.' She unlocked the cuffs on Barbara's ankles and let them dangle from the short chain. When she unbuckled the seat belt,

Barbara had trouble swinging her cramped legs out onto the ground. Neither of them helped her. Eventually she stood, swaying slightly. Phillipa grasped the chain connected to her handcuffs and yanked on it. Barbara was pulled stumbling into the house by her manacled hands. The velvet gloves were most definitely off.

She guessed that the roughness was calculated to let her know that this visit would be different from the last one – as if that weren't already clear enough to her. The house at least looked the same. There was a fire burning in the big fireplace. Somehow it didn't look as welcoming as it had on the last occasion. She was pulled over to it but Phillipa told her curtly to stand when she made as if to sit on the couch.

'I didn't give you permission to sit. You can rest after you've had a wash. We'll take care of that in a minute.' Turning to Frank, Phillipa went on, 'Take the car back to town and turn it in to the rental agency. You can use my car to get around in. You know what you have to do. Come back in three days.' For Barbara's benefit she added. 'I'll have her housebroken by then.'

Frank left without comment. Barbara heard the car start up and drive away. She was alone in the house with Phillipa, but which Phillipa was it to be, the one who had beaten her, or the one who had soothed her cuts with salve and then made love to her?

Phillipa beckoned her to come along to the bathroom, tugging Barbara up the stairs by her chain. As the tub was filling up Phillipa unlocked the handcuffs and set them aside. She helped Barbara unbutton her coat and unwound the scarf that concealed the tape. She pulled the sticky tape away from Barbara's mouth and told her to get undressed.

Dully, Barbara obeyed. She stepped into the tub at Phillipa's gesture and sank gratefully into the hot water. Phillipa washed her like a child, paying special attention to her breasts and labia. The seductress was back on duty.

'I'm going to wash your clothes. You soak some more, or wash your hair. Or both.' She indicated a bottle of shampoo on the shelf nearby as she began to gather up the soiled clothing.

Barbara did both. Phillipa took her time with the washing. When she came back she carried a bottle of champagne and two glasses. She poured the frothy wine for them both and handed a glass to Barbara. 'To our reunion,' she offered the toast, smiling slightly. 'You know, you really shouldn't try to avoid me. Not returning my calls was . . . unwise, shall we say? But never mind. Now you're here we can smooth over our differences.'

Barbara pondered the implications of that last phrase as she drank the wine slowly. She saw Phillipa looking at her nude body with something like hunger. In spite of the menacing situation she was obscurely pleased to be the object of this beautiful woman's desire. She only just restrained herself from arching her back and parting her legs.

Phillipa broke the tableau by pulling the plug to let the water drain away. She motioned for Barbara to stand and wrapped her in a voluminous bath towel. 'Go and sit in front of the fire. I'll be along in a moment.'

Barbara did as she was bidden. Inside the towel she felt less vulnerable than she had while naked to Phillipa's gaze, but she knew that it was an illusion. Nevertheless she was grateful for it, and for the warmth of the fire.

Presently Phillipa joined her, bringing another towel and several bottles and boxes along. She set about drying Barbara's hair, first towelling it vigorously and then using a brush to straighten out the tangles.

Barbara found herself relaxing under the soothing influence of the fire's warmth and the gentle brush strokes on her hair. Phillipa offered her another glass of champagne and urged Barbara to lie down on the couch with a gentle pressure on her shoulders. The towel fell open, but when Barbara tried to close it again Phillipa stopped her.

'I like to look at you naked,' she said. 'And that's not something I say to too many people. But I had another motive as well.' She chose a box of scented powder from the selection she had brought from the bathroom, and began to powder Barbara's legs. She moved up to her sex, playfully dusting the labia and touching her clitoris briefly. 'Did I touch a sensitive spot?' she asked innocently when

Barbara gasped. She continued to dust Barbara's stomach and breasts without waiting for an answer.

When she had finished Phillipa set the powder box aside and began to apply a skin cream, beginning with her feet. Phillipa rubbed and massaged the cream into her soles and heels, between her toes and into the arches of Barbara's feet. It was soothing and erotic without the urgency that told her it was time for sex, and Barbara relaxed more fully, surrendering herself to this new sensation and letting Phillipa pamper her. There were odd echoes of the time Frank had sucked her toes and massaged her feet in this same room.

Phillipa bent her knees so that she could work on her calves, then the backs of her knees. Next the cream was massaged into her thighs. Barbara mewed softly when Phillipa's hand brushed her labia.

'Not yet. Relax. There's plenty of time.' Phillipa shifted her hand to Barbara's stomach.

Once more the massage became soothing rather than arousing, but that stage lasted only until Phillipa reached her breasts. The gentle massage and the sporadic cupping of her breasts caused Barbara to catch her breath. Occasionally Phillipa squeezed the firm mounds, drawing a quick gasp from Barbara each time she did so. Phillipa moved on to the nipples, working the cream into them, pulling and stretching them until they were stiffly erect. Each time her nipples were squeezed, Barbara let out a long 'Ahhhh' of pleasure.

The aim now was definitely arousal rather than relaxation. Phillipa concentrated on Barbara's breasts, rubbing and squeezing them, catching the nipples between thumb and forefinger as if extracting milk from her. The soft 'Ahhhs' changed to sharper 'Ohhhhs' as Barbara became more excited. She wasn't even aware of it when her legs parted invitingly.

But Phillipa was. She moved atop Barbara so that she could continue the manipulation of her breasts while her mouth found the warm moist mouth between her parted thighs. When her tongue darted inside Barbara almost screamed. She felt as if her body was taut as a bow string, waiting for release. Her back was arched, thrusting her hips up and offering her sex to Phillipa's mouth. She was moaning softly, a sound that rose several octaves whenever the darting tongue found her clitoris.

Phillipa paused. The hiatus caused Barbara to cry aloud, 'Please! Don't stop. Go on!' The last words turned into a groan as Phillipa resumed her work. Barbara's hips began to rise and fall, her body twisting from side to side as she tried to present all of herself to those hands on her breasts and that busy mouth on her sex. And then she was coming. There was a knot in her belly that came untied suddenly. She writhed and jerked as the waves of pleasure swept through her, turning her legs to jelly and making her feel weak all over. But that passed, and another climax took her, and then another. No more thoughts about what Phillipa might do to her tomorrow. This was now, tonight, and it was shattering. When it was over, Barbara was limp and drained.

She wasn't aware of it when Phillipa rose and stood looking down at her. Her eyes were closed and she was drifting in and out of a most pleasant dream. She felt drowsy and warm and somehow safe. Finally she forced her eyes open and saw Phillipa looking at her with an expression of satisfaction on her face. Was she satisfied because Barbara had come so often, or because she had demonstrated her control over the younger woman, or for some other combination of reasons? Phillipa's smile gave no clue, and Barbara didn't have the energy to pursue the matter.

She felt Phillipa's hand raising her head, and a glass of something cool being pressed to her lips.

'Drink this,' Phillipa urged.

Barbara opened her mouth and drank the champagne, fighting the urge to sneeze as the bubbles got up her nose. She thought she really shouldn't drink any more, but Phillipa was urging her. She drank the rest of the wine. Phillipa let her sink back against the cushions, and she drifted in and out of sleep. Each time she woke she was aware of the other woman sitting on the floor beside her, and several times she felt her hands caressing her face and breasts. Once she asked drowsily if Phillipa would like to be done as she had been, but the other woman shook her head.

'There's plenty of time for that later. Plenty of time for everything.' Barbara was not reassured by her assumption that this would go on for an indefinite time, but she was getting sleepy from the warmth and the sex and the champagne. She slept.

And woke bound to a chair in the kitchen. That knowledge didn't come all at once. Barbara wanted to brush the hair from her face and found that she couldn't move her hands. She pulled, and felt the familiar bite of rope on her wrists and upper arms. She was seated in a wooden chair with a wide low back. Her arms were tied behind her back at elbows and wrists. More rope circled her waist, holding her firmly against the back of the chair. She discovered that her ankles had been crossed and tied together. They were pulled back under the seat of the chair and tied to the rung that ran across between the back legs. And she was gagged once more. This time something had been stuffed into her mouth before the tape was applied, and she was unable to shift it.

There was an uncomfortable sensation of fullness in her anus, and she realised that she was sitting on a dildo of some sort that seemed to be fastened to the seat of her chair. She couldn't lift herself off it or make it move. There was another one in her vagina, but this one wasn't fixed to anything.

Barbara had been dimly aware of Phillipa moving her about, but she had been too drowsy with the effects of the drink and the warmth and the lassitude that followed the prolonged erotic play to protest or question what was being done to her. Now it seemed that Phillipa's other side had emerged fully, and that she was going to have a very unpleasant time of it shortly. She didn't know if she could stand much of the sort of pain she remembered from the last time. At the same time the recollection of how Phillipa had made love to her afterwards caused her sphincters to tighten around her plugs in anticipation.

There was no sign of Phillipa. She had probably gone out in order to let the idea of what was going to happen to her grow on Barbara's mind as she sat helpless in the silent house.

Barbara pulled fiercely at the ropes on her wrists and elbows, but there was no give. Phillipa knew her business. She felt a rising panic as she struggled. For a few minutes she lost her head completely, jerking at the ropes like a mad thing. The chair creaked as she threw herself from side to side, and she became breathless. When she finally became quiet, sweating with fear and exertion, she was still securely tied. And she realised that the chair was somehow fixed to the floor – doubtless to prevent it falling over when its occupant (herself) tried to escape the double penetration and whatever else Phillipa had in mind. Her heart was hammering against her ribs, and she felt a tight knot of fear and anticipation in her stomach and chest.

She couldn't understand why Phillipa felt it necessary to threaten and subjugate people, but then she couldn't understand why she herself was so deeply thrilled by the idea of having sex while bound helplessly. Some dark side of her nature drove her to it, just as something in Phillipa made her want to dominate and even hurt people. Barbara remembered the thin stripes and raised weals on Phillipa's back – the ones she had kissed as she peeled the tight leather corselet from her body. Maybe she had been tortured by someone else, and was passing on to others the pain she had suffered. Not logical, but then these dark urges seldom are. And in any case all the analysis in the world wouldn't alter the fact that she was Phillipa's captive, or deflect her from whatever she wanted to do.

It was a bright cold day outside. The wind was making a low moaning sound as it swept across the farmyard. The last leaves skittered before it. There was no one in sight. Even the animals seemed to have gone indoors. The sense of her isolation and helplessness was reinforced by the emptiness of the windswept landscape – doubtless as Phillipa had intended. Phillipa seemed to know as much about psychological torture as she did about the other sort. She wanted Barbara to realise that there was no escape from whatever was coming, and that no one was going to interfere in the play between torturer and victim.

Phillipa must believe that she could make Barbara into a slave, a possession, by inflicting pain on her, with the threat of more if she resisted or disobeyed. That would be a long process and would necessitate keeping her under lock and key twenty-four hours a day. Phillipa had chosen her time well. If it weren't holiday time, Barbara would be missed at work, and there would be a search sooner or later. But now Phillipa could take whatever time she thought necessary to break Barbara's will to escape – either by threats or by instilling in her a desire for more harsh treatment, so that she could be allowed to go out on her own with the assurance that she would return to Phillipa at the end of the day to receive whatever pleasure or punishment she cared to mete out. Sarah had done something like that before the beating that had changed things forever.

Barbara thought she could resist the impulse to become Phillipa's slave, but there was (she well knew) a desire to submit buried deep in her. Maybe Phillipa could twist that desire to her own ends, make herself the object of it, so that Barbara would remain with her. And maybe she *could* be tortured to the point where she became a willing slave. And there was always the prospect of more sexual play as a reward.

The kitchen door opened and closed again, admitting Phillipa and a gust of wind. Barbara shivered in the chair as the cold air touched her naked body. Phillipa carried a riding crop.

'It's a nice day for a walk,' Phillipa observed. 'Now that I've had one we can get back to the business of you.' She swung the crop casually in the air as she moved toward the chair to which Barbara was bound.

Barbara tensed herself for the slash of the leather on her body. Bound as she was, the lash had to fall somewhere on the front of her body. Her breasts suddenly felt very exposed, and she remembered the last beating. Phillipa had threatened to lash her there, but hadn't. It looked as if she were going to do so now. Barbara was shaking her head in denial. She twisted on the chair, once more tugging in panic at the ropes that held her. The strangled noises that came through her gag were loud in her ears.

Phillipa raised her arm as if to strike, but she only touched the upper slopes of Barbara's breasts lightly. She moved the stiff shank of the riding crop under the exposed mounds, lifting them and making them more prominent.

Barbara felt the sweat of her panic running down her rib cage while Phillipa held her breasts up as if presenting them to an invisible audience. With a low laugh Phillipa bent and kissed the nipples, teasing them with her tongue and lips. She nipped at them gently with her teeth.

In spite of her panic (or maybe because of it) Barbara felt her nipples growing taut and erect, her breasts becoming heavy as they filled with blood. And at the same time she felt the first stirrings of excitement. There was a moment of lucidity in which she wondered again if there was anything that would inhibit her sexual response. Not even the fear of a beating or some other torture could put her off. The moment passed as Phillipa kept up her erotic play. As she always did, Barbara surrendered herself to the pleasure of being aroused by an expert. Her muscles tightened around the plugs inside her. Barbara's response was as much to the danger she was in as it was to Phillipa's mouth and lips. The arousal was only heightened by the threat of pain.

Phillipa seemed to be well aware of what was passing through Barbara's mind, for she suddenly withdrew and administered a stinging slash to the breasts she had been suckling.

Barbara's cry of pain and surprise was hardly uttered before she felt herself coming. As before, when she had experienced this close conjunction of pleasure and pain, she had been unable to separate the two. And so it was again. Phillipa had woven them so closely together that each impulse seemed necessary to the other. And, as she admitted later to herself, each had reinforced the other.

So Barbara came, crying out, her unmistakable cries of pleasure muffled by her gag. She hunched herself as far forward as the ropes allowed, pulling her knees up as if to huddle herself about her pulsating sex. She was tightly clenched around her plugs as she tried to prolong the orgasm.

Phillipa let her go on. When it was evident that she was finished, she returned to the attack. This time she placed herself behind Barbara's chair and reached over her shoulders to fondle her breasts. Her forearms were resting on the tops of Barbara's shoulders and her hands cupped her breasts. Barbara moaned softly as she felt the fingers close on her once again. She leaned back in the chair, offering her breasts to Phillipa's touch. Her head was thrown back and the tendons in her throat stood out. Her eyes were closed as if to blot out everything except what was happening to her breasts and between her legs.

This time Phillipa used her mouth to plant small kisses on Barbara's eyelids and the corners of her eyes and in the angle of her jaw. She nibbled gently at Barbara's earlobes and blew softly into her ears. She kissed her captive behind the ears and on the pulsing artery that lies just beneath the skin there.

And always her hands were busy stroking and cupping Barbara's breasts. She caught the nipples again between her thumbs and forefingers, alternately squeezing and stroking. The pressure became more insistent as she felt Barbara begin to stir under her hands.

To Barbara the soft kisses and the warm breath in her ears felt like butterfly wings moving over her face and neck, touching her and moving on. The soft touches on her face were counterpointed by the insistent manipulation of her breasts, which Phillipa heightened by an occasional pinch, or by digging her finger-nail into the sensitive flesh. Her soft moans became louder as the arousal continued. Once more she felt her muscles clenching around the two plugs.

Phillipa was both relentless and expert. Once she was certain that Barbara was on the brink of another orgasm she stopped long enough to deliver two quick slashes to the breasts she had been fondling. Barbara gasped and jerked in pain and surprise. Then Phillipa resumed stroking. Her mouth was busy once again on her victim's eyelids and ears and throat.

The sudden contrast, the flashes of pain, once more drove Barbara over the edge. She felt Phillipa's hands resume stroking her affronted tits, soothing the sting away. She twisted wildly in the chair, the plugs sliding inside her as she clenched herself tightly. Her strangled, urgent cries sounded loud in her ears.

This time when she was finished Phillipa let her rest. Barbara let her head drop forward and closed her eyes. She felt limp and sweaty and almost indecently sated. She also felt as if she could sleep for a week, and wished Phillipa would untie her from the chair so that she could stretch out on the couch, or a bed, or the floor. She wanted to be horizontal. But Phillipa left her tied. She seemed to be busy with other things in the kitchen, for Barbara could hear her moving about. The sounds were curiously distant, as if they had nothing to do with her. She might have been part of the furniture.

But Phillipa came back. She took Barbara's chin in her hand and raised her head until she could look into her face. When Barbara opened her eyes, Phillipa smiled down at her and asked how she was feeling. The question was clearly rhetorical since Barbara was gagged, and in any case only a blind person could have missed the effects.

Barbara felt exhausted, but Phillipa wasn't done with her yet. 'One more time,' she said. 'Third time pays for all.' Barbara shook her head weakly in denial, but Phillipa paid her no mind. 'Are you really a tit-person? You seemed to get a great deal out of it when I played with your pretties. But maybe some other areas are feeling left out? The greedy little mouth between your legs, for instance?' she suggested. 'It does look rather pretty and pink. And warm and moist too,' she said as she stroked Barbara's labia.

As Barbara had done on another occasion, Phillipa brought her hand to Barbara's nose and she smelled the odour of her own arousal. But still she shook her head, no.

She was still too tired. She wanted to rest. 'Nnnnggghh, she said.

'I'll take that as a yes,' Phillipa said with another smile. She went to fetch a low stool which she set down near Barbara's chair. From that position she could easily reach the target area at the apex of Barbara's parted thighs. She placed her hand partly on Barbara's belly and partly on her mons veneris. When she moved her hand, she massaged the sensitive area and caused the dildo inside Barbara's sex to shift tantalisingly.

Once more Barbara shook her head in denial. And once again Phillipa ignored her.

This time it took longer to arouse Barbara, despite the steady caressing of the labia and the quick darts of Phillipa's finger to her clitoris. But Phillipa was patient and seemingly tireless. Through her fatigue Barbara could feel the familiar signs of her growing excitement. A part of her stood aside in amazement, as if waiting to see if it were possible to do this again so soon after the last time. The rest of her was heading toward orgasm. Unstoppably. She received another push in that direction when Phillipa substituted her mouth for her hand. The hot tongue darting inside her and scraping her clitoris was irresistible. She was tensing in the chair, feeling the wave building in her belly and flowing down her thighs.

Phillipa chose that moment to spring the surprise she had prepared while Barbara was dozing. When she felt Phillipa draw back, Barbara prepared herself for the lash, hoping it would drive her quickly over the brink as it had the last two times.

Instead of the lash Phillipa began to manipulate the dildo in Barbara's sex, holding her down on the chair against the one in her bottom at the same time. Barbara moaned in time to the thrusting inside her. Only when she was sure Barbara was on the brink of orgasm did Phillipa use the lash again, this time across the tops of her thighs, threateningly close to the centre of things. She struck again and again, using her full strength, striking the occasional blow to Barbara's exposed breasts.

The blows stopped abruptly and Barbara was left breathless with the pain. Yet as she drew breath after shuddering breath, she felt herself coming, the waves spreading from her sex, down her legs, into her belly, loosening the clenched muscles and filling her with a wild pleasure she thought would burst her. This time she jerked at her ropes in mad release.

Later she had time to consider how the agony had been transmuted into this wild pleasure, but just then she was too wrung out to care about anything. Phillipa let her rest in the chair for a time, and then Barbara felt herself being untied and lifted off the rod that had been thrust into her backside. She was half-walked, half-dragged up the stairs to the bedroom. Phillipa laid her on the bed where she lay twitching for a time before dropping into exhausted sleep.

When she became aware of her surroundings once more, Barbara saw that she was in the same bedroom she had shared with Frank on her first visit to this house. While she was unconscious she had grown leg-irons, the steel bands locked around her ankles. There was a steel collar locked about her throat, to which her handcuffed wrists were joined by a short chain. She tugged experimentally and discovered that her hands were held closely under her chin and she couldn't use them for anything. A chain from the back of her collar was locked to the headboard of the bed.

She was tired and sore. And intrigued by her response to what could only be called torture. Strange are the uses of pain, she mused as she lay waiting for Phillipa to return. She realised that she was very hungry, having had nothing since the previous day. She hadn't thought of that while Phillipa was working on her. Barbara had recovered enough of her poise to be faintly amused by the way sex – even the bizarre and painful variety – could banish hunger. Tie me up and make me come and I forget everything else, she told herself wryly once more.

She lay quietly, drowsing and trying to ignore the rumblings from her stomach. Phillipa would have to come feed her since she couldn't do anything for herself. And sometime later – in the early afternoon – she did. She unlocked the chain from the bed and used it as a lead to conduct Barbara downstairs.

From the front room Barbara could smell the food in the kitchen. Her stomach rumbled so loudly that Phillipa smiled.

'Hungry, are we?'

Barbara nodded, then added hurriedly, 'Yes, Mistress.'

Phillipa nodded in a satisfied manner and led Barbara into the kitchen. The table had been laid for two. There was a salad and an omelette which smelled heavenly. Wine and coffee to drink. The chair to which Barbara had been tied earlier stood to one side, a reminder of what had been done to her.

Barbara ignored it, intent on the food. Phillipa pulled out a chair and helped her seat herself. Then she unlocked the short chain between Barbara's handcuffs and her collar. However, she didn't remove the handcuffs.

'One thing you'll find essential in polite company is the art of eating while handcuffed. Like all worthwhile skills, it takes some time to learn, but once you've mastered it you'll be welcome – even sought after – in any circle composed of B&D types.'

This was said with a straight face, and was so ridiculous that Barbara burst out laughing. When she stopped, she realised that she couldn't have been seriously injured by the earlier torture. And that was vaguely worrying. Was she becoming addicted to this sort of sex? From Phillipa's point of view, that wouldn't be so bad. From hers it was rather frightening. There was always the chance that Phillipa might go too far and injure her seriously. The whip was not something to play around with. Phillipa seemed to be unworried, but that might have something to do with the fact that she wasn't on the receiving end. If she were, she might well change her mind.

Phillipa served them and Barbara began to eat. The handcuffs made it awkward but she managed. Phillipa smiled approvingly.

'It's not so hard, is it? By the way, I have to tell you that the collar will go with you wherever you go. I threw the key away after I put it on you. I suppose that means you'll become famous for wearing high-necked blouses and jumpers everywhere you go. But you and your co-workers will soon become used to it, and some of those fashions are quite smart. On the positive side, keeping your neck covered may make it an object of erotic speculation among men. And you'll be safe from vampire bites as well.

'Later we can think of having you erotically pierced. I'd like to study you in more detail before deciding what to do with you. I don't know if nipple rings or labial rings would suit you better. Or,' Phillipa said musingly, 'we could go for a ring through your septum. Nose rings are becoming quite fashionable. Another possibility would be to have your tongue and the inside of your cheeks pierced. In that way you could be gagged undetectably merely by joining the rings. That might be good discipline for you. You'd be silent while everyone else was speaking. You might even gain a reputation for wisdom thereby.'

Barbara was taken aback by the matter-of-fact way in which Phillipa had assumed ownership of her: the collar with no key; the casual discussion of having her pierced; the unstated assumption that Barbara would offer no objection. Her hands rose to touch the collar. 'You expect me to wear this from now on?' she asked incredulously.

'Well, yes, I suppose that is rather what I had in mind,' Phillipa said mildly, as if explaining something to a stubborn child.

'But suppose – just suppose,' Barbara said ironically, 'that I object, and want to remove it?'

'Well, that would be rather difficult. As I told you, I no longer have the key. I threw it into the river while you slept,' Phillipa explained. 'Still, I suppose you could go to the fire brigade and ask them to cut it off with a pair of their heavy bolt-croppers. Or maybe you could find a clever locksmith to remove it for you. It might raise some embarrassing questions, but it could be done. But why on earth would you want to remove it. I think it looks rather handsome. And if nothing else, it would make a fine conversation piece.'

'Well, if you think it's so handsome, why aren't you wearing one?' Barbara retorted.

'Why would I want to wear one? I'm not the slave.' Her tone suggested that she was growing weary of silly questions. If Barbara persisted in trying her patience there might be unpleasant consequences.

But Barbara couldn't let the matter drop. She had already decided that she didn't want to be a slave, especially not this woman's slave. 'What did Sarah say to you when you told her she was going to be pierced?'

'Ah, yes. Sarah. Dear little Sarah. Running away was really in very poor taste. Well, to answer your question, I didn't tell her why I was taking her in to the clinic, so she never had the chance to formulate any serious objections. When she found out, she didn't seem overjoyed, but she went along in the end. Did she show you her rings? I thought they were rather pretty.'

The devil of rebellion made Barbara press on. 'Ran away? I understood there was more to it than that. There were sausages involved too.'

Phillipa's face grew red and angry. 'I know she told you about that because you brought it up on an earlier occasion. I wasn't pleased then. I see you haven't learned yet to keep your mouth shut.'

'Don't try it,' Phillipa warned as Barbara tensed herself to spring for the door. 'You wouldn't outrun me even without those leg-irons. And running around naked in this weather isn't such a good idea. Hypothermia is no respecter of persons. In any case, I won't kill you. Things can be unpleasant in the short-term, but I can make that up to you after you've learned better manners.'

Phillipa rose and fetched the coffee pot back to the table. She offered a cup to Barbara as if they were discussing nothing more controversial or startling than the weather. 'Finish your omelette. You can't go without food forever.' She appeared to consider Barbara's remarks for a time. Then she went on, 'I'm not such a terrible companion. You enjoyed what I did to you this time. Well, most of it,' she said with a chuckle. 'I imagine the last bit was stressful, but you even managed to enjoy that. And that sort of thing won't happen every time. For one thing, I don't want to blunt the effect.'

Barbara ate her food, forcing it down past the knot in her throat. Phillipa moved restlessly about the kitchen. She appeared to be trying to decide what to do in the face of Barbara's recalcitrance. She came to stand behind Barbara's chair, letting her hands rest on the younger woman's shoulders. She fingered the collar, turning it slowly on Barbara's neck. The touch was gentle, surprisingly so after the irritation she had shown.

Barbara tensed, knowing how mercurial this woman's moods could be. But Phillipa only said, 'Come along now if you're finished. I expect you'd like to use the loo.'

Barbara didn't resist as she was led to the toilet and then afterwards back to the bedroom.

'I have to go out for a while,' Phillipa explained as she brought Barbara's hands up to her collar and fastened the short chain to her handcuffs. She indicated that Barbara was to sit on the bed, and when she had done so Phillipa locked the chain from her collar to the headboard. 'You'll be all right here,' she said. 'I won't be away long, and Frank will be back soon as well.'

'Where is he now?' Barbara asked.

Phillipa consulted her watch before answering. 'He should be through his appointment by now. I sent him to be pierced in a rather intimate fashion, and he should be coming out to show me the results. After he's healed, I'll be able to leave you two alone without fear that he'll get at you. Sex will be impossible for him unless I consent.' Phillipa seemed to find that fact amusing.

'Then he *is* your lover,' Barbara said. She felt a kind of release as she said this.

Phillipa frowned. 'I wouldn't call him my lover exactly, though I occasionally allow him access. He's really my slave. He likes the role, as you will, I'm sure. It didn't take him long to become accustomed to living under my terms. You're a bit more trouble, but we'll get there in the end,' she added with a smile. 'Lie down now and get some rest.'

Phillipa drew the covers up over Barbara and tucked her into bed.

After she had gone Barbara lay awake thinking of how she could escape this woman. Even if she managed to get away from this house, Phillipa would find her again. She gave serious consideration to Sarah's invitation to move to Glasgow. Phillipa couldn't follow her everywhere. She dozed, never really falling asleep because there was so much to consider.

It was getting toward evening when Phillipa returned. Barbara heard her moving about downstairs, and shortly she came up to the bedroom. She carried a riding crop.

'Time for a bit more fun,' she said cheerily as she stripped the bedclothes off and landed a slash across Barbara's bottom.

She squealed and jerked against her chains. Phillipa struck her again.

As she raised her arm to strike another blow, the door banged back against the wall. Sarah stood in the doorway, her face a mask of fury. 'Phillipa, stop that at once and let her go!' she said in a commanding voice. She strode into the room and moved determinedly toward the older woman. Sarah no longer looked soft and small.

Barbara screamed, 'Sarah!' There was a note of relief in her voice.

Phillipa reacted more practically. She turned on the intruder and began to lash her with the crop she had been using on Barbara. Sarah raised her hands defensively before her face, so that the blows struck her forearms and her breasts and stomach. But she kept coming. Phillipa dropped the lash and used her fists against the other woman. She struck Sarah once in the stomach, winding her. Sarah dropped her arms to protect herself and Phillipa struck her in the face. The younger woman went down and lay unmoving on the floor.

Barbara was tearing at her chains like a madwoman and screaming, 'Sarah! Saarahhh!' as she tried to get to her friend.

Phillipa turned on Barbara with a look of fury on her

face. She struck Barbara twice across the face with her open hand. 'Shut up!' she hissed.

Barbara paid her no attention. She continued to fight her chains, trying to get to Sarah. Phillipa might as well not have been there. In her frenzy she slipped to the floor and the chain on her collar came taut, almost strangling her. She felt herself losing consciousness as she tried to help Sarah. Phillipa struck her once again but she didn't feel it.

Finally Phillipa realised that Barbara was strangling herself. She picked the smaller woman up and laid her back onto the bed so as to get some slack in the chain. At that moment a tigress sprang through the door and flung herself at Phillipa.

Elspeth landed on Phillipa's back and carried her down to the floor. She locked her arm around the blonde woman's neck and tried her best to strangle her. She was sobbing and crying, 'Sarah! Sarah! Hold on. I'm here.' To Phillipa she screamed, 'You bitch! You've hurt Sarah and I'm going to kill you!'

Phillipa recovered from the first fury of the attack and began to fight back. Her hair came loose, and she looked more like a Valkyrie than ever as she clawed Elspeth off her back and flung her to the floor. She made a lunge for the riding crop, intending to beat off this fresh attack.

Elspeth caught her legs and she crashed to the floor. The fall seemed to stun her, and Elspeth gave her no time to recover. She was on the larger woman at once, kicking her, punching her in the face and stomach, anywhere she could land a blow.

Phillipa struck back but couldn't dislodge the Fury that sat astride her body and struck her again and again.

Barbara had recovered consciousness and was once again jerking madly at her chains.

Sarah made a choking sound from where she lay on the floor. Elspeth looked up to see how she was doing. It was a mistake.

Phillipa seized the opportunity and backhanded the smaller woman across her face. Elspeth was knocked sideways, and Phillipa struggled to her feet. She was dishevelled and her clothing was ripped. There was a smear of blood from her mouth where Elspeth had punched her, and one of her eyes was closing. But Barbara thought she still looked beautiful. And dangerous.

In time the fight could have only one outcome. Phillipa's greater weight and strength gave her an advantage that would tell against the fury of the smaller woman. Sarah might recover in time to help, but there was no way to be sure she would. And Barbara was *hors de combat*, chained to the bed.

But the cavalry arrived on schedule. A tall blond man entered the room and seized Phillipa from behind, twisting her arm behind her back.

She cried out in pain and fell to her knees. He continued to apply pressure until she screamed hoarsely. But still she struggled. 'I'll break it!' he warned her. The fight seemed to go out of the blonde woman all at once.

Barbara later remembered that it had taken two people, one of them a man, to subdue Phillipa. That made her feel somewhat better about her own lack of resistance.

Elspeth crawled across to where Sarah lay. She cradled Sarah's head in her lap and smoothed her hair. With her other hand she wiped Sarah's face. She was weeping and crying Sarah's name softly as she kissed her.

Sarah opened her eyes and reached to touch Elspeth's face with her fingertips. 'Thanks, tiger. I don't think I could have rescued the damsel in distress without your help.'

'You idiot. Look what you've done to yourself. You should have waited for me,' Elspeth said in fond remonstrance.

Now that the excitement was over Barbara felt both excluded and embarrassed. Colin was standing guard over Phillipa. Elspeth was busy taking care of Sarah, and looking as if she needed some attention herself after Phillipa had landed her backhanded swing across her nose and cheek. And Sarah had taken the full force of Phillipa's attack. Barbara knew what that felt like. She was the only one who had taken no active part in her rescue – for that is what it was. She sat on the field of victory naked and in chains, for all the world like the prize for which the battle had been fought. Which in a way she was. That fact did nothing to lessen her embarrassment and sense of obligation.

Thankfully, no one was paying much attention to her. If she had been able, she would have crawled under the bedclothes, or sunk through the floor, done anything to feel less conspicuous and fought-over. But with her handcuffs joined so closely to her collar she could do nothing to cover herself or help in the aftermath of battle.

It was Sarah who broke the spell. She managed to get to her feet with Elspeth's help. She came shakily over to the bed and looked at Barbara.

'Poor Barbara,' she said softly. 'If I'd known you were in the hands of this harpy I'd have come straight away. Why didn't you tell me?' But there was no reproach in her voice. Sarah put her arms around her friend and held her tightly. She drew back long enough to kiss her softly on the eyelids.

Barbara was reminded of how Phillipa had kissed her there, but with Sarah there was no sense of menace and (this time at least) no erotic overtones. Just worry and concern. And love. Yes, that too. Barbara made as if to embrace Sarah but her chains prevented anything but the merest touch with her fingertips.

Sarah stepped back and assumed command. She asked Barbara where the keys were.

Barbara nodded in Phillipa's direction, and Sarah glared at her erstwhile lover. 'Elspeth. Colin. Would you get the keys off Madam so I can get Barbara unlocked.'

Elspeth said, 'Gladly. The sooner we get Barbara out of her chains and her (in a tone of scathing contempt) into them the better I'll like it.'

Between them she and Colin made Phillipa hand over the keys. Barbara's handcuffs and leg-irons were removed, and the chain attached to her collar was unlocked from the headboard of the bed. Elspeth strode over to Phillipa with the manacles. Colin pulled Phillipa's arms behind her back and Elspeth locked the handcuffs onto her wrists. When she bent to fit the leg-irons to Phillipa's ankles, the blonde woman kicked viciously at her. Elspeth darted aside and, when she had recovered her balance, planted her foot in Phillipa's stomach with as much force as she could muster.

Phillipa's face went white, then red, as she struggled to draw breath. Elspeth's kick had winded her completely, and all the fight went out of her in an instant. Elspeth measured the distance and kicked her again. While Phillipa drew in great shuddery breaths Elspeth locked the leg-irons onto her ankles.

'That was for Sarah,' Elspeth told her. 'I ought to kick you again for Barbara.' Looking across the room, she asked Barbara, 'Do you want me to let her have it again? It's no trouble. In fact I'd enjoy it.' From the tone of her voice there was no doubting that she wanted to do something painful to Phillipa.

Barbara shook her head. 'That wouldn't help. It's over now, and I'm glad just to be free of her. I have to thank you all, and I don't know how to do it.'

'Never mind,' said Sarah. 'I'm only glad I came when I did, and I'm sure Elspeth is too. Colin can speak for himself. Or at least he can once I've introduced you properly. Colin, meet Barbara. She's the one wearing the bright red all-over blush, over there on the bed.'

Barbara felt herself grow hotter and redder under his level stare. It felt like sinking-through-the-floor time again.

'Glad to meet you at last, Barbara,' he said quietly. 'Sarah's been bending my ear about you for a couple of weeks, and I'm glad to say she didn't do you justice at all.'

Elspeth said, 'You're making her blush, Colin.' To Barbara she continued, 'Don't pay any attention to him. He says that to all the women. He even said it to me, and I believed him.'

'Why, Elspeth, I meant it. I always mean it.'

'Then you shouldn't be saying it so often,' she retorted with a smile.

The light banter had relieved the tension, and Barbara

found herself able to smile once more, though she still felt embarrassed.

Once again it was Sarah who took charge. 'Barbara, where are your clothes? We need to get you out of here without making the cows blush or giving you pneumonia.'

'She took them,' Barbara replied, nodding at Phillipa.

At once Sarah turned to the tall blonde woman and demanded the clothes. 'And while you're talking, tell me where the key to Barbara's collar is,' she ended.

Phillipa glared at her. 'Being away from me hasn't improved your manners, I see. But that's probably due to the company you're keeping now.' When she saw Sarah's anger, Phillipa changed tack. 'You'll find her clothes in the laundry room downstairs. The key to her collar is at the bottom of the river. I imagine Madam will be wearing that collar for a long time.' This last was uttered in a triumphant tone. Phillipa was regaining her self-confidence.

'I don't mind the collar,' Barbara said to Sarah. 'I'll wear it as you wear your rings.' That brought another glare from Phillipa, but Barbara didn't care. She was free of her now.

Without saying anything to anyone Elspeth strode over to Phillipa and lifted her skirt. With some tugging, Phillipa resisting all the while, Elspeth got her pants off, ripping them to get them past the leg-irons. She stuffed them into the blonde woman's mouth and tied them in place with a scarf from the dresser drawer. None of the others interfered.

Colin went to fetch Barbara's clothes. She was grateful he had volunteered himself. As the only male in the rescue team, he was making the rescued damsel alarmingly aware of her nakedness and of the uses to which that nakedness could be put if there were no others about. I'm incorrigible, Barbara told herself without reproach. Nothing can distract me from thoughts of sweaty sex.

As he went out, Sarah burst out laughing 'Your face,' she said in answer to Barbara's inquiring glance. 'You were undressing him as he stood there, and you just after being from a fate worse than death. I wonder how the poor man felt. But,' changing tack abruptly, 'he *is* gorgeous. And he likes you. I could tell from the way he looked at you. And from the bulge in his trousers. That's the surest sign of a man's admiration. And he knows all about your deepest secrets and fantasies. I told him *everything* about you. And he does some of the best B&D in Glasgow.'

Barbara felt more naked than ever. But no one else seemed to care. Elspeth was smiling at her. She decided to ignore them. And see how things developed. Maybe this was her Mr Right. Hope springs eternal in the female sex, she thought, with another silent apology to Pope's ghost.

Colin came back with her clothes, somewhat wrinkled but clean and dry. He started to leave the room again so she could get dressed.

'You might as well stay,' Barbara said. These were the first words she had spoken directly to him, and she tried to keep her voice steady as she went on, 'You've already seen me naked, so watching me get dressed is bound to be an anticlimax. Or at any rate I hope it is.' Her sense of humour was returning.

When Barbara was dressed Elspeth raised the question of Phillipa. 'I suppose we could leave her here and call the police to come collect her after we're away. But I hate to repeat myself, and there may not be any salami in the larder this time.'

This reminder of the ignominious picture she had presented when Sarah had run away drew another glare from Phillipa.

Barbara now knew how much the tall blonde hated to be embarrassed, so she appeared to give some consideration to Elspeth's suggestion in order to make Phillipa uneasy. Her sense of mischief was recovering nicely. 'I suppose we could find some substitute if we looked around. There's bound to be something suitably phallic lying about. Or we could leave her tied to the chair downstairs with a dildo up the Khyber Pass.'

Barbara saw Phillipa grow pale at the prospect of being found once again in such circumstances. There was some satisfaction in that, but Barbara wasn't the vengeful type.

After allowing Phillipa to dwell on the indignity, she went on, 'There's no real problem. Just leave her as she is until her male slave gets here. She told me he's due later today.'

Phillipa looked relieved, but Elspeth was far from happy. 'She deserves more pain and trouble than that, surely,' she said with a glance at Sarah. She didn't mention what Phillipa had done to her.

Colin suggested, 'Let's go downstairs and get something to eat. We can discuss what to do with her in private. She might even enjoy the surprise.'

They went to the kitchen, where Elspeth volunteered to make the sandwiches. Barbara found a fresh bottle of champagne. As they ate they talked of their plans for the holidays. They decided to travel to Glasgow by train on Monday. Unless Barbara shed her collar and chain somehow, flying was out of the question. She would never get past the metal detectors, and a search would reveal her unusual taste in costume jewellery. Sarah and Elspeth had already had trouble with their rings, though sometimes they would get through. It was embarrassing when they couldn't, but they had learned to deal with that. It was decided that they would take the overnight sleeper train from King's Cross.

Barbara and Sarah were making plans for a last-minute shopping trip on Monday morning. 'Twas the season to be spendthrift, and Barbara needed a supply of high-necked tops to go with her collar. Colin gallantly (but without much enthusiasm) volunteered to accompany them.

Sarah whispered in Barbara's ear, 'He hates shopping, like most men. He just wants to be with you. If you want to make him happy, buy something daring in the lingerie line and hint that you're buying it for him to see.'

Barbara went pink, but she was nonetheless pleased. Colin appeared ready to make a considerable sacrifice just to be with her.

Sarah went on, 'You two can share a sleeper compartment and get acquainted. Don't worry about us poor girls. We'll make do with a hovel next door. Just don't scream too loudly when you come or we'll be envious.'

As they talked, Elspeth excused herself, saying she had to go to the loo. She was gone a long time before anyone noticed her protracted absence. Sarah was saying how lucky it was that Barbara had managed to leave so many clues for them when Phillipa had abducted her. Upstairs Phillipa suddenly screamed, 'No! Don't do that! Naaaoooohhh!' The last scream became an inarticulate howl and was accompanied by loud thumping noises.

They jumped to their feet and Sarah shouted, 'Elspeth! What are you doing?' As they reached the top of the stairs the noises subsided for a moment, then another agonised scream came from the bedroom.

When they reached the room Elspeth was holding Phillipa's riding crop in a shaking hand. She was crying, but there was a determined set to her face, as if she were seeing to a painful but necessary job. She had ripped Phillipa's blouse away to expose her breasts and was lashing them with all her slender strength. Phillipa was throwing herself about in an attempt to escape the blows. She was screaming wildly, at the top of her lungs.

Sarah rushed to Elspeth and took the crop away from her. Elspeth didn't resist. She was looking at Phillipa, whose convulsed body began to relax now that the beating had ended.

Sarah said gently, 'Elspeth, you didn't have to do that. You're only hurting yourself.'

Elspeth spoke as if she hadn't heard Sarah. 'It took me a while to work up the courage, and all the time she was looking at me and smiling in that superior way of hers. She probably thought I didn't have the courage to do it.' To Phillipa she said, 'Fooled you, didn't I?' Elspeth's voice sounded dull but determined. ' Took off her gag as soon as I was ready. I wanted her to scream, but I couldn't let her do it too soon and bring you all here before I could do her.'

Phillipa moaned softly.

Elspeth seemed to shake herself out of the mood, and when she spoke again her voice was nearly normal. 'She had it coming. And more. After what she did to you, Sarah, and to Barbara, I thought she should be made to realise how badly it hurts. She screamed when she realised I was going to hurt her. She lost her nerve when she found herself on the receiving end. And would you just look at her? I think she's wet herself. Anyone would think a woman of her age would be better toilet trained.' This last was said with a tone of amused contempt, more like the old Elspeth.

Sarah said once again, 'Oh Elspeth, you shouldn't have taken this on yourself. You didn't need to hurt yourself for me.' And she kissed Elspeth softly on the mouth.

They held one another for a long time. Barbara found herself a bit teary as well – not for Phillipa, but because of the naked love and trust between Sarah and Elspeth. She felt somehow lost and alone. And terribly envious.

Something of what she felt must have shown in her face, for Colin moved across to her and took her in his arms.

Barbara hid her face against his chest. Nor did she object when he put his face down and kissed her softly on the top of her head. She turned up her face to be kissed properly. This looked like turning out right after all, she told herself hopefully. In her hopeful mood she could even look on Phillipa with pity and a wistful affection.

When next she spoke, she felt better than she could remember feeling in a long time. 'I think we can leave Phillipa here. She struck me as the fastidious type, at least insofar as she herself was concerned. So it won't be very pleasant waiting for Frank to come for her. But she won't suffer any permanent harm.'

Phillipa said nothing.

Seeing the other woman's impassivity, Elspeth adopted a broad Glaswegian accent and said in a rough voice, 'Ach, cud I no' be haein' anither wee go at her, jist tae be gaein' on wi'?' She was grinning now, recovered from her earlier mood.

Phillipa heard her, as she had intended. And she reacted as Elspeth had hoped. 'No! Please! I . . . I can't take any more. Please don't let her hurt me!'

The break in her voice finally broke the spell she had had over Barbara. She turned away and went downstairs.

Elspeth stayed until last, and the last words Barbara heard from her erstwhile 'Mistress' were a scream, 'Take her with you, please! Don't leave me alone with her! Oh, God, please! Please don't hurt me!'

When Elspeth rejoined them, she said, 'It's amazing how her manners have improved. Have you ever heard so many "pleases" from her, Sarah? I only had to pick up her toy whip to make her sing.'

Barbara went out with them to the rental car her rescuers had arrived in. Sarah drove and Colin and Barbara sat in the rear seat together. Elspeth turned round to face them and with an impish grin said to Sarah, 'Wud ye jist be lookin' at them! He canna keep his hands aff her. He'll be haein' her pants doon richt here an' noo.'

On the Monday they went shopping. Colin stuck by his promise to go along with them. Barbara made a point of buying some see-through bras and pants, as well as some more of her favourite crotchless tights. Colin stood by the lingerie counter with the women, looking faintly embarrassed as men always do in that part of the store.

Elspeth didn't make it any easier for him by saying in a stage whisper, 'How d'ye like them, laddie? I'll bet ye canna wait tae tear them aff her.' To the salesgirl she explained, 'He's jist cam' doon frae th' Isle O' Skye, where the Wee Frees dinna e'en pairmit them tae think o' sic' sinfu' garments.' Sarah shook her surreptitiously. 'Do you think you could drop that Och aye, see you Jimmy accent? Your parents spent a fortune on your education.'

They went back to Barbara's place and made the task of packing for the holiday into a party, Sarah and Elspeth taking it in turns to make lewd suggestions about what to take along. Sarah insisted they take along her collection of B&D gear. 'If we're going on holiday, we ought to take along the recreational items. You won't be able to nip off and buy any of this stuff at the station buffet if you get the urge between here and there.'

Barbara was turning over the idea of not coming back, and making tentative lists of what to take and what to leave behind. The idea of making a fresh start with her friends was appealing.

Finally everything was packed and it was time to get dressed for the trip. Barbara drew Elspeth and Sarah into the bedroom on the pretext of helping one another get dressed. She was planning a surprise for Colin and wanted the others in on it. Borrowing the idea from Frank, Barbara planned to wear her coat with nothing else under it. Elspeth approved. Sarah suggested she wear at least some of the new lingerie she had bought that day. 'It's for Colin anyway, isn't it? And anyway everyone knows that a bit of clothing is more provocative than total nudity. At least for men.'

So Barbara put on a pair of the crotchless tights and one of the see-through bras. Even Elspeth was impressed. Paraphrasing the first Elizabeth, she said admiringly, 'Were I crested and not cloven, ye'd have me standing proud.' Sarah dissuaded her from wearing pants. 'Spoils the effect,' she declared.

'How do we let Colin know about me?' Barbara asked. 'I had it in mind to let him know sometime before we get on the train so his imagination can get to work.'

'Leave that to us,' Elspeth said. 'We'll have him stepping on his tongue and his trousers will be too tight for him by the time we get to the station.'

Barbara put on her coat and wound a scarf around her neck to conceal the collar. They were ready to go, and she felt like a girl being let out of school. Colin took charge of the small but heavy bag containing Barbara's collection. From the look he gave her, she knew that he was aware of what it contained. Barbara felt the familiar stirrings of excitement. What a lovely way to begin a holiday, she thought.

They were a noisy party at the station, attracting stares from the crowds of staid homeward-bound commuters. Barbara caught Colin looking at her with a questioning look in his eyes. Sarah or Elspeth must have told him something already. When they sat down at the station bar to have a drink before boarding the train, she contrived to let her coat fall open so that he could see clear up to her crotch. She hoped no one else had seen, but didn't worry much if they had. This was a holiday, and she felt a bit drunk even before the first drink.

She was sitting next to Colin by design. When her coat fell open he saw immediately but said nothing. Instead he slid his hand under the table and found the top of her thigh. He rubbed her leg gently and gave a little squeeze that made her go hot all over. She flushed but managed to say, 'Where *is* that train? I can't wait to get going.'

'Neither can I,' he said.

They had adjoining double compartments on the train. As they squeezed into theirs, Sarah asked Barbara if she'd ever made love on a train.

'No, I'm a railway virgin.'

'You're in luck, then. It looks as if you're standing next to the ideal person to help a lady get over that embarrassing condition.'

'I'll do my best,' Colin said modestly. 'I'm looking forward to opening my Christmas present early, so if you two schoolgirls can find it in your hearts to give us a little privacy, I'll get started.'

'Excuse me already,' Sarah said as she withdrew through the connecting door. 'Don't make too much noise. You'll make the neighbours envious.'

As the door closed Barbara felt her heart hammering. This is it! she told herself. Alone with Colin at last, and she was feeling like a schoolgirl meeting her first undergraduate.

Colin noticed her agitation. 'Relax,' he said. 'There's no hurry. What I told Sarah was for public consumption. If you're nervous we can wait as long as you like.'

'And am I for private consumption?' Barbara asked. She was unbuttoning her coat with one hand and unwinding her scarf with the other. 'And what if *I'm* in a hurry?' Her voice shook slightly and she felt the familiar looseness in the knees and tightness in throat and belly. As her coat fell away she was pleased to see his eyes widen in admiration. And the tent pole was up. I guess he likes me, she thought with relief.

But Colin was touching her collar, turning it so that he could see the lock. Barbara had let the chain dangle between her breasts under her bra. The free end was wrapped round her waist and tied with another scarf.

'I have an idea,' Colin said. 'I'll get this collar open before we start. Then I'll have a key made in Glasgow. I know several competent burglars and locksmiths who could do the job. If you're half as good as you look, I'll give it back to you and keep the key.' He was working at the lock with a stiff piece of wire as he spoke, frowning with concentration.

Barbara stood still, feeling herself flushing hot and cold as she inhaled the aroma of healthy male right beside her.

There was a click, and the steel band on her throat loosened and fell away. Colin untied the chain and withdrew it from under her bra, lingering, she thought, rather longer than necessary as he touched her breasts. She wanted to reach up and hold his hands against them but she forced herself to stand still and keep her hands at her sides.

Colin laid the collar on the top berth and turned back to Barbara. 'You'll be able to earn it back by good works, as they say in church.'

'Can I start now, sir? Please, sir? I'm dead keen, and I learn quickly.'

'Yes, I think we can begin now. Start as we mean to go on.' Colin opened the bag containing her bondage gear and brought out the thin cords she had bought. 'Sarah told me all about you,' he reminded her, 'so we'll begin with your favourite fantasy. Turn around, Barbara.'

She did, bringing her hands behind her back without being told. This was as familiar to her as her own body. She had dreamed of this often enough. She crossed her wrists and felt the cords tighten around them. Then he bound her elbows, drawing them closely together behind her. She was beginning to shiver with anticipation.

'Steady now.'

His voice in her ear, his breath on her neck. Then, as he finished tying her, his hands took her breasts from behind, cupping them through the sheer cups of her bra, rubbing her nipples, making them harden. Barbara was shaking now, her legs weak and rubbery. She leaned back against him, glad for the support of his arms around her. Barbara let her head fall back against his shoulder. She felt his lips on the side of her throat, nuzzling her ears and her hair.

This felt entirely different from the time with Phillipa. That had reminded her of butterflies' wings. Colin's mouth on her was hot and the skin of his face felt raspy on hers. There was all the difference between a man and a woman, and Barbara voted for a man. For this man in particular.

He laid her down on the bed and began to undress. His stiff cock was the supreme compliment when it sprang free from his trousers. She stared at it steadily as he approached. 'For me?' she said in wonder. 'Come into me now, please!'

Colin lay down on the bed beside her. It was cramped. British Rail had not planned these berths for double occupancy. He lifted Barbara atop him and then guided himself between her parted thighs. He sighed gratefully as he found her wet and slippery, ready for him.

Barbara cried out softly as she felt him enter her. This was the fantasy at last. Everything had been more or less a preparation for this moment when she lay atop a man, bound helplessly and with his cock stiff inside her.

Colin held her still, letting her feel him and enjoying the sensation of her muscles clenched tight around his cock. When he began to move, sliding in and out, Barbara thought she would burst with the excitement. She came very soon, crying out and thrashing wildly, trying to get more of him inside her. Her breasts were crushed against his chest and she was rubbing them on his raspy hair.

He was patient, letting her come again and again. Then when she paused he resumed. This time he went more slowly.

The edge had been taken off her need. Now she could appreciate the different smells and sounds of him, the texture of his skin, and the way he breathed into her open mouth when he kissed her. Barbara moaned softly, feeling herself rising to another peak. This one was not as urgent, but it was a longer series of spasms that racked her. When she felt him tensing inside her she knew he was about to come. She heard herself urging him on: 'Come now. Come with me. Now, now noooooowww,' she cried as he tensed and then spurted inside her.

He groaned and held her fiercely against him, as if to prevent her flying away.

Barbara ground her hips against his pelvis, pumping up and down like a mad thing.

When they were spent they lay together for a long time, breath slowing and bodies cooling. The train was moving, rocking gently from side to side as it picked up speed on the journey north.

Colin got up eventually, moving carefully so as to leave Barbara lying on the bed. She lay half on her side, her bound hands in the angle between the berth and the side of the carriage. Her hair was damp and clung to her cheeks and neck. There were dark stains on her bra and down the legs of her tights. She felt the cool air touch the sweat, drying it slowly.

Colin moved the hair away from her mouth so he could kiss her. Barbara pushed her face against his. She felt dizzy and breathless when the kiss ended.

Colin said, 'I like to watch you breathe. It does interesting things to your breasts.'

Not half so interesting as the things he did, she thought, but she was glad of the compliment. We try so hard to please, and sometimes we succeed, and then it's all worthwhile.

'There's more,' Colin said. 'We have time for plenty more before we get to Glasgow. And we have two weeks after that to try as many of your fantasies as you can stand. I'll have time to make some interesting leather gear for you – taking my measurements right from the model.' As he spoke he collected more of the cords from Barbara's bag. He had her sit on the edge of the bed while he tied her legs together at ankles, knees and thighs, just as she had done in her solitary fantasies.

But this was the real thing at last, the B&D groupie's dream. As the cords bit into her flesh Barbara felt herself getting excited again. But there was more. From his own bag Colin took a leather helmet which Barbara recognised from her examination of Phillipa's bondage gear.

'Consider it a parting gift from Phillipa,' he said as he showed it to her. 'We got it from her place when we were looking for you. It's a small enough price for all she did.' Colin stuffed a scarf into Barbara's mouth and buckled the helmet on her head.

Barbara was shaking with excitement as she sat in the dark, unable to see or speak while her dream lover made her his captive. His hands on her shoulders pressed her down and back into the berth. She felt herself being rolled over until she was lying on her side. Then he fastened her wrists to her ankles with a short length of cord, bending her knees back. Oh, God, he's done it, I can't get free, Barbara thought as she tugged at her bonds. She was hot all over, panting with excitement.

She heard him getting dressed and grunted an inquiry. Where was he going? There was no reply.

Then he was beside her. One hand found her breasts while the other slid between her bound thighs, touching her wet sex. Barbara moaned and tried to heave herself closer to him.

'Slowly, slowly,' he said. 'Remember that we have plenty of time.' Then he was gone. The door closed behind him.

Barbara was living her fantasy now, hot and sweaty and helpless, lying bound and gagged in a locked compartment on a speeding train, waiting for her demon-lover to return to her.